I0599976

Baby, It's You

Nicole Mikell

Copyright © 2025 by Nicole Mikell

All rights reserved.

No part of this book may be reproduced in any form or by any electronic or mechanical means, including information storage and retrieval systems, without written permission from the author, except for the use of brief quotations in a book review.

This is a work of fiction. Names, characters, places, and incidents either are the product of the author's imagination or are used fictitiously. Any resemblance to actual persons, living or dead, events, or locales is entirely coincidental.

First edition

ISBN: 979-8-9992297-0-0

Editor: Danielle Barthel

Cover Design: Gowtham T

The characters and songs in this book are a love letter to my life.

This one is for you G.B.

Being deeply loved by someone gives you strength, while loving someone deeply gives you courage.

— Lao Tzu

Contents

READERS NOTE:

Music plays a huge role of importance in this
novel. I listened to music the whole time while I
wrote this book and I want you to be able to
immerse yourself in the music as well.
I made a free Spotify playlist with all the songs
that are mentioned throughout the book.
I hope you feel moved by the music.
-Nicole

On the next page is a scannable QR code for the
playlist.

QR code

Baby, It's You

Chapter 1

Olive

I startle awake to the sound of tires screeching, and then a large crash, followed by someone shouting, *"You cheater! Ass."*

Rolling over to my bedside table, I click on my phone screen and groan when I see the blinding, bright 3:48 A.M. Great, it's not like I need sleep to function after working a twelve-hour shift on my feet, managing the bar. Who needs sleep?

I rub my eyes with my hands, then swing my feet over the side of my bed and head to my apartment window to see the commotion that woke me from my hour of blissful slumber. What I see is no surprise: my downstairs neighbor and best friend, Ivy, is standing in front of her boyfriend's car with a bat, swinging it around like she is Tiger Woods's ex-wife. His black Camry's front windshield has a huge shatter mark across it from her first blow, aka the culprit that woke me.

"I should have known. When that cocktail girl at Slots R Us introduced herself to me as *Tiffani with an I*... Who cares how it's spelled!" she continues to scream.

1

Her boyfriend, Dennis, who is a six-foot-two "professional" poker player who looks like a young Mark Ruffalo—if he stuck his finger in an electrical socket and became the slimiest person on the planet—leans out the driver's side window.

"Baby! Tiffani with an I is just a friend! Her texting me that she wants to suck my chips again was just a joke! You know you're the only girl for me." He throws his hands up in protest.

Groaning, I step away from my window. I wish I could say this is something I've never seen from them, but that would be a lie. Ivy and Dennis have been together for four years, and in that time, he's cheated six times, and she's taken him back six times.

Knowing the cycle is about to start again, I rub my eyes and walk to my fridge to uncork a bottle of chardonnay, knowing that soon I will hear her run up the steps to my place. Sighing, I look around my apartment and begin to pick up pieces of my work uniform that are strewn across the floor from me yanking them off over my head, tossing the outfit and my shoes without care, and collapsing into my bed the second I walked in the door after my shift ended.

Loud, muffled back and forth continues outside and at this rate the whole complex will be awake soon. This is why I don't date—I don't trust men and I never will. Between my parents' constant arguing and my father's short fuse growing up—that led to a divorce when I was young—and now watching Ivy's toxic relationship, I will never allow myself to get in a position where a partner makes me feel less than or causes me to lose myself.

The stress I have watched the women in my life go through because of a man's bad decisions and emotional intelligence is something I don't want for myself. I have watched my spunky strawberry blonde best friend go from someone who lit up a room when she walked in, to someone who can't even hold a conversation without checking her phone anxiously to see what Dennis is doing. I saw my mother cry time and time again because my dad called her another horrible name and stormed out of the house, going god knows where.

Eventually when I was twelve, he left and never came back. His leaving caused something inside my mother to snap, and she was never mentally right again. After he was gone, my mom dated one horrible guy after another, constantly causing chaos in not only her life, but mine. The nausea I feel in my stomach every time I think about the slamming of doors and the voices raising, followed by abandonment...I would choose to be alone over a "love" like that, always.

Ivy and I have been best friends since we were sophomores in high school, when her nomad parents decided to move here, to Clairesville, a town on the outskirts of Tennessee, after throwing a dart at a map. Literally, they packed up everything they had and moved here on a whim, decided by one single dart.

Freshman year I was kind of a loner; I had a few friends that I would eat lunch with, but no one I would spend time with outside of school. Sophomore year that all changed. This wild-eyed girl barged into my first period class with pigtails, a tie-dye shirt, and bell bottoms. She loudly introduced herself to everyone as Ivy Penny and tossed her bag down next to me in the front row. Once the teacher started talking about the syllabus, she turned to me with a big smile and immediately started talking to me like we had known each other for years.

She told me about how her dad burnt breakfast and it started a fire and the fire department came to their house and the firefighters were so hot. She enthusiastically told me this all happened that morning before her first day of school. I sat there absorbing her story and laughed along with her. I had never felt that kind of natural connection to anyone before, and we became inseparable after finding out how many things we had in common. We both hated mustard, appreciated all boy bands, had an aversion to jean skirts, and most importantly, cried every time we saw an old person eating alone at a restaurant. We also cried every time we thought of an old person eating alone at a restaurant.

I'm tearing up right now.

Glancing at the clock, I see it's now past 4 A.M. and she still isn't up here yet. I smell my armpit and cringe. I was too tired to shower when I walked in the door but now that I'm up, I must handle my stench. I head to the bathroom without unlocking my front door—Ivy already has a key, and I watch way too much *True Crime* to leave my front door unlocked, even for a minute.

I flick on my bathroom light and look around my dull bathroom. Chipped tan tile floors and a flickering florescent light stare back at me. My apartment is old, and the complex needs a serious update, but I stay because it's close to work and let's get real: I'm not raking in the cash. I basically live at the bar, but that's how I like it.

Cranking the shower handle to the hottest setting it can produce, I decide this will be an "everything" shower, because my legs are hairy enough to knit into a scarf. Mentally preparing myself for the next twenty-five minutes of washing, exfoliating, and shaving, I connect to my wireless speaker, turning on my "All my Vibes" playlist at a low volume. I make sure to respect my sleeping neighbors, of course, and step into my standing tub. "Zero" by The Smashing Pumpkins starts to play in the background as the steam from my scalding hot shower clouds my vision and relaxes my aching muscles.

Every bar shift leaves me drained but happy. I enjoy my job at Whiskey Jane's. I love the regulars, and my tips are usually fairly good. Even though I'm the manager, I'm also the bartender most days since our staff is extremely limited. It doesn't bother me, though, and every day I leave happy, even when I don't make much money.

That is until recently. I can't stand the guy currently in charge of the bar. He blows.

"OLIVE!" I hear Ivy whine from somewhere in my apartment.

"In here," I call.

Ivy opens the bathroom door with a whimper, and I peek my head outside the shower as she plops onto the shag rug by the sink and buries her mascara- and tear-smeared face in her hands.

"So, what happened this time?" I ask, returning to my left leg shave.

"He cheated on me again! After all this time and all of the promises he's made me, the ass turns around and does it again," Ivy groans.

I roll my eyes as I go back behind the curtain. "Where did you get the bat from?"

"I think it was little Steve's from Apartment 12A. I passed him playing baseball with some friends yesterday by the pond. I saw it on the grass right by the sidewalk as Dennis pulled up in his car. It was really meant to be."

"How convenient," I say. "Don't do that again, though. He might get petty and call the police on you. How did you bust him this time?"

"His iMessage was logged into my iPad and all these texts from Tiffani came through."

"What an imbecile," I say over my music, and shake my head in disgust from behind the curtain. I open my cherry blossom scented shampoo and start to lather my hair up in suds.

I have been down this road with her so many times. I peek

my head out once more and say, "Kitchen, chardonnay, Damon Salvatore. I'll be out in five."

She nods from her puddle of sadness on the floor and gets up to begin the routine we have done time and again since high school. Let's pretend the chardonnay was apple juice when we were sixteen; we were good girls.

Our tradition started after Ivy's first heartbreak with Chad Miller junior year. She found him making out with Mackenzie McCray after his track meet by the bleachers. He smelled like a walking Axe body spray ad and had acne everywhere, but that didn't matter to Ivy. All she saw was the "love of her life" sucking lips with another girl and it was over. She wailed next to me the whole ride home and I promised her I would sleep over at her house.

That night we raided her mother's wine cellar. Yes, her nomad parents were wealthy enough to have a wine cellar. Thanks to Ivy's mom having an inheritance, we were intro-duced to our friend chardonnay. Half a bottle of wine deep, we decided to watch a show with our favorite hypothetical boyfriends, Damon and Stefan Salvatore, because everything was easier in fiction. This was where our heartbreak routine began. When a boy let Ivy down, we just watched hot men on TV and our troubles floated away, momentarily.

I towel off my hair when I'm done and throw on a green oversized T-shirt. Then I walk out to my grandma-style worn paisley couch from Goodwill and plop down next to Ivy. She tosses me a blanket and hands me the open bottle of wine. Then she clicks play on a rerun that we have watched a million times over the years.

There's no reason to try and convince her to block him or leave him. She knows what I think of Dennis, and I know she won't walk away from the relationship. We have learned this balance from years of friendship: take each other as we are. I want more for her, but she has to want more for herself to make a change.

After the episode finishes, I hear her start to sniffle next to me and know the tears are coming. I pause the intro to the next episode and open my arms to her. She lays with me on the couch, and I let her sob, knowing she just needs to let it out. After fifteen minutes, she finally stops, and only hiccups from crying so hard are left.

Ivy sits up and gives me a small smile so I take that as my opening to call him every name in the book I can think of. She laughs, forming a giant snot bubble by accident, which makes us both crack up hysterically. Ivy then reaches over and clicks the play button on the remote and we resume watching like nothing ever happened.

Eventually, we drift off to sleep, intertwined and dreaming of fictional men.

Chapter 2

Hunter

"Ah, man! I thought I had it that time!" Wes shouts, after attempting his eightieth (maybe not, but probably) try at a 360 hardflip.

"Let's take a break, dude," I say, putting down my camera as I watch him throw his board in frustration into the nearby bushes.

Chuckling because I know that feeling all too well— wanting to get the trick so badly but the more you think about it, the more you psych yourself out—I turn away to give him a moment to cool down. Suddenly, I feel my pocket buzz and look down to see a call coming in. The name on the screen is "Dennis." Because I'm a glutton for punishment, I answer.

"Hello, Dennis," I say.

"*Cuz!* How's it going?" he says, but before I can even respond he continues, "Hey, man, I need to ask you for a little favor. My girl kicked me out again over something stupid. Can I crash at your place?"

Rolling my eyes, I think about the last time Dennis stayed with me when he graduated college, "couldn't find a job"

8

(meaning he didn't want to), proceeded to eat all my food for months, and destroyed my place. I eventually kicked him out after catching him trying to kiss the girl I was seeing at the time, Cecily.

"Have you exhausted all of your other options, which is why you're coming to me after years of no communication?" I ask.

He lets out a half laugh in response. "Listen, man, if you're still mad at me for eating all your Cheetos and ramen back in the day, I can reimburse you now."

I look over my shoulder to see Wes digging through the bushes for his board and turn back to my call. "What? No. I don't care about that. If anything, I would be mad about the situation with Cecily."

"Who's Cecily?" he asks. Unbelievable. Then he continues, "Listen, bro, you're my favorite cousin. I always talk about how great you are to everyone. If you could just do me a solid and let me sleep on your couch for a few days until my girl calms down, that would be great."

I sigh and look off into the distance, deciding whether I want to be the good guy or the bad one. We used to have great times together as kids and Dennis stayed with us often growing up because his dad, my uncle, was in and out of his life frequently.

Feeling sympathetic because of his upbringing, I reluctantly comply. "Okay, yes. You can stay with me. *Just* for a few days, I mean it. I will be traveling for work starting Friday and I don't want anyone staying at my place while I'm gone."

"You got it, thanks, man. I owe you one. Text me your address," he says and then abruptly hangs up.

That's typically how our conversations go in our adult lives: he contacts me when he needs something and then disappears when he doesn't.

I text him my address, already feeling the dread of an unwanted house guest. Then I turn back to my equipment and put my phone in my back pocket. Wes has successfully retrieved his board from the nearby bushes and walks back towards me.

"Hey, dude, I think I'm gonna call it for today, my knee is starting to bug me. I don't want to end up having to wear the brace again," he says.

Wes has always been a skateboarding prodigy and started attracting attention at an early age when I began filming him doing tricks at an empty Big Lots parking lot behind our houses. I always messed around skating, too, but I mainly enjoyed filming my friends on my crappy phone as a fourteen-year-old. Then I would edit the choppy clips on iMovie and upload them to YouTube. As Wes's talent grew, so did my passion for filming, and one day some of the clips I uploaded of him went viral. This attracted attention from the skate community and that's where my career began.

I used to feel alive watching someone attempt a trick that they'd daydreamed about and then, when they finally pulled it off: magic. It was the greatest feeling knowing that I was the one to capture that moment in time for them. The electricity that hummed off the skater, the pride everyone else around watching had as they smacked their boards on the concrete in congratulations...there is no way to describe that feeling to someone that hasn't skated before.

"No problem," I let him know. "Hit me up later. I might want to go out with you guys tonight for Eddie's birthday."

Wes turns back from walking to his car. "The old man *actually* wants to leave his place and go out? I think hell will freeze over first."

"Yeah, yeah." I shake my head and accept his playful jab. "Don't give me a hard time or I will change my mind."

He chuckles and waves goodbye.

I am not known as the most outgoing. In my younger years when I first started filming and traveling with pro skateboarders, we would go out and party. But even then, I was the more introverted guy, never going out of my way to get attention and always too shy to ask a girl for her number.

I've always been told I'm conventionally attractive. I am tall and have a "*luscious* head of hair," my mom's sixty-five-year-old hairdresser, Barb, always says. I don't have the self-assured nature to back it up, though. I have always been shy and have decided it's usually easier to just be quiet than to say the wrong thing. It's rare for me to feel comfortable with people quickly; it usually takes years to show my true self.

I take the lens off my Sony FX6 and load it into my backpack, along with my extra battery pack and light. Wiping the sweat from my brow, I look up into the unforgiving heat of July and vow to take an ice-cold shower when I get home. Is that something people do? It's got to be. I feel like I've seen a TED Talk about it being good for you.

I manually unlock my old crew cab navy blue Ford F-150 that I restored a few years back with my father, and slide into the driver's seat. Dad always had a huge passion for cars but was never able to spend the money or time restoring them. When we found out that he was diagnosed with stage 4 colon cancer when I was twenty-four, that changed quickly.

I luckily had the financial means from my success on YouTube to buy an old truck he loved. I made it my mission for us to fix it up together. We spent a year working on the car every time I was in town and not traveling for work, customizing the steering wheel and restoring the old leather seats.

It was the greatest gift, the time I had with him before his passing. The truck really brought us together in the end. Every time I sit in the front seat, I can hear him muttering, "You got your good looks and your taste in cars from me. You're welcome, son," in the playful way he always did.

I plug my phone into the aux cord attached to the new stereo we added and then shuffle my playlist. The soulful sound of "Just Dropped in" by Kenny Rogers begins to flood from my speakers. I roll all my windows down and take off along the winding, tree-lined road, back to my house.

Chapter 3

Olive

I have a slow start to my day after my eventful night. I can't help but continuously hit snooze on my alarm until a whole hour of ten-minute reminders has gone by.

When I finally get out of bed, it's almost noon and I'm about to be late for work. I jump up, realizing I completely overslept, and throw on my work uniform. Then I run to my bathroom to put my hair in a bun, brush my teeth, and apply a quick coat of mascara. I grab a banana and fill my water jug, knowing I will be making and consuming a liter of coffee once I get to work to cope with my tiredness.

Stepping outside, my breath is at once taken away by the thick, muggy heat of Tennessee in the summer. I think humidity was invented to keep us humble. I would like to meet one person that looks good after two hours outside on a humid day. News flash, they don't exist.

I spot my car parked all the way at the outskirts of the parking lot. That's the problem with working late—by the time I get back to my apartment at 2:30 A.M., every nearby spot is taken by already snoozing residents.

Jogging over to my bright purple old Chrysler Sebring, I click the unlock button on my keychain three times, hearing nothing in response. Ugh, my battery must be dead again. I unlock my trunk and pull out my portable jump box. That's how often my battery drains—I had to buy a box to keep it alive.

Popping my hood, I hook up the cables and turn the box on, tapping my foot impatiently as sweat starts to form down my back. After waiting a few more seconds, I rub my steering wheel for good luck and talk to my car. "Come on, Barney, you've got this. I'm already late for work and I promise if you just turn on and drive, I will get you a new battery soon. The best battery I can find."

When I turn the key in the ignition this time, I let out a quick "yip" in relief when it starts. I hurry out of the car to close my hood and throw the jump box in my trunk.

Turning out of my complex, I begin to feel anxious, like I have every day lately. Tripp has been in charge this past month, and I feel like I'm walking on eggshells at work. A place that used to bring me solace and comfort feels like it's slipping away from me.

Whiskey Jane's was originally opened by a man named Seymour and his wife, Jane, who he loved more than anything. He always said that every kiss he shared with Jane was stronger than any whiskey ever made, hence the name of the bar.

They opened back in the late '70s with only a dream and each other. The bar became a local favorite on our side of town, and has been for over 50 years. Seymour passed away in 2003 from an unexpected heart attack and instead of closing the doors on her husband's livelihood, Jane continued to run the bar like the resilient woman she is.

When I turned eighteen, I was awkward, lanky, and

desperate for a job. I went down every strip of restaurants and bars I could think of in town. Eventually, I stumbled upon Whiskey Jane's and walked in. Jane stood behind the bar looking like a stylish mountain woman. Long untamed gray curls and large chunky teal earrings framed her sun-aged but gorgeous face. She looked like a backwoods Dolly Parton. She had beautiful silver rings on almost every finger and a fitted blue flannel that hugged her frame. I felt myself shrink in her presence and was intimidated immediately, even though she stood at half my height.

I self-consciously cleared my throat and then stepped towards her. I started giving her my pitch about why she should hire me and handed her my perfectly typed-up resume that I'd spent hours creating at the local library. She accepted the paper and waited for me to finish my spiel. Once I was done stumbling over the reasons why she should hire me with no experience, she smiled and crumpled up my resume, tossing it in the trash.

I stared at her open-mouthed, gaping like a fish, till she said, "Darlin', you're the first person I've had walk in here and apply for a job with a resume, while lookin' me in the eyes, in the past ten years. If you want a job, it's yours."

So that was it, I started the next day. That's where my bond and love for Jane began. She took me in as an awkward, inexperienced high school grad to fill ice bins and serve food. She transformed me into a confident bar manager. No to-go order goes without napkins on my watch. No Karen leaves pounding a negative review into her phone on Yelp. No piece of gum is found wedged under a table. I take my job very seriously and Jane's approval has always meant the world to me. She helped shape me into the strong woman I am today, after all.

The past few years at the bar have been the hardest I have

experienced. Four years ago, I started noticing that Jane would repeat herself multiple times during a shift. I originally thought this forgetfulness was just her age and being overwhelmed with the many tasks that there were to handle in a day. But her mental state continued to decline and after visits with a doctor, Alzheimer's was found as the cause.

There is nothing that can describe the pain of watching someone you spent years connecting with, slowly forget you. Every joke and experience you shared together is suddenly a one-sided memory. The past two years tumbled by with Jane slowing down and growing more agitated and confused until it got to the point that she could no longer drive or come to the bar. In the last months, Seymour and Jane's only son, Tripp, came here from New York to move Jane to a memory care facility since she is no longer able to care for herself day to day. He has never cared about the bar, and through the years, Jane always talked about how he would never visit them once he left town. So, when he walked in one day and told me he was coming back to Clairesville to run the bar, I was shocked.

Tripp started trying to make changes instantly at the bar. He said that it needed to have a "cleaner" and "refined" aesthetic to attract new customers.

To him, this means changing the charm and grit that created the bar. First, he told me there will be uniforms, which would have Jane in a *fit* if she saw them. Jane has always been about self-expression and always told staff to "come as they are" to work.

One time I showed up for a shift in a puffy, metallic blue '80s style prom dress that I found thrift shopping to play a prank on her. When Jane saw my outfit, she just shouted, "Hey! When did you raid my closet?! Now go over there and start marrying the ketchups." She didn't acknowledge my outfit again for the rest of my shift. The joke ended up on me because

I had to work the rest of my shift looking like a clown threw up on me. I must say, though, my tips were great that night.

Now Tripp has mentioned he wants to paint the bar and change up the interior, too. Whiskey Jane's has always had a tradition that you can draw and write on any wall in the bar. That means every inch is covered in things like scribbled drunken names, funny inside jokes from our regulars, and young hopeful couples marking their initials accompanied by the year in Sharpie hearts. The interior may be dated and lack beauty to someone like him, but to the locals that have come here for years and years, it feels like home.

Even as a child, Tripp hated spending time at the bar, Jane always mentioned to me. She said he resented it and hated having to spend time in a place that looked "poor" and run down growing up. He was always embarrassed by his parents' business. The day Tripp finished high school, he moved to New York, saying he needed to get out of this dump.

I could always hear the hurt in Jane's voice when she would talk to me about this. She always made excuses for Tripp, though, saying he was meant for bigger and better things than her and Seymour. Which is why I was extra shocked hearing that he had a sudden interest to move back and run the bar, now that Jane isn't able to. I have always been able to read people's intentions well, I think, and I know there must be an ulterior motive to his sudden interest in the well-being of the bar.

Pulling up in the bar parking lot with the mountain view I love so much, I see that Tripp's car is already here. I mutter, "Shit," to myself and quickly turn off my car. I am about to get a lecture for being late.

Checking myself in the mirror quickly, I realize that my mascara has smeared under my eyes from my battery jumping excursion, so I quickly wipe under them with my pointer fingers. Then I rush out of my car and give myself a pep talk. There is a bitter taste in my mouth, knowing I'm about to get chewed out by someone who just showed up here randomly and now acts like he knows what he's doing.

Opening the back door to the bar, I'm at once overtaken by the scent I've grown to love through the years. Real wood floors, French fries fresh out of the fryer, and a little bit of stale beer that lingers.

I see Rob, our cook, standing at the flat top getting ready to start some burgers. Rob is a six-foot-four beast of a man who started here as a bouncer back in the '90s, but quickly realized he was a teddy bear who couldn't handle sending people away. So, he trained to work in the kitchen and has been here ever since.

He turns to me in greeting, and I quickly put my finger over my lips in a "shhh" motion. He glances up at the clock and nods, then motions his eyes to the left indicating that Tripp is in the office. I thank him with an overdramatic sweeping bow and run past him to the right as he chuckles to himself.

Blasting through the kitchen door to the front of the bar, I see a few of our regulars are already munching on their sandwiches and burgers. I know then I'm in the clear. Rob must have taken their orders for me. I will have to run to The Mart across the street later to grab him a giant pack of Nerds Clusters as thanks.

Our locals would never complain to Tripp if their orders hadn't been taken. They would just sit at the bar, chat, and help themselves to the soda gun until I arrived. If he came out front and saw anyone empty-handed in the bar, he would only see dollar signs down the drain. The last thing I want is to get chewed out by Tripp and his never-disappearing coffee breath.

Thinking of coffee, I head to the pot on the burner behind the bar and pour myself a giant cup. After two big gulps of

18

what I realize is probably last night's stale coffee, I gag a little and set the cup down. I turn and grab my black half apron and tie it around my waist. Two of our regulars, Johnny and Rick, sit at the bar and give me a knowing glance.

"Rough night?" Rick asks. If you took Danny Devito and stretched him about six inches taller, that would be Rick. He has the compassion and warm smile that you would expect out of a Hallmark card, and I can always count on him to read me well.

"Probably partying after her shift like always. You know how crazy Olive gets. I heard the police were on the lookout for a streaker last night matching her description," Johnny teases, leaning in closer to me across the bar. "Where were you at four A.M., Missy?"

Where I can expect a sentimental moment and hug from Rick, I can also expect a dad joke and goof from Johnny. Just looking at Johnny, he's a character. Every single day he wears a black top hat. Seriously, every day since he started coming to this bar back in the '80s, a top hat has been on his head. I have no idea what's going on underneath that hat. It could be hair, no hair, or maybe even a rat controlling his arm movements. I asked him to see once, and Johnny's response was, "I am nothing without this hat and you can pry it off my dead body before I show you. *But* even then, you won't be able to see because I will super glue it to my head right before I die."

Today he's wearing a piano key tie, along with the top hat. A bold choice.

"HA-HA-HA, I've never heard that one from you before," I deadpan as I turn around and start stacking glasses. After a few minutes, I continue talking. "I had another rough night after a certain toxic boyfriend decided to sleep around again."

Rick shakes his head and tsks. "I will never understand why

someone like Ivy, who has everything going for her, chooses to date someone like Dennis."

"Women enjoy a-holes. That's why I had so many girlfriends back in the day," Johnny says. "Still do."

"Oh, please. You haven't had a girlfriend since 2006. What was her name? Debbie?" Rick asks.

"Doobie, and since I'm a distinguished gentleman," Johnny replies, while he motions to his top hat, "I don't kiss and tell, which is why you know nothing about my nightly encounters with my lady friends."

I turn around and look at Johnny. "Wait, what did you just say her name was?"

"Doobie." He responds with a blink like it's the most normal name in the world. "She owned a secret marijuana farm a couple miles up in the mountains."

"Wow," I say, trying to hold in my smile. "And whatever happened to Doobie?"

Johnny scratches his mustache. "She got arrested for embezzling checks and went to jail for a year. Asked me to take care of the farm while she was in the slammer and I accidentally burned it down one night when I had a bonfire next to her plants. She never spoke to me again after that."

Rick looks over at him, shocked. "Why would you have a bonfire right next to her plants?"

"I thought they were cold and needed some heat," Johnny responds, looking down full of sorrow. "I didn't even get to smoke them. Those poor little buds."

Rick and I share the look we do many times a shift hearing these stories. I never know what to expect from Johnny, but I always know his stories will make me snort or cause my jaw to drop. Rick and his wife separated years ago, so he spends most his time at the bar, and Johnny has never married but does have a daughter in her thirties now. I can expect to see these two almost every single time I come to work and that always makes me feel better.

I cut around the corner of the bar with a tray full of lemons and slam into Tripp, who's looking down at his phone while walking through the metal kitchen door. I let out a shriek as we collide and the lemons spill all over the floor.

Trip gives me a onceover and lets out an exasperated sigh. "Olive, I can see you're behind on your duties," he claims, looking down at the uncut lemons on the floor in disgust. "Yup, Tripp," I respond, "got caught up talking with the guys, sorry."

He looks over my shoulder at Rick and Johnny, who give him overly friendly smiles. They can't stand him, either. We are three gossips when he's not around.

I bend down and start to retrieve all the lemons. "I will be done cutting these in two minutes. Just got to go rinse them off now," I add, unable to keep some annoyance from my tone. "You know I have worked here for nine years now. Not to mention, I had been running this place on my own while your mom is sick. I can handle it. You don't need to micromanage me."

Tripp looks shocked by my blunt response and it takes everything in me not to stare at the balding shiny patch on the top of his head. He is only three years older than me and going bald? I have a theory that it's because he's so evil. Tripp is so horrible that even his hairline doesn't want to stick around.

Tripp steps closer to me causing me to retreat and knock my back into the bar.

"I don't care who you think you are or what you used to do here. I am in charge now. That's my mother's name on the sign." He points towards the front door. "I will be the one that calls the shots, always." He straightens his tie. "Also, you have a stain on your uniform. Don't let it happen again." He motions to my stuffy button-down shirt and then walks off. I look down at the stupid bow tie, suspenders, and white blouse that is now my uniform and groan at the big dirt stain from opening my car's hood.

Thanks to Tripp, I now spend every shift looking like a hipster from 2012 that just discovered her first handlebar mustache and banjo. I need to remember to do laundry next time I have a day off.

Chapter 4

Hunter

P ulling up to my house, I see a black Camry with smashed glass in my driveway with an "FBI: Female Body Inspector" sticker on the bumper. I guess Dennis came straight over here after I texted him my address.

I drive through my grass around his car and park in front of the big maple tree to the left of my house. Mentally preparing myself to be surrounded in all of his douche glory, I sit in my car for a minute and stare at the tree until I hear a knock on my window. Turning to look, I see Dennis's pale, hairy butt plastered up my window. He laughs like a hyena.

The second I got off the phone with him, I was already regretting letting him stay here, but I wanted to give him a chance. It took about .001 seconds of him being here to remind me of how much I can't stand him.

"Dude, get your hairy crack off my window," I say, shoving my car door open. He falls back, still cackling, and quickly jumps around while pulling his pants back up in one motion. "HUUUUUNNNNTTTER!" he yells out my name like an announcer at a baseball game and yanks me into a bear hug. I clap him on the back twice and maneuver out of his hold.

"Remember this is only for a few days," I tell him. "I am leaving on Friday, so you better have your stuff figured out by then."

He nods like his life depends on it. "No problem, man. My girl and I will be gravy by then. Just a little hiccup. A little bump in the road, you know what I'm saying."

"No. I don't," I respond, grabbing my equipment out of my back seat and heading towards my house. "I keep my place clean, so please don't disrespect my house while you're here. Dishes in the dishwasher, trash in the can, and for the love of god, flush the toilet," I say, looking back at him.

Last time he stayed with me, he thought it was funny to randomly leave what he called a "floater" in the toilet for me to find. Like I said, the guy is a douche, but I have given him one too many chances in life because I know the person he used to be. I always hope that he will wake up one day and shed his unruly behavior like a skin and act like a functioning adult.

"The whole YouTube thing must really be working out for you, bro. Look at this place!" he says, looking at my house in awe.

I look up at my home as well and feel a little pride well up inside. I worked really hard for this house. Many people think I just uploaded a few clips to the internet and made money instantly, but I had to consistently work with pro skaters and brands to grow my name to what it is now in the industry. For every filming gig I got offered, there were twenty I applied for that shot me down. I was motivated to make something out of my passion, and I sacrificed family holidays and milestones to travel with the pros for work. To prove myself worthy. Looking back, if I knew my dad was going to get sick, I would have spent that time differently, but I was a young guy with stars in his eyes and I didn't understand how fleeting time with family can be back then.

This house was my first big purchase. I used to always drive by it with my parents on the way to our house as a child and I loved how different it looked. The house is a dark wood A-frame cabin that has one side of giant windows that opens up to the forest behind. The front door is a weaving pattern of stained-glass flowers that connect at the bottom and the front yard has a full garden. There is truly nothing like this house in Clairesville and when the previous owner passed away, I knew I had to make it mine.

I unlock the front door and I'm immediately greeted by my little black Bombay cat named Dog. I bend down and give her a scratch behind her ears, and she purrs, rubbing herself against my ankle. Dennis clobbers in the door behind me and closes it with a thud, causing all the hair on her back to stand up before she runs off. *Good intuition, Dog, I wish I could run, too.*

I walk into my kitchen and set my bag on the island. Turning towards the cabinets, I ask Dennis, "Need any water or a snack?"

"Nope. Just had a burrito at Nacho Bay."

"Weren't they just busted by the health inspectors last week for multiple cases of food poisoning?" I ask.

"Yeah! I've been eating there almost every day since. If I get food poisoning there, I can sue and then I won't have to work for years. Work smarter, not harder, my friend," he responds, touching his temple, like it's the most obvious thing in the world.

I place my fingers between my eyes and pinch the bridge of my nose. "Alright, man. I'm headed upstairs. The guest room is off to the left. You have your own bathroom in there and the towels are under the sink."

I unzip my bag and grab my camera. He nods as I head out of the kitchen.

Taking my stairs two at a time, I jog upstairs to the master bedroom. Once I'm in my room, I close my door and quickly change out of my clothes into some baggy gray sweats to work out.

I was always an active skater kid growing up and was in shape, but never muscular. As an adult, I needed the endorphins from working out to keep my mental health in check after losing my father. Every time I lift weights or do cardio, I feel the tension and stress from work and everyday life leave my body like steam rolling off me.

I installed a home gym in my basement when I moved in. Since I travel often for work, there's no point getting a gym membership. I also have a crazy case of insomnia, so instead of sitting alone with my thoughts in the dark at 4 A.M., I work out.

I grab my camera and hook it up to my laptop so the footage of Wes from today can upload. Then I head back downstairs and beeline past the kitchen, where I hear Dennis snooping through my drawers, going to the basement.

When I get down there and click on the light, I feel like I'm in my safe space. The walls are covered with photos from my favorite moments with pro skaters and I have a wooden shelf full of my dad's collectibles and old records.

Walking over to one of the little model cars on the middle shelf, I brush some dust off the top. "I promise I'll shine you guys up soon," I say, looking over the pieces of metal that hold way more memories than value.

The loss of my father never gets easier. Some days the sadness feels smaller, and I think, "Hey, I'm coping pretty well now." And then the next day the loss will wash over me, consume me, and take all of the progress I thought I made with it.

Glancing at the clock, I get ready to start my thirty-minute warm-up on the treadmill and head to my speakers. *What will it be today*, I think to myself as I scroll through my playlists. The Strokes? King Diamond? No, I find the artist I'm looking for and smile. The sound of Cher singing begins to blast through my sound system.

Real men listen to Cher.

Chapter 5

Olive

"Crap," I say, slamming my trunk in the bar parking lot, realizing that I forgot my mask for tonight's themed karaoke night. Jane and Seymour always loved singing together so back in the '90s they started a weekly karaoke night with some kind of crazy theme that the regulars would go all out for. The theme all summer long was Mask or Task. If you didn't wear a mask, you would end up on stage having to do some ridiculous request that one of the regulars wrote on a piece of paper in the "Task" bucket that hung on the wall by the jukebox. The entire year, the bar patrons would laugh as they wrote something on a sheet of paper and threw it in the bucket, preparing for the summer. Some of them were *really bad*. I was not taking any chances.

This was one of Jane's favorite themes and she would always tell me how she got everyone to lie to Seymour about what day it was so he would be the only one without a mask and end up on the bar stage doing something ridiculous. Her eyes would twinkle as she laughed and described to me the time that he had to do jumping jacks and sing "Amazing

Grace" simultaneously. Or when he had to recite the Gettysburg Address from a piece of paper while wearing a pink thong and bra on top of his clothes. He was always a good sport about it, Jane would tell me, deep in her nostalgia.

I usually always kept a Halloween mask in my trunk. But last week, I sat it down on the bar at the end of the night and a drunk girl grabbed it and kept shoving it in her best friend's face telling her to "make out with Mike" and then I never saw the mask again. Imagine being so drunk you steal a Halloween mask and then the next day, you wake up with that on your floor. In *July*. I would pay to know what she was thinking that morning.

I check the clock on my phone and decide to run over to The Mart, which is across the street, since there is a lull in business at this time of day. Tripp left at 2 P.M. saying that he had a dentist appointment to "check his night guard," whatever that means. He also told me that he can't stand the theme nights and everyone's "drunken charades," so he won't be returning after. Thank god.

Crossing the street and stepping inside The Mart, a store I know like the back of my hand, I'm greeted with an ice-cold blast of AC. I wave to Mr. Ray at the counter as I head to the candy aisle to grab Rob his "thank you" Nerds.

"I'm having a mask crisis!" I shout over my shoulder.

"No more Mike Myers?" Mr. Ray responds.

"He was taken from me. RIP Mike, you saved me from many horrible tasks, and I will always remember you," I say playfully, putting my hand over my heart.

"Well, I don't know what you're going to find here to use, unless you're going to cover your face in Band-Aids and pretzels."

"Hmm Band-Aids...that's not a bad idea, actually. But so painful, right?"

"Depends how bad you want to get out of the dreaded *tasks*," he chuckles, opening his eyes wide for emphasis.

I keep scanning each aisle and say, "AH HA!" when I see a large box of cereal.

I proudly walk it up to the counter and Mr. Ray gives me a quizzical look as he scans my items. "Don't doubt my crafting abilities." I wiggle my finger at him. "I have an idea."

He puts his hands up in surrender. "Okay, okay, I believe you. Give this to Rob for me please," he says, reaching under the counter and tossing a small bottle of fresh honey into my hands. Mr. Ray's wife, Sonjia, has a bee farm in their yard, and she always gives Rob honey because he makes them takeout once a week, his treat. Rob doesn't expect anything in return and just likes cooking for them, but she always wants to show her thanks.

"You've got it, boss," I say, giving the cereal box a shake and heading out the door.

As soon as I get back to the bar, I go to the kitchen and find Rob reading while leaning against the grill.

"Honey. Candy," I say, and sit them down next to him on the prep station.

He looks up from his book and gives me a wide smile. "It was nice doing business with you," he states, grabbing the Nerds, then ripping the top open and shaking the bag into his mouth.

"Thank you for covering for me this morning." I lean against the opposite counter. "It was another long night with Ivy."

Rob gives me an understanding look. "You're a good friend to her. She will thank you one day for always being her shoulder to cry on."

I sigh. "I just want to shake her and tell her to *wake up*. I feel like she's under some spell and I hate the way he makes her view herself. I don't get it. I would never put myself in a position like that and I don't know why she allows him to hurt her. Repeatedly."

"Well, first off, you know everyone thinks differently. She is not you. People also give their partner too many chances sometimes when they think they have found love, even an unhealthy type of love. You also know that I stayed in a marriage way longer than I should have," Rob says. "The relationship was toxic and extremely painful for years. I spent many nights on the couch, looking up at the ceiling and wondering, 'Is this really what my life is supposed to be like?' but I felt trapped, and I thought she would change. So, I just stayed. When we finally decided to separate, I was so negative through the divorce and thought I couldn't go on. I was sure I would never open myself up to dating again. I closed myself off from any possible romantic connections."

"But then you met Missy." I nod, knowing where this story is going. Missy is Rob's wife. They met six years ago, when she applied to work at the bar as an extra bartender. She still fills in a few times a week so I can have a day off here and there, but she works as a librarian most days now.

"Right, then I met Missy. And I realized that I was just going through a bad season of life before. It's an amazing feeling to be in love. To have a best friend that's also your partner," Rob continues. "I'm sure Ivy yearns for that. Just because she is in the wrong relationship right now, it doesn't mean she will always be in it. Give her time and she will figure it out. Don't worry, you will get your friend back."

"Yeah, I know," I agree with him. "I know she's still in there."

Rob smirks. "And what I'm also trying to tell you is just

31

because you have seen bad relationships around you like Ivy's and your own parents, that doesn't mean you are guaranteed to have a bad relationship, too, if you give dating a chance." He slides a basket of fries towards me.

I roll my eyes. "Yeah, yeah. I've heard it all before from you," I say, swiping a fry from the basket and cramming it in my mouth as I walk through the kitchen door.

Everyone in my life wants me to find someone. I don't tell them that I never plan to.

Chapter 6

Hunter

I glance up from editing on my laptop at the sound of my phone buzzing. Wes's name, with the photo of him jumping off my roof on his skateboard, flashes across my screen. I pick up and answer the call. Instantly I hear bass thudding through the speakers on the other side, along with some garbled speech.

"Turn your music down," I say into the phone.

"What?" Wes asks. Drums and bass still blast in the background.

"TURN YOUR MUSIC DOWN!" I shout.

Suddenly there's silence on the other end. "Sorry, man," Wes chuckles. "My bad. I just picked up Eddie and we are headed to get you."

Shit, I think as I look over at my clock. I completely forgot I told him I would possibly come out with them tonight. To Wes, that means yes.

I shut my laptop and put my phone on speaker as I open my closet. "Where are we going tonight?" I ask.

"Just to a bar on the other side of town, a dive bar I found when I was searching for karaoke spots."

"And why were you searching for karaoke spots?" I question. The introvert in me wants to cancel already.

"Because I want to belt out some Creed for my birthday. Is that too much to ask? I'm twenty-nine now, and I've got to start acting like a responsible adult," Eddie says, jumping into the conversation. Knowing this is what he wants to do for his birthday, I can't back out now.

"Happy birthday, man," I tell him. "How much time do I have till you guys get here?"

Wes responds, "In three...two..."

I hear the click of the call hangup and the sound of "Pound Town" by Skream growing louder outside. Okay then, I guess they are here.

I grab a dark green snapback out of the top bin of my closet and toss a black T-shirt on. Pushing my unruly curls out of my eyes, I slide my hat on and grab my keys and phone. Running down the steps, I shout to Dennis that I'm leaving and hear a grunt from the guest room in response. I don't want to know what he's doing in there.

Dog waits for me at the door and I bend down to her level. "I'll be back, girl," I say, rubbing between her ears. She tries to tangle herself between my legs in protest and I give her one last scratch before standing up and walking out.

When I get outside, I see Eddie hanging out the top of Wes's jeep as the music still blasts. "I'm twenty-nine, bitches!" he screams, and shotguns a beer. Of course, he does this as my sweet old neighbor Mrs. Bodart walks by with her Shih Tzu, Pebbles.

I hold up my hand in an apology wave and give her a smile. "Lovely night we're having, Mrs. Bodart," I shout over the song. She just gives a look and walks on, much quicker this time.

I quickly hop into the back of the jeep before they can embarrass me any further. "Turn that shit down," I say.

"Sorry, dude." Wes turns down the music and looks at me through the rearview mirror. "Eddie did a little pre-gaming before."

"I can tell," I shout as we pull out of the driveway.

Eddie turns around to face me from the passenger seat. "I'm drunk because it's my birthday. Also, I'm having a midlife crisis," Eddie tells me, and then faces forward again. He puts his feet up on Wes's dashboard and Wes pushes them back to the floor.

"Feet off the dash. Also, you're twenty-nine, not forty," Wes says. "And you have accomplished more in twenty-nine years than most people ever have in their lives."

I nod my head in agreement. It's true. Eddie was a star college soccer player and then decided he wanted to give it all up one day to start his own app. One night he was sitting in his dorm room and couldn't find a show to watch while he ate his meal, so he just sat there scrolling through a million options and streaming services while his food got cold. That's when the idea struck him. He started an app that tells you what show or movie you should watch based on what you're eating, and it actually became wildly successful. Who knew people just wanted someone to tell them what to watch while they eat? The world is easier when we can just shut off our brains sometimes and enjoy a good bowl of pasta while watching *Breaking Bad*.

The app is called Watch What You Eat. So basically, Eddie is an immense success compared to most people, and his existential crisis is unnecessary. I think most adults feel that way every time their birthday comes around, though. I know I have gotten the birthday blues before, too.

The sun begins setting behind us as we drive around the

winding mountains to the other side of Clairesville. The wind is blasting us as we speed around each turn and I'm unsure how Wes is even able to drive with his long, blond hair whipping around his face. Girls have always loved Wes; back in high school they called him a Greek god.

He has never lacked in the dating department, and he's definitely the most outgoing of the three of us. I wouldn't even call what he does dating. More like dialing any woman's number out of his phone and having a hookup. He is always trying to convince me to go out with him to the bars and have casual hookups, but I just can't do it. I need to feel invested in someone to get to a place of intimacy with them. Eddie and Wes both give me a hard time about that.

"I'm starving. Let's grab something on the way," Wes shouts over the wind.

"Let the birthday boy pick," I respond.

Eddie looks up from his phone where he's suddenly in work mode, texting an employee about marketing. Even drunk he is still a boss, but thank god for autocorrect. "Obviously I want Bricks."

Wes nods. "Bricks it is, captain."

Bricks is a pizza spot that we have been going to since we were all fourteen. We used to skate around and find quarters on the ground to grab some one-dollar cheese pizza slices there every day after school. Looking back, those were some of the best times. Even Dennis used to come with us every once in a while. The guys agree that he used to be pretty cool back in the day. His dad's lack of fathering just really did a number on him. While we grew up with structure, he grew up with chaos.

Wes parks the Jeep in front of Bricks, and we all jump out and head inside the metal warehouse door that takes to you the front counter. Before it was a restaurant, it used to be an airplane hangar, so the inside of Bricks is huge. Bands perform shows here all the time after closing since the space is so large; it can get pretty wild. Wes hung from a ceiling rafter during a punk show once, fell, and broke his ankle. The owner, Brick Wrigley, was furious even though Wes promised not to sue. He was unable to skate for months.

"You guys go get us a table and I'll order," I tell the guys, making my way up to the counter.

Brick Wrigley's daughter, Savannah, stands at the register and gives me a huge smile when she sees me. The guys have always said she has a big crush on me, but I just haven't felt any interest in asking her out. Don't get me wrong, she is beautiful. She's blonde and has ocean blue eyes and an enthusiastic sense of humor. But I'm not going to waste a woman's time if I'm not invested in getting to know her. My dad always taught me to be a man of good intentions, and I stand by that, always.

"Hi, Hunter," Savannah says, looking up at me through her lashes. "I like your hair today."

I reach up and touch my hat. "Oh yeah, thanks. A hat is the only way to keep it under control."

"I love it. There's something about a man in a hat that really gets me..." She trails off, staring at me. After we stand in silence for an uncomfortable few seconds, I clear my throat. She snaps out of her trance and looks embarrassed.

I try to save the awkward moment and give her a sincere smile. "Hey, thanks, that's kind of you to say." I quickly change the subject. "Can I get six slices of pepperoni and three beers for the guys and I, please? We are in kind of a rush, hitting a karaoke night for Eddie's birthday."

She tucks her hair behind an ear and recovers. "OMG, sorry. Yes, of course! I'll put it in right now." She punches our order into the register and adds, "Tell Eddie I said happy birthday!"

"Will do. Thanks, Savannah," I say, as I hand her my card to pay.

She swipes it, gives me my receipt, and then pops into the kitchen with our ticket like someone just lit a fire under her. That thankfully puts an end to the awkward exchange.

When I get to the table, I can see the guys cackling, looking at me.

"Do I hear wedding bells in the future?" Wes teases.

"Dude, you're so red right now," Eddie chimes in.

I run my hands over my face. "Stop. I don't want to make her feel bad," I say, glancing back towards the counter to make sure she's not in earshot.

"I don't see why you just don't give her a chance," Wes says. "She's super-hot. I would go there."

"You already have." Eddie laughs.

Wes looks confused. "Have I?"

"Yes, you have," I tell him. Wes looks perplexed as I turn to Eddie and continue, "So what's the name of the place that we are going to?"

"Whiskey Jane's," Eddie responds. "It looks like kind of a shithole but those are always the best bars."

We quickly eat our pizza slices, chug our beers, and walk to the door to head out. I can feel Savannah staring at me from the register, so I turn and give her a quick wave goodbye before pushing the door open. Her eyes widen as I acknowledge her, and she gives me an overenthusiastic wave back. *Shit.*

It's now dark out and there are lightning bugs floating around in the Tennessee summer. I smile to myself, thinking of all the times I would catch them in my hands with my parents as a kid and pretend like I had magic. My mom still lives down the street from me in the house that I grew up in. I love being near her so I can be there to help since dad passed, but it always feels bittersweet going to my childhood home. I'm thankful for the memories it still holds, but I also feel like something is completely missing, being there without him.

I feel a thud on my back and turn to see Wes standing to my right. "Let's go, brother," he says, before heading towards his Jeep.

He knows I was lost in my thoughts and understands how the loss of my father has taken a part of me that I will never recover from. Since I am an only child, Wes and Eddie have always been like my siblings. They literally picked me up off the floor after losing my father and sat with me as I wept. We bust each other's balls and joke around, but at the end of the day we have each other's backs.

Eddie runs past me and yells, *"Shotgun!"* Like I even care about having to sit in the back seat. I laugh and hoist myself over the side of the Jeep and fall back into my seat as Wes peels out of the parking lot.

Not even ten minutes later, we pull up to a small bar with muffled music blasting from inside. There's a flashing sign hanging from an old pole that says Whiskey Jane's. A few of the letters flicker on and off; the place definitely needs some fixing up. Once Wes parks, we all get out of the Jeep. Walking up, I can see some of the wood is eroding on the building and the paint is chipping off on the front door.

"This place must have been here for a while," I say, as Wes takes the lead and pulls open the door.

As soon as he opens it, I notice two things. The first is that there is writing in every color you can think of on all the walls inside of the bar, and the second is that every single person inside is wearing a mask of some sort. Suddenly, everyone looks over at us and cheers.

Chapter 7

Olive

I'm bent over filling up the ice bucket when I hear everyone cheer at once. *What the hell?* I stand up and follow the patrons' line of sight to the door where I see three guys standing like deer caught in headlights. Johnny starts chanting, *"Task, task, task,"* and soon the whole bar has joined in. These poor guys have no idea what's going on. They probably think they just walked into a cult.

Rick gives a look around the bar and tells everyone to pipe down. I laugh to myself as I watch the guys walk in, confused as ever.

After speaking to each other in a huddle momentarily, a tall blond one with tattoos on his arms walks up to me at the bar.

He clears his throat, "Hey...Fruity O's?" he says, while motioning to the box on my face. For my last-minute DIY mask, I cut the cereal box in half and made eye holes and a mouth hole, finishing it off by tying some string around the back to keep it on my face. So needless to say, I look hot.

"That's Miss Fruity O's to you," I tease. "What can I get for you?" I gesture to all the bottles lining the bar.

40

The blond guy who looks like he was carved on Mount Olympus laughs. "Okay well first, are we allowed to be here or is this a private event?" He looks around at the bar guests, his eyes visibly confused. "What the hell is this?"

At that I laugh with him, knowing how insane we all must look. There hadn't been a single patron all night without a mask on before they showed up. Our regulars have been dying for someone to come in the door sans mask—which is why the aggressive cheering and chanting happened at their arrival.

"This is Mask or Task night at the bar. Basically, since you're not wearing a mask, you must draw a task out of that bucket over there," I say, and point in its direction.

He looks over at the blue bucket on the wall, full of papers, and turns back to me. "So, this isn't a karaoke night? That's why we came here, for my buddy's birthday."

"Oh, it's a karaoke night. We get wild. But first, you all must prove yourselves worthy to partake. This is the way," I say, mock seriousness in my expression, while gesturing back to the bucket.

He lights up. "I'm so in. This actually sounds fun." He looks over at his two friends standing together and then says, "Can I get six shots of Jameson first? One of my friends is a little shy."

I nod and pour them. Then I slide them in his direction and say, "Good luck."

He gives me a wink as he hands me a fifty-dollar bill and then walks off with the shots.

Before they can even take their first sip, Johnny, wearing a Ghost Face mask and of course, his top hat, goes over and introduces himself. I see the tallest guy, with tan skin and buzzed black hair shake his head and laugh at something Johnny has said. He's got to be at least six-foot-six; the guy towers over everyone else. Johnny looks up at him and makes a comment

41

that has all the men smiling now. He could make friends with a shoe; that's one of the things I love about him.

Slapping the guys on their backs one at a time, Johnny points to the stage and then to the bucket again. The blond guy downs both his shots and pretends to crack his neck. Then he walks over, digs his hand around the bin, and pulls out a slip of paper. You could hear a pin drop. He opens it and lets out a hardy laugh after reading the paper.

"Tell us what it says," a lady at a high-top shouts out.

Giving her a dazzling smile, he says, "Well, it looks like I will be giving a lucky lady who volunteers a lap dance tonight on stage. It also says the song is 'bartender's choice.'"

The regulars cheer and everyone turns towards me. I give a thumbs-up in response, knowing exactly what song I'm going to choose, and head over to the jukebox. The blond guy pushes his hair out of his eyes and yells, "Any volunteers to sit in the chair?"

Half of the hands shoot up in the bar and I laugh when I see Johnny has also raised his hand. I turn to the jukebox and shuffle the selection until I find the song I want. Then I punch in the number and wait. "Hocus Pocus" by the band Focus begins to blast out through the bar speakers and one of the three guys, the one with curly brown hair, lets out a laugh. *A man of good taste*, I think.

The blond guy takes Mrs. Frett's hand, a seventy-year-old widow who always wears cheetah print, and carefully leads her to the stage. Loud rock music blasts as he guides her to a chair on stage and he bobs his head, looking overly confident. He grabs the front of his tank top and begins to rip it in half just as yodeling plays through the speakers. He gives his friends a confused *what the fuck* look, but then shrugs after a moment and finishes yanking his tank in half. He flexes and throws the ripped tank into the crowd; someone cheers when they catch it.

He dramatically turns back, fully committing to the routine, and drops down on Mrs. Frett, grinding on her. She smiles as he quickly turns around and shakes his butt towards her face. She playfully spanks him while laughing and saying, "Look at that tush!"

No one in the bar can hold back their laughter at this point and I honestly have never seen her happier. After multiple minutes of dancing around like his rent is due, I put him out of his misery.

"Okay, this song is seven minutes long. You've paid your dues. You're done!" I yell out and begin clapping. He bows and gently walks Mrs. Frett back to her seat as the bar erupts in cheers. He joins his friends once more and the tallest of the three guys claps him on the back and says, "I'll go next."

Walking up to the bucket, he shuffles his hand around inside and pulls out a crumpled sheet. As he reads the paper, I can see his face fall. "Hell no," he says, and hands the paper to his blond friend.

The blond reads it and lets out a bark of a laugh, then says aloud, "Drink a shot of whatever liquid is in the bar mat."

The bar is full of *"ewwws"* and laughter. My stomach churns just thinking about it.

Mike Layner, wearing a ski mask, proudly stands up and says, "I wrote that one down!"

The tall guy shoots him a look. "Thanks, man," he says sarcastically. "It's my birthday today."

Hearing that, Rick, in a fox mask, pushes back from the bar and stands up. "I will do it for him."

Everyone turns and looks at him.

"I can't let you do that," the tall guy says.

Mike Layner pipes up again, "Well, someone's got to do it! It's a task."

I peer at Mike through my cereal box. "Oh shut up and sit down, Mike. Unless you're gonna take one for the team," I say.

At that he quickly sits back down. The tall guy runs his hands over his buzzed head and then rubs the side of his face, thinking.

"How about we do it together. Half and half?" he asks Rick.

Rick smiles back. "Great idea, son. What's your name?"

"Eddie."

"Eddie, I'm Rick." He reaches out to shake his hand and then looks over at me and nods.

I stare down at the bar before I pick it up, trying to think of every drink I've poured tonight as I turn it sideways into two glasses. Muddy looking liquid swirls in the two cups and the men step forward, together. The bar is completely silent. Why is this one of the most dramatic things I've ever witnessed?

"Cheers," Eddie says, holding his glass out to Rick's. They clink them together and throw the drinks back in unison. Both men make a sound, and Rick chokes out a cough.

"*Wheewwwwww*," Eddie shouts as he slams his glass back down on the counter and wipes his mouth. "You guys better have some Creed on karaoke to make up for that shit."

Laughing, Johnny walks over and reassures him that this bar has many nights of Creed serenades. Eddie smiles, falling into conversation with him once more. Everyone begins to turn back to their friends, the bar filling up with voices again.

Suddenly, someone yells from the other side of the bar, "There's one more guy!"

I turn to see the final guy with brown hair standing in the corner by the bar exit. His eyes are as wide as saucers when he realizes that everyone's attention turns to him.

Chapter 8

Hunter

Allll eyes are on me. This is literally my worst nightmare. I decided to step out of my comfort zone tonight, to be a good friend to Eddie and celebrate his birthday with him. Now look at where it's got me. I have a bunch of faceless, mask-wearing people glaring at me expectantly. I can't back out at this point; Wes has stripped for an old cougar and Eddie just drank mystery slush. As much as I would love to bail, I can't do that to my friends.

Giving myself a quick pep talk about how I never have to see any of these people again, I walk over to the bucket of papers and pull one off the top. *Perform a random talent on stage that no one knows you have,* the crumpled sheet says. *Great.*

"What does it say, kid?" the mouthy guy that was heckling Eddie shouts at me.

"It says I have to do a secret talent on stage," I tell the crowd.

The bartender—the talking box of fruit cereal, who is also wearing a bow tie—yells out, "Ooo! I put that one in!"

45

I give her a quick glance in acknowledgment and rub my hands together, trying to shake off my anxiety. The crowd parts as I head up to the stage, telling myself I might as well get this over with.

I step up and stand on the sticky platform and walk to the mic. I'm assuming this is where they do the karaoke if we ever make it to that point. I take a breath and lean in towards the microphone. It makes a sudden, horrible screeching sound that causes half of the crowd to cover their ears.

Clearing my throat I say, "Uh, sorry about that, folks. I, uh, my talent is..." I search for Wes and Eddie in the crowd and see them nod at me reassuringly. "I'm really good at balancing stuff on my head."

Crickets.

I continue, "I can balance a stack of books or a drink if you guys give it to me. I can basically balance anything."

The woman behind the bar snorts out a laugh. "*Prove it!*"

I give her a small smile. "I just need an object."

A man with a Batman mask near the stage hops up from his booth and hands me his beer can. "Balance this," he grunts out.

I look at him. "Done."

I take off my snapback and place the beer on my head. I take a few steps back and forth to show it's not going anywhere. The crowd lets out a cheer as I hand his drink back to him.

"Try this!" An older lady, adorned with a Betty Boop disguise, walks over and hands me an 8-ball she took off the pool table.

I grin back at her. "Easy peasy." This time I run in place with the ball on my head. Everyone *ooohhs* and *ahhhhs*.

I am starting to enjoy myself when the bartender lets out a

dramatic fake yawn and says, "That's light work. Show me something impressive."

She crosses her arms and although I can't see her expression under the box, I can assume it's a smirk. She's taunting me and I'm enjoying it.

"Damn, Fruity O's. Okay," I say in response, giving her a playful look. "Someone hand me that bar stool."

"Hell yeah!" Wes says, laughing, and Eddie has already gotten out his phone to never let me live this moment down.

The bartender walks from behind the bar, arms still crossed, and grabs a stool. She then walks it up to me and I bend down to grab it.

I flip the wooden stool upside down and place it on my head, starting to balance it. Everyone watching begins to count, "One...two...three..."

I'm starting to feel extremely confident by the time I hit thirty seconds. The crowd is hooting and hollering their approval. The idiot in me decides to take it up a notch and I start squatting up and down while still balancing the stool. Everyone goes wild and I hear the bartender laughing. It's an adorable belly laugh, and I tilt my head down a little bit to try and look at her out of the corner of my eye.

That's where I make my mistake. When I tilt my head, drawn in by her laugh, the stool falls off my head. Faster than I can grab it, it smacks into the bartender watching below, face first.

Chapter 9

Olive

"**F**uck!*" I yell out as I get smacked in the face with the wooden bar stool. I bend down and rip off my mask, grabbing my nose. I feel people begin to crowd around me as blood starts to drip through my fingers. I hear someone yell out for a napkin with urgency.

Okay, I'm bleeding. Badly. I see red drops hit the sticky bar floor. I don't do well with blood. *You're going to be okay*, I try to convince myself as someone pushes a wad of paper towels into my bunched-up hands. I throw out a general, "I'm okay! It's fine, I'm fine," to everyone around me and lift my head up. The regulars are looking at me in horror, so I smile while pinching the bridge of my nose, trying to reassure them that I am okay.

At that exact moment, I see the man from the stage before me holding out more paper towels and apologizing profusely. I couldn't get a good look at him before with my cardboard mask on, but he's hot. So hot. He looks just like Diego Boneta with long curls and facial hair. I continue to force a smile and start to tell him something along the lines of, "It's okay."

I glance behind him and do a double take when I see myself in the mirror on the wall. Blood is dripping from my nose into my smiling mouth and down the front of my white button-down.

Promptly, I faint.

Chapter 10

Hunter

Oh my god. I just saw the most beautiful woman I've ever seen in my life and now she's lying on the ground unconscious because I gravely injured her. She looks like Snow White with fair skin, dark hair, and full, red lips. But unlike Snow White, I'm not going to bend down and kiss an unconscious woman I just met. Whoever thought that was a promising idea for a children's story?

I quickly kneel next to her, alongside many other bar patrons.

One of them puts a cold beer on her forehead and the older man in the fox mask touches her arm gently saying, "Olive, Olive."

I keep looking around at everyone while apologizing. I couldn't feel worse right now, as a big mammoth of a man comes out of what I assume is the kitchen. He bends down next to her just as she begins to wake. As her eyes blink open, she glances up at him looking completely confused and dazed. He helps her sit up.

"You good, Olive?" the burly guy asks.

50

She nods a little while feeling around her face and wincing when she gets to her nose. Her gaze then shoots over to her right, and she's looking me directly in the eyes.

"You," she says.

"I am so, so sorry," I begin to say. "Please let me know what you need. I can drive you to the hospital right now. I will pay any medical bills. I am so sorry. I'm an idiot."

I stutter over my words and then trail off.

She holds up a hand to get me to stop talking. "It's okay. I fainted because I hate bloo—"

She begins to sway back again. Most likely from thinking about the state of her face right now. I swoop my hand behind her back at the same time as the big man to keep her from falling back again.

The guy that wears a big top hat, Johnny, walks over with a wet bar rag and tells her to close her eyes. She complies and he gently begins to wipe around her face, removing the blood that has crusted around her nose and lips. She winces slightly but thanks him.

I feel Wes's hand on my back and see that he and Eddie have moved to stand behind me. They realize how anxious I am right now. I look up from my spot on the ground, at Wes and Eddie, pleading with my eyes for them to help me figure out what to do.

Wes leans towards the bartender while she is still getting her face wiped off. "I just wanted to let you know that I've been skateboarding for years, and you took that slam better than most guys I'm seen."

I give him an "are you kidding me!" face, but to my surprise she lets out a snort and responds, "Well, I think the Fruity O's box protected me a little bit."

Eddie chimes in, "I'm supper impressed. Now every time I go to the breakfast aisle at the grocery store, I'll think of you."

At that she lets out a full-on laugh and begins to slowly stand up from the ground. I move towards her and reach out my hand to assist her. She looks at my hand like it's made of daggers.

"I'm fine," she says and stands without my help.

I could crawl in a hole and die right now. She won't even look at me and I can't stop staring at her. I feel like a freak. I have never wanted to meet someone for the first time again so badly in my life. I want to have a do over, to see her out in public and meet her in some normal way. Knowing that I physically caused this girl pain makes my chest feel tight.

She has her back to me now and is talking to an older gentleman and the giant man, reassuring them that she's fine.

"Please let me take you to the hospital, Olive," I say from behind her, my voice hoarse with concern. I have never wanted to reach out and comfort a person so badly in my life.

She whips her head around and looks taken aback. "How do you know my name?"

"Oh. Everyone was saying it while you were unconscious." I scratch at the back of my neck, feeling increasingly more awkward. "Also, you have on a nametag."

She looks down and laughs, "Ha, oh my gosh, duh!" Then she playfully slaps herself on the forehead.

I wince, not wanting her to cause any more damage to her face.

"I'm fine, totally fine!" she yelps out, but she doesn't seem fine as she quickly walks off through the swinging door the big guy came out of.

I wait for forty-five minutes, watching the door for her to come back out, but she never does. Instead, the big guy comes out and begins making the drinks. He apologizes to the crowds saying he doesn't know how to set up the karaoke machine, but everyone gets a shot on the house tonight for coming. The guests let out a cheer and don't seem like they mind the change, but I feel even worse about ruining the planned event.

Wes and Eddie try to start up conversation with me to make me feel better, but all I can do is stare at the metal door, wishing for and wanting it to swing open. Life does not prepare you for situations like this. Where was my "you just smacked the most beautiful girl you've ever seen in your life in the face by accident with a bar stool while balancing it on your head like a tool and now she disappeared" course in high school?

It's getting late, and the bar crowd begins to thin out. The guys tell me they are ready to leave but I can't get the feeling in the pit of my stomach to go away. I won't be able to sleep tonight because I will be replaying my interaction with her in my head, indefinitely. I do the only thing I can before we take off.

I grab a piece of paper and a pen that are next to the blue "Task" bucket and write a note. Then I hand it to the big guy behind the bar. I ask him—practically plead with him—to give it to Olive.

He must take pity on me because he looks down at the note and grunts out an "Okay" as he puts it in his pocket.

Chapter 11

Olive

I stare at my haunting reflection in the mirror and wince as I attempt to apply concealer to the dark purple bruises blooming around my nose and eyes. Last night was a shit show, to say the least. I decided to egg on and taunt that hot guy by teasing him to do something crazier than he was with the beer can and pool ball. Look at where it got me. Now I get to walk around getting concerned glances from everyone that passes.

I can't even imagine the crap Tripp is going to give me when he sees my face. *"That's not part of the uniform, Olive,"* I think to myself, his stupid, nasally voice ringing in my ears. After he hears about last night's debacle and the fact that we didn't even end up having karaoke at the *karaoke night* because I hid in the office until we closed, I know he will try to end that tradition, too. I was so embarrassed, though; I couldn't go back out while that hot guy was still there.

I exit my apartment and jog down the steps to Ivy's place below. Before I can even knock on her door, it swings open.

"Holy shit," she says, looking at my face.

"That bad?" I respond.

"I'm not gonna lie to you. It's bad. Are you sure it's not broken?"

"I don't think it is. I did an *is my nose broken* quiz on google last night and my results were *likely not broken*. Even if it is, there's nothing I can do about it. You know I have no insurance, and my car is eating at the little savings I have. The hole in my finances only gets larger every single time it breaks down."

"I still don't understand why you didn't deck that guy in the face after he threw that chair at you." Ivy puts her hands on her hips. She has always had a flair for the dramatic. She turns mole hills into mountains when she describes anything. I don't mind it, though; she keeps things interesting.

"One, I told you that it was an accident. Two, he didn't throw it at me. And three, he was mortified after. I had to get away." I called her last night as I was hiding out in the office and she lost her mind, wanting to come up to the bar and "fight the guy" for me.

"Still sounds suspicious to me," she scoffs, and then murmurs to herself, "What a creep."

I conveniently left out the part about how attractive he was, knowing I would never hear the end of it from Ivy if I did. I never find guys worth thinking about twice, so she would go bonkers if she knew someone caught my eye. Ivy is always trying to push me to go on dates. After how awkward last night was, I hope I never see him again. I smiled at the guy with *blood* dripping down my teeth. He was probably disgusted.

I try to change the subject and notice something in the background. I peek behind Ivy and see a bunch of cardboard boxes are out. No way.

"*Ivy?*" I say, my voice rising. "Are you *kicking him out?!*"

"Yup. I'm seriously done this time."

"Stop." I can't believe what I'm hearing. "I'm going to scream."

"I can't do it anymore, Olive, I mean it. I really am done. I'm done uprooting my life for a man that can't even spell orange."

"That's a joke, right?" I ask as I grab her and pull her into a hug.

"He really is *so* dumb," she whispers into my ear.

I pull away and hold the sides of her petite face in my hands. "I have wanted this so badly for you. You are going to thrive without him!"

"I know," she says confidently. Then she pulls back from me and straightens her sports bra. "Now I just need someone to come get his shit. I refuse to let him step foot back in this place. I'm not going to give him a chance to gaslight me again."

"I'm so proud of you."

"Yes, I know." She smiles at me.

Suddenly, I hear my *ten minutes till shift* alarm blare in my pocket. I look down at my phone and realize I'm yet again about to be late for work. I don't know what's been going on with me recently, but I need to get it together.

"I hate to leave you hanging like this but I'm about to be late," I tell her.

"Go!" she responds, and begins to shoo me away. "You can text me later."

I give her a quick second hug goodbye and then I sprint to my car.

When I pull up to work, I am pleasantly surprised that Tripp isn't here yet. I smile to myself, thinking about how this morning has been great so far. No more Dennis and temporarily no Tripp.

I whistle to myself as I get out of my car and walk in the

back door. I greet Rob, who is slicing tomatoes and also does a double take when he sees my face.

"Not a word about *it*," I tell him and he reluctantly complies.

"I do have something for you. Not about 'it'," he says, while motioning a circle around his own face. "But in regard to that situation."

"Huh?" I ask him.

Rob reaches into his pocket and pulls out a small sheet of paper. He hands it to me and I give him a confused look as he nods for me to read it.

Hi,

It's me. The piece of shit who accidentally knocked you out. I swear I don't usually do things like that. My name is Hunter and I'm going to include my number on here so you can contact me if you have any medical bills. Please do not hesitate to make me pay. Again, I'm so, so sorry. You can also contact me if you wish to throw a bar stool at my face and I will humbly accept the punishment.

I'm an idiot,

Hunter

P.S. I'm also sorry I ruined karaoke night for everyone.

I flip the paper over and see his phone number in large letters on the back. I snort but feel myself wanting to smile at the note. He really was so cute, and the note is kind of endearing. The edges of my lips start to tip into a grin as I ponder the note again.

I feel eyes on me, and I look up to see Rob smiling at me with one brow raised.

"Good note?"

I immediately drop my smile and shove the paper into my pocket. "Back to work, please," I say. "Tripp is going to be here any minute."

And just like I summoned the devil, he walks through the back door, accompanied by an old man in a suit.

Chapter 12

Hunter

I'm finishing my final set lifting weights when I hear a sudden commotion upstairs. I place the weights back on the rack and wipe the sweat off my brow when I hear yelling again and decide I need to figure out what's going on. When I get to the top of the basement steps, I see Dennis pacing back and forth in my living room. He is arguing into his phone, almost spitting the words out.

"You can't kick me out! I'm on the lease."

There's a garbled response that I can't hear on the other end of the line. "Okay. Well, then I'm going to *demand* to be on the lease now so you can't kick me out."

More ineligible talk in response.

"I mean it, Ivy. I don't want to leave. I love you. Please, baby. Let me come back home, it will never happen again. I promise this time."

I roll my eyes knowing that he must be referring to some type of cheating. Dennis has always been a serial cheater. I have never seen him stick with a girlfriend without finding someone else on the side. Even in high school, he would find a way to juggle girls. Not well, I might add. He always was caught within weeks but would just start the cycle again.

"Please don't hang—" Dennis looks down at his phone and then yells out in frustration. "UUUGGHHHHH!" He then chucks his phone at my couch, where it bounces off the leather and smacks onto the wood floor, accompanied by a cracking noise.

I start to quietly walk past him so I can head up to my room for a shower. I don't want to deal with his crap. I almost make it to the bottom step before he stops me.

"Wait. Hunter, I need a favor, cousin."

I tap my hand on the banister of my stairs and sigh at the fact that he is weaponizing our relationship. Then I slowly turn back towards him.

"What's up?" I ask, already exasperated from what's to come.

"Can you swing by my apartment later and grab a couple boxes of my stuff? My girlfriend said she's going to throw everything away in the apartment dumpster if someone doesn't come grab it today."

"If she's throwing all of your belongings away, I don't think she's your girlfriend anymore," I respond.

"Semantics," he chides. Then he continues, "I just need someone to do it for me. She won't let me near the apartment, and I don't want her throwing out my laptop or Nikes."

"I think your priorities are off, man," I tell him.

"My laptop equals me being able to gamble, which equals me being able to get out of your place sooner."

Wait, what? "I told you that you only have till I leave Friday morning to get your shit figured out."

"Yeah, well, I may need a few more days now that I know I can't go back to my place."

Would my conscience be okay with putting Dennis out on

the street? Unfortunately, no. I wish I didn't care and could tell him to eff off but that's not the case. I have been known to give people one too many chances before.

"Okay, fine. I will get your stuff," I concede. "But this is seriously it. You have to figure out your next step. It's not my responsibly to take care of you." He nods his head as I continue, "Tell me where and what time. I'll work it into my schedule today."

He quickly thanks me and gives me the address. Dennis tells me to swing by at any time because Ivy will be there all day, since it's her day off. I'm sure Ivy, whom I've never met, is going to have a great first impression of me. The cousin of her cheater boyfriend. I'm housing the enemy.

After I get to my room and have a steamy shower, I stare at myself in the mirror. The older I get, the more features I share with my father, and it's a little uncanny to see the man looking back at me. I still feel like that dumb sixteen-year-old inside that would ding dong ditch my neighbors, and play "hey, mister" with my friends outside the gas station till someone bought us beer.

It unnerves me that one day we go from being children who have no responsibilities to suddenly having to figure everything out on our own. I guess that's why I take pity on Dennis. Where I had a dad that cared and got on my case when I messed up, he never did.

I remember looking at my dad as a boy and thinking *man, he's so brave*. I thought nothing could ever scare him. That he was untouchable. The first time I ever recognized fear in his face, it was at the thought of dying and having to leave my mother and me. I tried to step up before he passed, show him that I could take over. That I could handle everything that life throws at me, but sometimes I don't think I can. I don't know what to do most days and feel like a phony trying to act like everything is okay without him. I need his advice and supportive nods when I mess up.

I wasn't always a great kid. I made stupid mistakes like most teenagers and I know I disappointed him at times. As an adult, I want to make him proud; I hope to make him proud.

I love my job most days and I know I have a great life. I can't lie to myself, though, and say I don't feel like something is missing, something with depth. I work and then come home and repeat the cycle over and over. I'm starting to feel lonely, honestly.

I would like companionship beyond friendship. Ever since I lost my father, I haven't been able to date, though. I tried to go on a few dates this past year and I found myself wishing I was at home with Dog instead every single time. I have become quite the hermit when it comes to women, not wanting to even put the time in to get to know someone...which is why last night hit me like a freight train.

I can't stop thinking about the woman from the bar, Olive. Her trying to smile and assure everyone that she was okay with blood dripping down her face. I cringe at the thought of what happened. I tossed and turned all night long, unable to sleep every time her image popped into my head, replaying the moment I tilted my face down to glance at her, all the way to when she hit the ground. I haven't been able to stop thinking about her chocolate brown eyes and lush lips. How even with an injury she was still the most beautiful woman I have ever laid eyes on.

After many skateboarding slams, I'm no stranger to bruising and I know her face must be black and blue today. That thought alone causes nausea to churn in my stomach. The guilt is consuming me. I left the note for her but I'm sure she will never reach out to me. I'll need to find a way to make it up to her if I ever see her again.

Chapter 13

Olive

Tripp looks over at me and his jaw drops. He then clears his throat, trying to quickly recover.

"This is Olive, the bar manager," he tells the man he's standing with, and then looks at me. "I am going to show Mr. Cronline around."

The two of them completely ignore Rob's presence, which is impossible because he's huge. It instantly makes me dislike the situation. Tripp, I expect this from. But for this stranger to come into our kitchen and not even acknowledge someone else in the room makes anger bloom in me.

The old, lanky gentleman leans towards me with an eerie salesman smile. "Hi, little lady. I'm Ted Cronline with B&B Investments. I can't wait to look around. That's quite the nasty bruise you've got on your face."

Rob makes eye contact with me and then grabs the trash out of the bin and exits through the back door. I mentally try to tell him to *get back in here*, but my attempt doesn't work. Mr. Cronline holds out his hand for me to shake. I look at his hand and then his yellowing teeth. A piece of something brown is stuck between two of them. Maybe it's a piece of bread? No. Maybe it's a seed? A nut?

Realizing I've been standing there staring at his mouth while he holds out his hand, I quickly recover and reach mine out to finish the shake. I plaster on a fake, overly friendly smile. "Sorry. I'm feeling a little under the weather." I lean into Mr. Cronline like I'm telling him a secret and whisper, "Head trauma. Tripp hit me with his car yesterday."

The man looks taken aback and Tripp steps forward. "She's kidding," he tells him and then shoots daggers at me with his eyes. "Olive, why don't you take the day off? Recover." He narrows his eyes with disgust.

"No, I'm fine!" I respond cheerily. I feel satisfied that I pissed off Tripp in front of this businessman, so I begin to turn and to head to the office. Tripp grabs my wrist. I look down at it in shock—who does he think he is?

"No. I insist. Go home for the day," he grits through his teeth.

I look at his sweat glistening on his bald patch and pull my wrist out of his grip, sharply. "Fine." I smile. "I wanted to go visit Jane today anyway."

"Great. Have a good day," he responds with a smirk. He's not even phased by the mention of his mother. Tripp turns back to the man and continues to speak like nothing just occurred. To him, I'm the scum of the earth.

Rob walks back into the kitchen, having missed the whole interaction. I tell him goodbye and he looks extremely confused. I point to my phone, so he knows to check his in a minute. He acknowledges with a single nod and then walks to the sink to wash his hands while Tripp continues to lead Mr. Cronline around. I know he will be listening in on their conversation for me.

As soon as I get to my car, I shoot him a text telling him to let me know when he figures out what that guy is doing with Tripp at the bar. I'm not even going to bother telling him about Tripp grabbing me; he would be livid. I don't want Rob to lose his cool and get fired. There is a bigger fish to fry right now.

I stretch my arms out and try to shake off the emotions running through me. Tripp is the bane of my existence right now. I loathe him, and I will never understand why he has always been so nasty. When he moved out of state, he was a stockbroker. Jane always said he was doing well and busy with his job. So something obviously didn't pan out as far as I can tell. I don't think he would come back to Clairesville unless he was out of options. He has always treated the bar like a chore. Something to get over with as fast as he can, forget about and move on to the next thing.

I could never look at Whiskey Jane's that way. It's more of a home to me than my apartment. It's the only sense of stability I've ever had in life.

I look behind me to make sure the road is clear before backing my big purple car out of the parking spot. I'm thankful she was at least reliable today. I don't think I can take anything else bad happening right now.

At least my face matches my car.

Too soon?

Twenty minutes later, I pull up to the memory care facility, Hills Pointe, that Jane lives at now. I park my car in one of the front spots, next to the small man-made pond with ducks floating around. Peering at myself in the mirror quickly, I see how bad my face looks, even with makeup. I search through my tote until I find my large knock off Ray-Bans to try and distract from my black eyes and nose swelling.

When I get out of my car, I see a bush of magenta petunias and do a quick glance around before I run over and pull a handful of flowers off the plant. I stuff them in my purse like I just robbed a bank and walk to the entrance. Jane deserves to have something beautiful to look at and petunias are her favorite flower.

The memory care facility has a sterile feel to it. The walls are drab with generic landscape paintings of the ocean and shells and there's always a lingering scent of urine in the air. I hate that she's here. I'm not her family, though; Tripp is. Where she lives is his choice since he's her only living relative.

I walk past the front desk, greeting the receptionist who is always smacking gum around in her mouth, but she barely acknowledges me over her game of Candy Crush. Guess I didn't even need the glasses. I walk the route I have done so many times in the past few years: down the hall, turn left, go past the cafe, turn left again, three doors down, and then arrive in front of Jane's room. The door is always open; all the patients' doors are. I knock three times and lift the sunglasses off my eyes as I walk in.

Jane is sitting in her favorite blue velvet chair in front of the TV. She has always been a stylish queen and though her health has declined, her fashion has remained. It's interesting how she has lost many of her core memories at this point but still holds onto her strong taste without knowing it.

One time a new nurse on the floor tried to make her wear a hospital gown temporarily after she helped bathe her and Jane threw a fit. As she swatted the nurse away, she yelled, "Get that shit away from me, I'm not an old lady!" The poor nurse was so confused.

Luckily, in her moments of lucidity, one of the other nurses told Jane the story while joking with her. Instantly, Jane demanded to see the new nurse so she could profusely apologize. The new nurse, Jojo, and Jane are thick as thieves now.

Jane is wearing head-to-toe sparkles today: a glittery teal top with spandex silver leggings, accompanied by big chunky beaded earrings. I can't help but giggle to myself when I see Jane has on pink bunny slippers, though. A queen of comfort.

I walk up to her and place my hand on her arm.

"Hi, Jane!" I say, mustering as much enthusiasm as I can, but I am anxiously waiting to see if she recognizes me today or not.

She looks up at me and says, "Hey, Olive, you look like shit."

I blow out the breath I had been holding and sit across from her on a stool. "Yeah, well you should see the other guy," I tease.

Then, I begin to recount the story of what happened last night, making sure to include every detail because I know she gets bored sitting around here all day. She smiles and laughs along as I describe the three guys. She asks all about their appearances, and I quickly describe them as attractive, not making a big deal about it. I make sure not to mention that the last guy made me nervous in a way that men never do. He was beautiful.

Jane looks at me for a long time after I finish talking. It feels like minutes have passed when she finally says, "When is Tripp coming to town?"

I can see she's starting to slip into an episode, which saddens me, but I don't want her to get confused.

"He will be coming soon!" I tell her enthusiastically.

I never tell her how I really feel about her son; I don't want her to worry about me or her bar while she sits here, hopeless. On the days that she remembers well, I want her to be happy, not stressed.

"The bar is doing great! Rick and Johnny ask about you all the time. I'm sure they will be paying you a visit soon."

She brushes off the comment, not really acknowledging me.

I can tell she's slipping further away, so I say, "Let's watch something together!" and click on her favorite show, *90 Day Fiancé*.

We have been watching TV for an hour when Jane lets out a hacking cough. I hurry to find her some water. A few months ago, Jane got pneumonia from a bad cold. Due to her Alzheimer's, she hasn't been able to care for herself like someone normally would when they are sick. It was scary at first and I spent many mornings before work sitting with her, always trying to help her drink broth or explain to her how to blow her nose.

On the days where her mind isn't coherent, it's like teaching a child how to do things for the first time. She gets really frustrated with herself and it's difficult to watch a woman who was once so strong and independent deteriorate before my eyes. We are all vulnerable when we get older. It doesn't matter who we were in our youth. Everyone gets to a point where we can't take care of ourselves anymore and that's hard to cope with.

I lean down and hand her a water bottle I found in her black mini fridge. She takes a long sip and her cough clears for a moment. I push back her grey hair and give her a small kiss on the forehead as she drinks more.

After she's done, Jane looks up at me, grabs my hand, and brings it to her cheek. "Thank you, my dear," she whispers.

"There's no one more important to me in the world," I tell her, meaning it with all sincerity. Jane gave me the stability that my mom never could. Without her hiring me, I never would have been able to move out on my own and create a healthy routine for my life. I owe a lot to her.

Jane lets out a yawn and I know all the coughing has made her weak.

"I'm going to head out so you can nap. I've got a lot of

laundry to do at home," I let her know, and she nods and leans her head against the chair, still looking up at me.

"I don't ever want to forget you," she says, with tears in her eyes.

I will never tell her that there are many days where she already has.

"Are you kidding me?" I respond playfully. "I won't let you forget me. I will harass you until you remember. Don't you worry!"

I give her a smile.

She grins back. "Okay, dear, thanks for coming to see me. I love you."

I hug her and head towards the door, turning back for one last look to see her still watching me. I wave again. "I'll come see you next day I'm off. I promise."

With that, I walk out to the parking lot and hold back the tears until I shut my car door.

Hugging myself, I hold in a sob, wishing Jane never got sick. My time with her is slipping through my fingers and I'm terrified.

After a moment, I lay my head on my steering wheel, accepting the fact that this is the way our relationship will be. Her slowly getting worse and me watching it happen.

Suddenly, I hear my phone vibrating and lift my head up. I grab it out of my tote and click on the screen to see two text notifications from Rob.

I know why Tripp had that man here.

He just told me he's going to sell the bar.

MOTHERF—

Chapter 14

Hunter

I park in front of an older-looking apartment complex with a beige stucco exterior and dated roofing. Each unit is only two stories high but there must be at least 150 apartments in this area alone. It looks like it's about to rain and the wind is picking up by the minute, so I hope I can load everything up before I get caught in the storm.

I walk up to the apartment with the number that Dennis gave me and knock on the door. It swings open almost immediately and a petite, muscular girl stands in the doorway, looking extremely confused.

"Who are you?" she asks me, her arms crossing skeptically.

I clear my throat and stammer, "I'm Dennis's cousin. He asked me to come grab his stuff from you. I'm letting him crash on my couch, temporarily...so here I am...to get it." I rub at the back of my neck, feeling extremely awkward.

She smacks her hands down at her sides and lets out a huff of breath. "This is actually insane. How does my boyfriend—*ex*-boyfriend," she corrects herself, "of four years have a *cousin* that lives in the same town, and I had no idea?" She points her

70

finger at me accusingly. "That piece of shit never told me anything. He probably lived a double life the whole time."

Not knowing how to respond, but feeling responsible for his bad actions, I say, "I'm sorry. I haven't talked to him in years, seriously." I continue, feeling like I need to explain myself, "I'm only letting him stay a few days. I would just feel bad leaving him homeless when I have an extra room at my place." I shrug slightly.

"Let him be homeless. Play stupid games, win stupid prizes," she deadpans. "Anyway, I'm Ivy."

"Hun—" I reach forward and shake her hand, but she cuts me off before I can even finish saying my name.

"You're super-hot. No wonder why Dennis never mentioned you." She shakes my hand back.

I instantly flush. I always feel uncomfortable when I get complimented. Clearing my throat I respond, "Thank you," and break eye contact. I just want to grab his stuff before it starts raining and I'm mentally counting down the seconds till this awkward exchange ends.

"I have the best idea," she says, leaning forward. "How about we go to my room and get a little *revenge* on Dennis, eh?" She winks at me suggestively. Now I know I'm redder than a tomato. I just stand there in shock.

After a few seconds that feel like an eternity, Ivy starts laughing hysterically. She smacks me on the chest, playfully. "I'm kidding, relax! I would literally never hook up with someone related to Dennis. I'm not asking for bad karma in life."

"Oh, okay." I force a small chuckle in return, relieved that she was just messing with me.

She gives me quizzical look. "I do have a super-hot best friend, though. I should introduce you." Then she taps her finger to her lips in thought.

I shift my weight from one foot to the other. "That's kind but no, thank you. I'm not really dating right now."

"Bummer."

Trying to move this exchange along, I give her a small smile and say, "If I could just grab his stuff quickly, that would be great. I don't want to get caught in the rain with all of the boxes."

"Yeah, of course! Let me get out of the way. Everything is in the corner next to the couch." She motions behind her.

"Awesome, thanks," I tell her.

"He should be the one thanking you," she murmurs. "If I had to stare at his stuff for one more day, I was going to list everything on Facebook Marketplace so I could get some money out of the breakup." She begins laughing once more and I'm not sure if she's being serious or kidding about selling the stuff. I wouldn't blame her, though.

Ivy steps aside to let me into the apartment and I walk to the corner that is jampacked with overflowing boxes of clothes and random items. There are two boxes that say "porn" in huge marker letters. I turn and look at her.

"Sorry," she says, "I thought one of his loser poker player friends would be coming to grab the stuff, so I wanted to mess with them."

"Gotcha." I scratch my neck. "No problem."

She continues, "I'm going to my room to shower. Just shut the front door for me when you're done."

"Will do," I say as she goes to her room and closes the door. Avenged Sevenfold begins blasting a few seconds later. *I bet the upstairs neighbor loves her,* I sarcastically think to myself. She's a little kooky, just leaving a man she doesn't know alone in her living room. I mean, I'm a decent guy, so she has nothing to worry about, but does she do this with everyone? Is this how she ended up with someone like Dennis in the first place? She trusts easily, I'm assuming.

I lift the two boxes labeled "porn" and turn the writing so they face my stomach. Then I rush them to the back seat of my truck. I jog back to get the next few boxes, trying to beat the storm.

Fifteen minutes later, I finish loading everything, my back seat stuffed with boxes. I wipe my sweaty forehead with my white tee and then reach down to grab my phone out of my pocket. I don't feel it and I realize it must have fallen out while I was moving Dennis's stuff. I quickly walk back to the side-walk and look up and down. I notice it right next to the curb by the street and feel relieved the screen isn't cracked since I must have dropped it while moving the boxes.

As I reach down and pick it up, I hear someone cry out. Shoving my phone in my pocket, I turn around. I see woman about thirty feet down the sidewalk with a giant laundry basket that's fallen over, clothes blowing down the street from a strong gust of wind. I run over to help her and hear her sob as I get closer. She has her back to me, and I grab a shirt and towel that are on the ground near my leg.

"Excuse me, miss. These are yours, I think," I tell her and walk closer.

At that moment, she turns around and mumbles, "Thanks," while reaching out her hand. I sharply intake a breath when we make eye contact. I feel like lightning has just struck me.

It's Olive.

Chapter 15

Olive

I look up to see Hunter, the guy from last night, in front of me. *You have got to be kidding me.* I hold back my tears and reach my hand towards his, taking the clothes that he picked up for me. He then runs around the parking lot and retrieves my other items that have blown across the street before I can compose myself more to help. Hunter sets the last few things in my laundry basket and looks at me.

"Thank you," I murmur, giving him a quick glance. A left-over tear falls down my cheek and I quickly swipe it away, hoping that he doesn't notice.

"No problem." He gives me a soft smile and tilts his head down towards me.

"How are you always here to witness me at my worst?" I groan and look away. "Well, my worst twenty-four hours," I add. Then I realize how insane it is that he's here right now and turn back to face him. "Also, what are you doing here...where I live?"

"To be fair, I caused what happened to you yesterday. If I wasn't at the bar, that never would have happened to you." He

74

pulls at the hem of his white shirt that sticks to his torso with sweat. "Also, I promise I'm not a stalker." He laughs. "I just came here to pick up some stuff for a family member."

"Cool, cool," I respond, trying to appear nonchalant as I grab my basket. I want to get out of this conversation quickly, so I muster up as much enthusiasm as possible before saying. "Well, thanks! Bye!"

I can feel him staring at my bruises as I walk past, and I ignore the urge to meet his eyes. The universe has to be laughing at me right now. Putting this man in my presence again after last night is basically comical. I'm just waiting for a sinkhole to open and swallow me up at this point.

"Wait," he calls out from behind me. I keep walking but he jogs to meet up with me on the sidewalk anyway. Once he is next to me, I stop and turn to him.

He bites his lip lightly, and I can tell he wants to say something.

"Yes?" I ask him, while struggling to keep my tone from sounding impatient. I glance at the sky behind Hunter and see heat lightning dash across it. *Great.*

He pushes his hair back from his eyes and I can tell he seems nervous. "I am so sorry about the bar stool. I feel like the biggest asshole in the world." I stare at him as he continues to speak. "Is your nose okay?"

I shrug. "Yeah, I think so."

"Do you want me to take you to the doctor?"

"No," I quietly respond and sit my laundry basket down.

Feeling suddenly exhausted and defeated from the day, I slump down and sit on the pavement. "I think it's fine, honestly. It seriously doesn't hurt as bad as it looks. Don't even worry about it." I look up at him and huff out a laugh. "You accidentally smacking me in the face with a bar stool is actually only the third worst thing that's happened to me in the past day."

I'm unsure why I even said that to him; like a stranger needs to know about my day.

He looks at me for a moment and then sits down next to me on the ground. I can feel his body heat close to mine on the sidewalk and it feels oddly intimate. I twirl a strand of my hair with my finger to distract myself as he turns towards me.

"Do you want to talk about it?" he asks.

I shake my head no.

"That's okay. If you do want to, though, just know I'm a vault. Whatever you tell me will stay with only me."

Strangely enough, I believe him when he says this. I stare at my shoes for a moment before deciding, *what the hell, sure.*

"You really want me to tell you my problems?" I ask, raising an eyebrow.

"Yes, I do." He looks at me earnestly. "The least I can do is try to be a friend after the physical pain I've caused you." He looks at my bruises and winces at the thought.

"Alright. Fine," I tell him and stretch out my legs. I unclip my fake bow tie from my uniform and toss it in the laundry basket. I feel like I'm suffocating in my work uniform after what I found out earlier.

"Well, for starters, I found out that the place I love more than anywhere in the world is going to get sold by an evil dictator."

Hunter looks at me, concerned, "And the place you love is?"

"The bar. Whiskey Jane's." I point to my uniform.

"The place we were at last night...where you work?" He looks surprised and continues, "I didn't see a for-sale sign. Why are they selling?"

"They, as in the owners, would never want to sell, but their son, Tripp, is currently in control of the bar and hates it." The thought of him getting rid of the place that I hold so dearly in my heart causes a wave of nausea to churn in my stomach.

"How would he be able to sell it if he doesn't own it?"

"Because his father, Seymour, the man who built it from the ground up, passed away years ago. And Jane..." I stop and take a breath. I hate having to explain her condition to people. It makes it real. "Jane, his mother, has been running the bar alone ever since his dad died. She has Alzheimer's now and isn't doing well."

"I'm sorry to hear that," Hunter responds. "Watching someone you love suffer is the worst feeling in the world." He goes quiet and I can tell by the sincerity in his eyes that he means it. I momentarily wonder who he has lost in his life.

I nod my head. "Yes, it is."

"So, their son works at the bar?"

"Kind of. He has never cared about the bar before a day in his life, but now suddenly he has interest in it because he wants to sell it."

"That's messed up," Hunter says, shaking his head.

"Yeah, I agree. He's their only child, though, so there's no one to override him."

"But I don't think he has the right to sell it. It's not his business and if his name isn't on the deed, I doubt he can legally do that," Hunter tells me, his voice trying to sound reassuring.

I shrug. "I'm not sure, I don't know any of the details yet. I just found out a few hours ago...after I left from visiting Jane at the memory care home."

"Oh," Hunter says, "I'm sorry. I'm guessing that was another hard part of your day."

I nod and watch an ant crawl onto my leg from the pavement. I gently move it back to the ground as I say, "It's bittersweet every time I see her. I love being with her, but I also know our time left is limited. On the days she doesn't remember me, it's extremely difficult."

I feel his eyes on me again. "How was she doing today?"

"She was okay. She remembered me, which was great, but she tires easily now. Her mind and body aren't reliable anymore."

"That must be tough," he says, and picks a small yellow flower from the grass. "I'm sure she loves your visits, though, even when she might not recognize you."

"Yeah. She does," I agree.

Hunter twirls the little flower between his thumb and index finger. Then he begins to reach it out in my direction, like he's going to offer it to me.

At that moment, rain starts to drop on us rapidly and I glance at my pile of clothes.

"Shit! I just washed all of this," I tell him and jump up to grab my laundry basket.

"Let me get that for you." He drops the flower and jumps up, reaching forward and taking the basket from my hands. "Point the way and I'll take this to your place for you." He motions to my clothes.

I look at him playfully as rain pelts down my back. "I'm not telling a stranger where I live."

"If you have Amazon Prime or Uber Eats, you literally tell a stranger exactly where you live every time you order something." He laughs.

We are both soaked now from the drops.

"Wow, I've never thought about that. You've really opened my eyes." He smiles as I shrug. "Well in that case, follow me, stranger." I take off running to lead him in the direction of my apartment.

He laughs from behind me and jogs to catch up, stepping in

front of my path. "Am I still considered a stranger if we are on a first name basis?" he asks while looking down at me.

"I don't remember your name," I tease, as I go around him and walk ahead again. "I have amnesia from yesterday."

Rain falls on us in buckets now. I pick up my pace.

I hear him groan. "I am so sorry. I will apologize indefinitely about that, Olive."

I stop when I hear him say my name. It's like he's letting it escape his lips, finally, breathlessly. I turn and look back at him. "I accept your apology, *Hunter*." I really put emphasis on his name in return.

He stops next to me and responds with a dazzling smile, his eyes crinkling in the corners. I find myself staring at his mouth and can't seem to look away.

"That's more like it," he says, leaning in closer, and I smell *man*. Literally, just an all-encompassing man smell. Woodsy and powerful, but also something soft and sweet, like jasmine. Hunter smells like he could carry me on his back through the snow and then make me a cup of tea after.

God, he's hot. I hate this.

We quickly climb up the steps together trying to get out of the storm. When I get to my apartment, I stop at my front door. "Thanks for the help."

Hunter looks down at my laundry and grabs a dish towel. He rings it out over the ground and looks at me, sympathetic.

"I think you will have to dry this stuff again."

"Yup." I exhale and continue, "Thank you for carrying my basket for me, though. Looks like we are even now. I got hurt yesterday, *but* you helped me today."

"Not even close." Hunter pushes back a stray damp curl. "I owe you once again. I struck up a conversation with you while you were just trying to do your laundry. You were obviously busy. My mouth ruined your clean clothes and got you all wet, too."

My eyes almost pop out of my head at the comment, and he instantly turns red, realizing what he said.

Stammering, Hunter quickly adds, "The rain," pointing towards the sky.

I let out a little laugh and cover my mouth with my hand. "Yes. I know."

My thoughts do wander for a second. His shirt looks like it was painted onto his body after being in the storm. I can see his abdominal muscles peeking through the cotton fabric.

"Anyway," he continues, snapping me out of my thoughts. "I still owe you one. So I'm going to find a way to make it up to you." He bites his lip. "And you can hold me to that. I'm a man of my word."

I roll my eyes playfully. "Okay, *Mr. Man.*"

I try to be funny and reach out to squeeze his muscle in a teasing way, but I get momentarily stunned when I make contact with his skin. His arm is toned and warm, with cool drops of rain stuck to it. The skin-to-skin contact causes a shiver to go through me. Hunter looks at my hand touching his arm, so I quickly pull it back before he can say anything else.

"Well, thanks for the help. Bye, Hunter," I say, abruptly cutting him off before he can continue our conversation.

He looks confused but gives me a nod. "Sure, no problem. It was nice talking to you." Then he recovers quickly with a smile. "Bye, Olive. I'm going to come visit you at the bar soon."

I give him a tentative smile back and unlock my apartment. I step through my doorway and suddenly decide to do a goodbye curtsy. I bend down awkwardly and then realize *wtf am I doing* so I quickly get back up and close the door before I can embarrass myself more.

Did I *seriously* just *curtsy* goodbye? Did I have a stroke for the past five minutes? I do not know that woman.

Now I'm praying that he doesn't come visit me at the bar. Hunter makes me feel so flustered and not my usual composed self. The last thing I need on top of the chaos in my life right now is to be distracted by a guy with a great head of hair. Better yet, I refuse to let it happen.

I silently vow to myself that I won't see him again. Then I throw the wet laundry basket aside and I walk into my bedroom. For the next thirty minutes, I stand under the fan until the heat from touching him has finally left me.

Chapter 16

Hunter

I get into my truck dripping wet and stare out at the rain hitting my windshield. Realizing that I'm smiling to myself like a madman, I reach for the spot on my arm that Olive touched, wishing that the moment had lasted longer.

I can't believe I ran into her. The fact that she lives here is mindboggling. What are the chances that I would ever see her again, not to mention the next day? This stuff doesn't just happen; seeing her today feels like fate. I know I can't just walk away now and pretend she never existed.

Looking into her beautiful brown eyes as she held back her sadness, I just wanted to reach out and wipe her tears way, to sweep her into my arms and fight off anyone that has ever hurt her. I now have beef with a guy named Tripp that I've never met. I want to help her in some way so she can keep the bar she loves so much.

But what can I do? I just film skateboarders. My job doesn't provide me with the qualifications to help in a situation like this.

I hate this feeling. The helplessness. I felt this way the

whole time during my dad's fight with cancer; it ate away at my soul. I'm not going to be the person who sits and hopes things get better for Olive. I'm going to *make* her situation better. I won't let her lose something she loves dearly.

I open my phone to turn on some music for my car ride and see I have over ninety-nine new notifications on YouTube. I uploaded some new footage of a sixteen-year-old pro, Max Beacon, earlier and the video has quickly gone viral. That's thanks to my large following on YouTube.

After recording years of skateboarding content and camera equipment tutorials, my audience has grown significantly. So, no matter what I upload, it gets tons of views now. That's one of the reasons brands like to work with me, because they are familiar with my filming style already. Subscribers seem to really love the videos where I film documentary-style. I like to switch between asking the skater questions, showing them in their everyday life, and then also showing the footage of their tricks. The audience loves a story where they can connect with the person on screen.

That's when it hits me. I know exactly what I'm going to do to help Olive save the bar.

Chapter 17

Olive

One week later

The past week has been a nightmare at work. Tripp has random people in the bar left and right taking dimensions and talking about what they could transform the space into. He is planning to sell the land for at least a million dollars due to its *scenic location,* he said. Tripp told Rob that this bar was going to become an absolute "gold mine" for him.

I spoke immediately with Tripp when I went back into work on Thursday. He told me that yes, he is selling the bar and that has been his plan for a while. When I asked him how he thinks he's going to do that when he doesn't own Whiskey Jane's, Tripp smirked and quickly walked to the office. He came back moments later and shoved a paper at me.

The document was the deed to the property, with his name on it. It was dated five years ago and had Jane's signature at the bottom. Sneering, he told me, "My mom signed this place over to me years ago. She knew she was getting older, and it was best for me to make the decisions."

I stared at the document in shock that day. Jane never mentioned any of this to me. Why would she just sign the rights of the bar over to Tripp without even talking to me? I know he is her son, but she has always mentioned his distaste for Whiskey's, whereas I adore it.

He told me, "I'm getting rid of this craphole as fast as I can," and with that, he had yanked the deed back out of my hands and slammed the door once he made it to the small office.

I had never wanted to smack someone so badly in my life. I ran to the bathroom and cried for at least an hour, knowing I have no one to turn to about the bar, no one to help with this situation. I'm the manager, and Jane is so sick, I would never bring this up to her in her condition.

I've been a mess ever since. The bruises have gotten better under my eyes, but now large circles from lack of sleep have taken over. I toss and turn all night, having nightmares about Tripp knocking down the bar with a giant wrecking ball, dressed like the Monopoly man.

Johnny and Rick have noticed the change in me and have been trying to cheer me up by playing my favorite songs on the jukebox throughout the day. Right now, "Sunny" by Boney M plays and still, the upbeat tune doesn't lift my mood.

Johnny even brought me sushi today from my favorite spot, Happy Rolls, as a surprise. I did get a laugh when he described trying to order from the menu and having absolutely no idea what he was doing. I ended up with random raw fish over rice and a California roll.

I pull up a bar stool so I can sit across from the guys at the counter and dig into the food.

"Have you ever had one of these things?" Johnny asks me,

pointing to the California rolls. He's stuck a white feather on the outside of his top hat today; he looks like Steven Tyler.

"Yes." I laugh. "Those are the most popular sushi rolls ever made, I think." I pick one up with chopsticks and make him try it. His face contorts at first, but by the end of the bite, I can tell he is pleasantly surprised.

"Man, that's good." Johnny smiles. "I've got to go get myself one of those Californer rolls."

"California," I correct him playfully.

"That's what I said." His brows draw together.

I turn away from the bar at a noise and peek through the kitchen window to see Tripp walking in through the back door.

Rick mumbles from behind me, "PowerTripp incoming."

He gave him that nickname after he found out that Tripp is planning to sell the bar. I didn't know Rick had that kind of sass in him. The name couldn't be more fitting.

I slide my sushi under the bar counter, not wanting to deal with his wrath since I'm eating on the clock. Tripp pushes through the kitchen door like a tornado. He's wearing a salmon polo shirt and sweat is glistening on his head. He looks like a shiny pig.

I will never understand how Seymour and Jane, both extremely attractive and loving, gave birth to this evil naked mole rat. I think sometimes when two people are so gorgeous and perfect, it cancels out when they have a child.

Tripp walks up to the bar and slams his hand on the counter in front of me. "Good morning."

I jump at the noise and mumble, "Hello."

"Just letting you know the man from B&B will be stopping by again today, to talk shop." His expression is almost taunting as he says this.

I narrow my eyes at him. "Do you not see how cruel it is to

sell off the place your parents built and cherished, without a second thought?"

"Sorry for being a realist. This place is a money pit" he smarts back. "I have to make moves. Every day I sit in this dump, another dollar is down the drain."

What he's saying isn't completely true. Yes, business has slowed down over the years since Jane has been sick, and improvements need to be made to market the business to a younger crowd. I've had to basically run everything alone and can't do it all myself; I'm running on fumes. I'm also not the owner so I can't sign off on any changes to improve the bar at this point. "Jane would be devastated if she knew what you were doing," I tell him, crossing my arms. "She didn't put you in charge so you could throw the bar away like it means nothing to you. Have you even talked to her about how you're selling?"

He glares at me, sharply. "Not that it's any of your business, but one of the doctors from the facility called me a few days ago and told me they will be transitioning her to hospice with my approval." He snaps, "This is *my* decision. She doesn't need to know I'm selling the bar."

"What are you talking about? I just saw her Wednesday, and she was doing fine."

"Her cough has gotten much worse and she's back on oxygen. Another lung infection," he says, while having the audacity to seem bored by the conversation. Tripp acts like we are talking about the weather. "I'm going to visit her later, not like it matters. She won't remember it anyway, and she's heavily medicated With her mental state, it's pointless."

What a vile human being. I have no words.

"I have to go sign the hospice paperwork, since I am her medical proxy."

I look at him for a long time and then say one final thing. "I hope that no one ever treats you the way you treat your mother. Though I can't say you wouldn't deserve it."

I turn my back to him, busying myself with restocking napkins.

With that, he scoffs. "You better watch what you say to me, or I'll put you out of a job before I even sell this place." Then he storms to the office.

I exhale a breath as Rick quietly says behind me, "I will never understand what has caused that boy to be filled with so much anger in life. He's been like that for a long time now."

I shrug. We have talked about this a lot over the years and there's nothing to justify Tripp's actions. He grew up with two parents who loved and supported him. Some people are just selfish and there's no excuses for their behavior. Reasoning with him is like trying to resolve conflict with a brick wall.

I hear the main door to the bar *ding* as it opens, and I turn to greet the new customer. I'm shocked to see Hunter walking towards me with a huge smile planted on his face. He is in a blue- and black-striped shirt and a backwards hat. His curls peek out from underneath his hat, and he looks handsome as ever. *Fantastic.* Even though he mentioned visiting when I saw him at my apartment, he hasn't stopped by all week. I thought I was in the clear, that he'd forgotten about me.

"Look, it's bar stool boy!" Johnny exclaims.

I watch Hunter cringe at the nickname and lift his hand in recognition.

"Here I am. In all my glory," he says, nodding to Johnny. "I almost didn't recognize you without your mask. Thank god for the top hat."

Johnny pretends to be offended as Rick cracks up at Hunter's quick dig in response.

"And you must be the fox that did shots with my buddy, Eddie?" he asks Rick.

"The one and only. That shot sat in my stomach like a rock that night," Rick responds, shaking his head. "Can't say I regret it, though; didn't want to leave your friend hanging on his birthday."

Hunter chuckles with him. "Yeah, Eddie said it was the worst thing he's ever drank." Then he meets my eyes. His own are shining with apology.

I point at him playfully. "Hey, no more saying sorry. I mean it."

He puts his hands up in surrender. "I know, I know. *My apologies* that I haven't come by the bar until now. I was traveling for work."

I brush off his statement, not wanting to admit to him that I didn't want him to come at all. "It's fine, no problem."

"I'm here now though," he continues, "and with a solution to your problem."

"What are you talking about?" I half laugh.

He leans forward and does a drumroll with his hands on the counter. "I'm going to help you save the bar."

I really laugh now. "Oh yeah?" I say with a disbelieving look. "And how are you going to do that?"

"I'm going to help you raise money so that you can buy the bar from Tripp." He says it like it's some simple thing.

"Yeaaaah, riiight," I tell him sarcastically, dragging out each word.

Hunter looks at me, as serious as can be.

"I'm not joking, we will raise the money."

I glance at Rick and Johnny and then lean in towards him. "Listen, Hunter. It's really sweet that you want to help me. But a couple car washes and bake sales aren't going to raise the million dollars needed to save this place."

He doesn't even seem surprised by the amount I mention.

"You're right. Those things would never work to raise that much money. But I know something that will."

"Okay, let's hear it. I'm all ears," I tell him, not even allowing myself to feel hopeful.

"So, I am a filmer. I work for skate brands and I also have a YouTube channel where I upload content. It's kind of popular." He looks bashful as he continues, "The videos get a lot of attention and shares."

I give him a small smile to be kind, but I don't understand how this information helps my situation. "Well, that's really cool, but what's that have to do with the bar?"

He looks around the bar, excitement in his tone. "I thought I could make a series that I upload to my channel about Whiskey Jane's to raise money for the bar. With your help, of course. You know the bar and regulars way better than I ever could. We could set up a funding page that people could donate to and my videos are also monetized so I will add the money I make from the YouTube series to the 'Save the Bar' fund."

I am surprised by his suggestion, but I can't say the idea doesn't intrigue me a little bit.

"How would that even work?" I ask him. "I doubt there's enough information to share about the bar that you could turn into a series."

"You know that's not true." Hunter smiles brightly. "From the first second I walked in here, it was like a place I'd already been. I'm sure there's tons to film. I mean the themes alone," he recalls, pointing towards the "Task" bucket, "are an experience. There's lots to talk about."

Johnny chimes in, "Yeah, and look around at the walls. There are a million stories to be told, just in the memories people have scribbled down."

Hearing that, Hunter walks over to a Sharpie drawing by

the men's bathroom of a bug sitting on a cloud, eating a bowl of cereal. Then he moves over to a spot with the names Doris and Glenn in a heart, the date 1988 written in beautiful script.

"You're right," he says, looking back at Johnny, his voice almost breathless. *"That's the idea."*

Then Hunter walks towards me, growing more excited by the second. "We should choose some of the names, jokes, and drawings and track down the stories behind them." He smiles at me. "Each video of the series could feature one of the things. People watching would love it, and learning the history of the customers would really help people fall in love with Whiskey Jane's!" He puts his hands together. "We could film one a week and that would cause people to anticipate each new episode and give us plenty of time to find out each of the stories."

Rob pops his head from the kitchen window and speaks up before I can say anything. "I think that's an amazing idea." He looks at me. "You should do it."

Johnny nods his agreement and chimes in, "Give it a try, Olive. What do you have to lose?"

I rest my left hand on my chin as I think it over. Hunter is staring at me like a kid on Christmas morning.

"Why would you even want to help with this and give us the money you make from the videos? That's a lot of work for you for nothing in return." I drop my arm. "We also don't even know if we can locate these people; many of the things were written before I worked here."

"We can help with that," Rick pipes up. "We've been coming here basically since the bar opened. As you know, we're old." He chuckles. "Which is an advantage right now, because Johnny and I know a lot of the history."

Johnny grins. "Yup, this is all true."

"What if people don't want to talk on camera?" I shoot back.

Rick responds, "Trust me. When it comes to saving Whiskey's, they will. People care about this place and most importantly, they care about Seymour and Jane's legacy."

"Missy and I can cover for you behind the bar while you guys go and film the stories if need," Rob adds. "I'm usually just back here reading anyway."

Hunter nods earnestly towards each of them. "That would be awesome. Thank you." He looks at me next. "As for why I want to help you with this, I can't explain. I just need to. So please let me. I haven't had an idea make me excited like this in a long time." He looks at me shyly through his lashes, his brown eyes full of hope.

He speaks up again, more confident this time. "Will you do this with me? Let's save the bar, Olive."

I let out a deep breath. "Alright, fine. We can try."

All four men let out a cheer in victory.

Chapter 18

Hunter

I walk out of the bar fifteen minutes later and put my hands in the pockets of my Levi's. Looking around, I take in the mountain view that was behind me and smile to myself. Somehow, I just convinced Olive that we can save this place together and that means I will get to spend a lot more time with her.

We decided to meet here tomorrow morning before Whiskey Jane's opens for the day. That way I can shoot some footage of the atmosphere, and I can pick something written on one of the walls that jumps out to me for the first video.

I unlock my truck and hear someone yell for me to wait. I turn to see the big guy that works in the kitchen walking towards me. I step away from my car and meet him halfway in the parking lot.

"Hey, man," I say.

"Hi. I never formally introduced myself. I'm Rob."

"Rob," I reply, looking up to him. "You're massive, dude. Has anyone ever told you that you should play football?"

93

He snorts. "Yeah, I've heard that a few hundred times in my life before. I hate sports, though. Not my thing."

"You don't say." I laugh.

"I just wanted to catch you before you left and let you know that I really appreciate what you're trying to do for the bar."

"Yeah, no problem. I want to help if I can. The bar seems really special."

He looks back at me quizzically. "Yeah, well, I wanted to let you know the *bar* is a tough nut to crack. It can be intimidating and stuck in its ways but if you are worth it, the *bar* will notice."

I stare at him and give a small smile. This guy is on to me way too quickly. "Listen, I only have good intentions with the *bar*. I promise. I just want to make the *bar* smile."

"Her smile really does light up a room, huh?" he replies.

I raise my eyebrows in response.

"I mean the *bar*, of course." Rob chuckles. "It's been alone for a long time, and I think it's lonely. No one wants to be lonely."

"Yeah, I feel the same," I say.

Rob leans in towards me suddenly and says in a low tone, "And you better not do anything to hurt her if she does end up liking you. Olive is like a little sister to me. You hurt her and I will hurt you."

Oh shit. He switched up quickly. "Makes sense, man," I respond, putting my hands up in surrender.

"The only reason why I'm even talking to you right now is because I have a good feeling about you," Rob continues. "My intuition is usually right."

"Thank you," I tell him. It feels nice to know that Rob is rooting for us in some sense.

"Alright. Well, I'm headed back inside, bud." He claps me

on the back. "Appreciate you talking with me. I'll see you tomorrow."

"Sounds good, thanks again, Rob."

He nods a final time and heads back towards the bar. I turn away and walk to my truck. The dude is intimidating to say the least. He has nothing to worry about, though. The only thing I want is to make Olive happy; she owes me nothing in return.

When I get back to my house, I'm relieved to see that Dennis's car isn't in the driveway. The last thing I want is his company when I'm trying to edit skate footage today.

As soon as I unlock my front door, Dog is there to greet me. I pick her up and give her a kiss on the top of her head, but she quickly leaps out of my arms and saunters off. That's her social battery for today.

Suddenly, my stomach rumbles and I realize I never ate lunch, so I walk to the kitchen to make something. Once I get there, I see a note sitting on the kitchen table. I scoop it up and read.

HUNTURD,

WENT OUT TO MEET WITH MY BITCOIN GUY. I DON'T HAVE A PHONE STILL AFTER IVY CAUSED ME TO SMASH MINE. WILL BE BACK LATER TONIGHT, MAYBE WITH A CHICK? DON'T WAIT UP.

I roll my eyes and throw the note in the trash. He is the human version of a fedora. I don't understand how any woman sleeps with him.

Also, Dennis trying to blame Ivy for him throwing and breaking his own phone because of his poor anger management

95

skills? Ridiculous. Ivy seemed pretty normal from the few minutes that I talked with her. So, what kind of spell did he put her under? If Dennis is her taste in men, I'm kind of scared of what her taste in best friends is. I shake off the thought of a female version of Dennis.

My phone rings in my back pocket and I see Eddie is calling. I hit the accept button and rest my cell on my shoulder while opening the fridge door.

"Hello?" I answer.

"Hunter! How's it going, man? Are you back in town?"

"Yup, just flew in last night," I respond, sniffing some takeout on the middle shelf. I gag at the smell and toss it in the trash.

"How was Skate Park of Tampa?"

"It was sick. Nice to have an indoor park to film in."

"I bet. I saw the new video of Colby Brunn you posted today. Dude is insane."

"I know, the kid is oozing talent. I felt lucky to film him." I grab some yogurt and accept the fact that I just need to go grocery shopping.

"Who are you filming next?" Eddie asks.

"I'm actually going to be staying in town for a little while. I have a new project I'm going to work on here."

"Oh, cool. Why so mysterious?"

"I just worked out the details today," I say. "I'm going to make a documentary series about a local bar that's at risk of closing."

"That's something new for sure," he agrees. "What made you decide on that?"

I clear my throat. "I just liked Whiskey Jane's when we went and when I heard they might be closing, I wanted to help the bartender save it."

"Wait, they're closing? You're trying to help the bartender?

The one you knocked out? Is she okay? She wants to buy it?" he asks rapid-fire questions then stops. "Oh shit, you like her."

I can feel his smile on the other end of the line.

"Did you take your Adderall today?" I joke. Eddie has a serious case of ADHD.

"No, of course not. Don't change the subject. When did you spark up a conversation with the bartender about them closing? We were with you the whole time."

"I ran into Olive the next day. It was insane, man." I run a hand through my hair. "It feels like something special."

"Awwwwww, *Olive*," Eddie teases me. "Hunty is in love."

"Oh, shut up, don't make it weird, Eddie," I say.

"Okay fine, but I'm going to still make jokes about it occasionally. I have no self-control."

"Yeah, I know that." I snort.

"This is so exciting!" Wes yells out.

I look down at my phone to check that this wasn't a three way call this whole time. Only Eddie's name is on the screen. I should have known they would be together.

"Hey, Wes, what are you guys up to?"

"On the way to Basil Tattoo. I'm adding to my left sleeve," Wes responds.

"What are you getting?"

"A duck wearing a suit."

"I'm glad to hear that your tattoos always have meaning."

"Yeah, the meaning is I like a classy duck."

I laugh.

"Hey, we just pulled up to the shop," Eddie says.

"Alright, I'll let you guys go. Text me later."

I hang up the call and chuckle to myself. I can always count on the two of them to act like my brothers, reliable but usually busting my chops.

Today really has been the best day.

First, I got to see Olive and look into her mesmerizing doe eyes this morning.

Second, my house is Dennis-free right now.

Third, I have friends that support me and get me.

I throw away my empty yogurt and head upstairs to my room. I set down my phone and keys on my bed and then I walk to my master bathroom so I can relieve myself. Standing over the toilet, I begin to unzip my pants when I look down and see a fucking "floater" in my toilet.

That's it. Dennis is out tomorrow.

Chapter 19

Olive

Early the next morning, Ivy looks at me across the table at our favorite cafe, Violet's Cup, utterly confused.

"So, you're now going to make YouTube videos with the guy who dropped the barstool on you? The weirdo that you don't know?" she asks for the tenth time, bouncing around on her side of the booth. She has way too much energy for it being seven in the morning right now.

"Oh my god, you make it sound so bad." I roll my eyes at her. "He is going to try and help me raise money for the bar. That's it. You know what that place means to me."

She nods and sighs dramatically. "Yes. We both agree that Tripp is a huge ass and Whiskey's needs to be saved. Buuuut, I think it's a little extreme to let some creepy old dude make videos with you."

I scoff. "Well, when you say it like that it does sound creepy. But he's not old, why would you assume that...I told you he makes skateboarding content."

"I just thought if he was at the bar, he was old." She shrugs.

"No offense but you know there is usually an older crowd at the bar."

"None taken." She is right and that's probably why the bar isn't making money like it used to. Many of the longtime patrons don't drive in their older age now or have passed away; as morbid as that is, it's true.

Ivy continues, "I just want to make sure you aren't getting too invested in this idea. That's a lot of money to raise and probably a short amount of time."

"I agree, I'm just going to see what happens."

"If you think this is going to help Whiskey's, I will help in any way I can."

"Thank you," I tell her. "I will let you know if I need your aid with anything."

She takes a big sip of her coffee and I change the subject. "So have you heard anything from Douchey Dennis?"

"Surprisingly, it's been radio silent on his end," she responds, while picking at the edge of her lid. I can tell it bothers her that he isn't contacting her.

"That is good news, Ivy. Any contact with him will just open that wound again and you will have to start over with your healing."

"I know." She nods. "It just really sucks to see someone I wasted years of my life on truly not give a shit."

I feel sad for her in this moment. She wants love so badly.

"Want me to go slash his tires? Just say the word and I will," I tell her. "Actually, you don't even have to say a word, just blink and I will do it. I will go to jail for you." Leaning forward I take her hand. "It would be the honor of my life to destroy him for you."

She yanks her hand away. "Oh, shut up. I get it. He sucks."

"That he does."

"I don't want to think about him anymore."

"That makes two of us. So how has work been?" I ask her.

"Pretty good." She sighs. "But I'll never get to wear my dream dress now."

Ivy works at a bridal store as a consultant and helps brides find their perfect gowns for their big day. Just like in the show *Say Yes to the Dress*. This means she is constantly yearning for when it will be her turn to get married. She has already picked out her dream gown, of course, and tries on the sample dress every chance she gets.

"You would not want to marry him anyway." I stare at her. "That would be an absolute nightmare."

She nods and then looks down at her lap, unable to hide her lip tremble as she tells me, "I just want it to be my turn. I see love around me every day at work and it's hard sometimes. I want someone to think I'm special enough to marry. I want someone to cherish me."

I can't fault her for that. Deep down, I wish I could find that, too, someday. My guard is up so high when it comes to men, though, that I don't think I will ever let someone in as a potential partner.

I get out of my seat and slip into the seat next to her. Her teary blue eyes meet mine. I grab both of her hands and squeeze them.

"You are so special to me, and I cherish you. I understand you want a romantic relationship and that will come when the time is right. But know that in the meantime, you always have me. I will always be your companion, and I am always on your side."

Ivy sniffs and wipes her nose. "Why can't you have a penis?" she jokes. "You would be a perfect boyfriend."

I laugh. "Yeah, right. I'm emotionally unavailable, and don't you remember when we lived together? We were ready to kill each other daily. We would never work, even if I was a man."

She laughs along with me as we recall the two years we lived together that almost ended our friendship *multiple* times. We used to fight over everything. Stealing each other's clothes, her partying and coming home drunk, slamming the cabinets when I finally fell asleep after a long shift at the bar; we even fought over whose turn it was to clean the bathroom. Maturing taught us that we are the best of friends, but can't live under the same roof, and that's fine. We have lived in our apartment complex one floor apart since then and it's the perfect amount of distance for us.

Ivy finishes off her last gulp of iced coffee and gets up to toss her cup in the trash can. I check my face in the reflection of my phone screen, starting to feel nervous about having to see Hunter. The other three times I saw him were not in my control. He just popped up in front of me, so I had no time to think about it in advance. But now that I know I'm going to see him, I feel anxious.

After he left Whiskey's yesterday, I went into full-on creep mode on the internet and searched "Hunter, skateboard, YouTube" and was able to immediately find his channel. He has a big following. Over two million subscribers and millions of views on his videos. I spent way more time than I should have watching playlist after playlist of skateboarders and his tutorials for aspiring filmers. I couldn't look away from his smile as he explained equipment parts in his videos, his eyes sparkling with excitement. I couldn't care less about learning about cameras, but I watched his videos like I would be getting a pop quiz today.

When she notices that I'm analyzing my reflection, Ivy squints her eyes at me in suspicion. "Wow, you must like this not old, not creepy bar stool guy."

I scoff. "Yeah, okay."

"I mean, you made yourself look cute today," she points out.

"You always dress cute, that's not a dig at you, but you know what I mean. Not usually before a work shift..."

I get up from the table. "Yeah. It's in case I'm on camera," I respond defensively.

She's right, though. Today I put some extra effort into my appearance. I was able to cover my leftover bruises with some amazing concealer. They completely disappeared. I also put waves in my mid-length dark hair and applied a little extra blush to my fair cheeks. I'm wearing a red cardigan with a black mini dress and my white converse. I even pulled back some loose strands of hair with a red bow. I brought my uniform to change into before Tripp comes to work, so I don't even really know why I dressed up. Now that Ivy mentions it, I'm feeling a little self-conscious. I don't want to give off the wrong impression because the last thing I want is for Hunter to think I am interested in him.

Ivy interrupts my train of thought. "Well, once they see you on camera, I'm sure plenty of men will be asking for your number. So be prepared, babe." She raises an eyebrow. "You're a hot tamale."

I ignore the comment and put my phone in my tote. "Okay, thanks."

"Let me know how it goes," she continues. "Text me after work."

"Will do." I give her a hug and walk off to conquer the day. Once I get to my car and put the key in the ignition, I silently cheer when my Barney car starts. I really need to get that battery; I'm pushing my luck.

Chapter 20

Hunter

I'm sitting outside the bar's front door at 8:30 A.M. with my film equipment, listening to the song "Snap Out of It" by Arctic Monkeys on my headphones, when I see Olive pull up in a bright purple car. *Interesting choice in vehicle color*, I think while chuckling to myself. Not what I expected from her.

She glances over at me while she parks and then steps out of her driver's side. As she starts walking towards me, I swear time slows. She's wearing a dress that shows off her pale, smooth legs, which look like they go on for miles. I find it hard to swallow and tug a little at the collar of my button-up Dickies shirt. This is the first time I've seen her that she wasn't in her work uniform, and I can't look away. Olive gives me a wave, and I smile back at her, trying to be respectful with my gaze. I take a few steps closer to her and pull my headphones out of my ears.

"Hi, Olive, you look really nice." I sheepishly grin. Why do I feel like an alien in my own body right now? She makes me feel so intimidated.

She looks down at her outfit. "Oh, this old thing? Just something I threw together." She quickly brushes off the compliment.

"Well, you look great," I reiterate, as she walks by me to unlock the door.

She turns back towards me, gives a small smile, and quietly says, "Thank you." Then she pulls the door open, and I reach out to hold it, motioning for her to go first.

I follow her through the doorway, my eyes adjusting to the dark, empty bar after standing outside in the sun. She sets her flower print tote on a stool near the counter and turns towards me.

"So," she says, "where do we begin?"

"I could just search around real quick and see if there's something that really stands out to me on the walls? If it catches my eye as a newbie to the bar, I'm sure it will interest the audience, too."

"Okay, clever idea. I agree." She nods.

I put down my equipment bag on a low wooden table and begin my search. Every wall has so much writing that it's almost overwhelming to make the words out. I can't imagine how many stories there must be in here. Thousands, easily.

I feel Olive looking at me out of the corner of my eye and turn to meet her gaze. She's chewing on her bottom lip and she quickly looks away when we make eye contact. I can feel the situation getting awkward, so I decide to switch it up.

"I love the vibe here," I tell her.

She lets out a breath and scans her eyes around, too. "Yeah, me too. I've worked here for going on ten years and I always find something new to stare at."

I walk over to my camera bag and screw my lens on my Sony. "I changed my mind. I'm going to film some shots of the atmosphere first and then I will figure out what to focus the first episode on," I let her know. "Just some artsy clips of the bar before customers get here."

"Good idea," she responds. "I'll go stand in the kitchen to get out of your way." She points to the metal door that leads to the back.

"No, stay," I tell her quickly. "You're part of the atmosphere."

Olive half laughs. "Okay. I'll go stand in the background like an NPC."

Laughing with her, I explain, "No, just do what you normally would in a morning. Like I'm not here."

"Okay. That I can do."

She takes off her red sweater and as she shimmies out of it, I notice a tiny tattoo on the inside of her arm. It looks like a flower of some sort. She meets my eyes and I quickly look down at my camera, adjusting the settings to accommodate the dark bar. I press record and begin to walk around, taking different angles of the signs and tables. I then pan the camera up towards Olive and see that she's over at the jukebox, clicking through the options.

"I always turn on my favorite songs while I prep the bar for the day. Do you mind?"

"Absolutely not," I say, not telling her I will probably have to change the audio if I use any of these clips, so I don't have to deal with copyright issues. I just want to see her in her element. I hear a joyous beat start to play through the speakers and instantly recognize the song, because my mom played it all the time when I was a child. It's "9 to 5" by Dolly Parton.

"This is my cleaning song," Olive shouts out over the music and begins to sing along. She's not the least bit in tune, but somehow that makes it even better. I appreciate it when someone isn't the best singer but belts it out anyway. That's a confidence everyone should aspire to have.

I film her as she grabs a towel from behind the bar and dramatically wipes the counter with it, swaying her body to the beat. I watch her through my screen, unable to look away. Her dark hair swishes across her face and she flips it back with her empty hand. I walk closer to her, feeling like a voyeur watching something intimate, a routine she usually does alone. The song ends then and she looks up at me and lets out a laugh.

"How was that?" Her cheeks are red with excitement.

"You're perfect," I quietly respond while setting my camera down on a nearby table.

"What?" she asks.

Thankful that she didn't hear me, I recover quickly. "I said 'perfect.'"

"Alright, great!" She smiles and nods. "Now what?"

"Now I will look around."

I put my hands behind my back and turn towards a wall. I read some names and random words and laugh at some drunken scribbles. Then I stop in front of a giant pink Sharpie drawing of a bumblebee with the words "I came for a beer and left with bees" underneath it.

I chuckle and point at it. "I choose this one."

Olive walks up to stand beside me. "Perfect, because I know that story." She turns to smile at me. "And it's a good one."

I look down at her and match her grin. "Let's do it."

"Right now?" she asks.

"Yup, we are good to go." I pick up my equipment bag and sling it over my shoulder.

"Well then, we will need to visit a friend of mine across the street. Follow me."

She grabs her keys, slips her cardigan back on, and begins to head through the kitchen door. Quickly, I jog to catch up with her.

"Has anyone ever told you that you walk very fast?" I ask her.

"All the time. It's my long gazelle legs," she responds, her dress swishing, but she still doesn't slow down.

I use all my self-control to not look at these long gazelle legs as she walks ahead. I love the fact that she's tall and carries herself with confidence.

We cross the street and walk over to a small store called The Mart.

Chapter 21

Olive

We step into the store and Mr. Ray sits behind the checkout counter, where he reliably rests on his stool and stares at his tiny TV. You can always count on him watching golf or a trashy court show where ex-couples fight over who gets to keep the pet in the breakup. Sometimes while I'm at the counter paying, the episodes are so juicy that I will stand there with him and wait for the verdict before I leave the shop. Today he's watching the pet court show.

When he sees me, Mr. Ray lights up. "Olive! *Pet Paternity* is on! This couple is fighting over who gets to keep their Betta fish. The guy is crying."

I walk over quickly. "No way! A real tearjerker." I lean over the counter for a better view to watch the drama unfold.

After a few minutes, Mr. Ray looks behind me and clears his throat. I realize Hunter is standing behind there. Wow, I'm so rude. I was sucked in by the glitz and glamour of reality TV and forgot about the whole reason why I walked in here.

I turn towards Hunter. "I'm so sorry. We have a mild obsession with this cheesy reality show." I glance back at Mr. Ray.

"Mr. Ray, I would like to introduce you to Hunter, a badass skateboarding filmer who has graciously decided to shoot a series about the bar."

Hunter flushes slightly at my compliment and reaches out to shake Mr. Ray's hand. "It's nice to meet you, sir," he respectfully says, his voice deep and strong.

Mr. Ray hastily extends his own hand to meet Hunter's. "It's great to meet you, too." Then he turns towards me. "So are the rumors true? Everyone has been talking about Tripp wanting to sell Whiskey Jane's."

"Yes, unfortunately it's true," I tell him, rolling up the sleeves of my cardigan. Why did I wear a sweater when it's ninety-two degrees outside?

"Wow, word travels fast on this side of town," Hunter exclaims.

I laugh. "Yeah, we have this kooky, old, top-hat-wearing man who spreads gossip like it's air."

He smiles. "Let me guess, is his name Johnny?"

"The man, myth, and legend."

Our eyes linger on each other.

Mr. Ray looks back and forth between us before breaking the silence. "So, what are you going to film at the bar?"

Hunter and I explain everything to him. I finish the story off by saying, "And this is why we are here now. Hunter chose the bee drawing first."

Mr. Ray has a huge smile. "What a strong start." He looks at me. "Drive on over. I will call her and give her a head's up that she will have visitors soon."

"Thank you!" I clap my hands together. "I'm excited to see her." I turn to Hunter. "Get out that camera out, my friend. We are hitting the road."

Hunter lifts his bag. "I'm ready!" he replies enthusiastically.

We tell Mr. Ray a quick goodbye and he holds up his hand in a wave. When we are almost to the door, I hear him playfully murmur to himself about how he didn't get to see who got the custody of the fish because we were all talking.

Hearing this, Hunter glances back towards him. "No one ended up getting custody. The Betta fish died during the episode, probably stress from being put on the stand."

Mr. Ray and I both look at him, shocked.

Hunter shrugs. "I watch a lot of late-night reality TV reruns because I have pretty bad insomnia. I think I've seen every episode of *Pet Paternity*."

I continue to stare at him in shock as Mr. Ray begins to laugh hysterically. His whole body shakes as the raspy laugh overtakes him.

I'm still looking at Hunter as he begins to open the door and motions for me to go first. I walk out and as I go, I hear Mr. Ray talk to himself once more. "Now, I like that kid," he says. "I really like that kid."

Chapter 22

Hunter

I turn to Olive when we get outside the store and ask, "Okay, whose car are we taking?"

"Definitely not mine," she quickly says. "Barney is not reliable."

"Barney?" I laugh.

"Yeah. That's my big purple car's name. Every car has a name." She says it as if it's a matter of fact.

"Mine doesn't," I tell her.

She looks at me as if I'm insane. "Are you kidding me? You haven't given your car a name? That should be reported as a crime. Your car *deserves* a name."

I grin down at her. "Okay, then you give it a name."

"No way." She shakes her head. "Only the owner can choose their car's name. It wouldn't be right; I don't have that kind of relationship with your car."

I tilt my head back and laugh at that as she continues speaking.

"I'm serious. By the next time I see you, you better have a name for it."

"Okay, I will," I promise her.

She holds out her pinky and I stare down at it momentarily. Olive smirks. "Everyone knows a pinky promise is a legally binding contract."

I chuckle and shake my head slightly before I link my own with hers.

Since our cars are the only two there, she automatically heads over to my truck. I walk to her side first and unlock it, opening the door for her. She almost seems a little taken aback at the gesture as she slides into the passenger seat. I walk to my side of the car and wonder if she's not used to someone opening doors for her.

I get in the truck and start it up, the engine loud and commanding in the silence between us. The smell of roses and orange blossoms drifts to my nostrils. I realize it's Olive; being this close to her makes me feel drunk on her scent.

I lift the aux cord towards her. "Want to choose the music for the ride?"

"Although I am highly honored that you just offered me your aux cord," she teases, "I want to hear what kind of music *you* like. I'm curious."

"Okay. Where to start..." I say, feeling temporarily vulnerable. She might as well have just asked me to get naked. What if she hates my taste in music? Music compatibility is a big thing, I don't care what anyone says. You have to enjoy the same music to coexist with someone. Imagine if you married someone that only enjoyed listening to bagpipe ballads all day. Nightmare fuel.

I scroll down my playlist and click my favorite band. "Enjoy the Silence" by Depeche Mode begins to play around us. I glance over and watch Olive's face for cues to see what she thinks. She listens intently and I see her fingers start to tap her thigh as the melody continues. After thirty seconds, she turns towards me.

"I like this song."

"Good. Me too," I respond. "Windows down?"

"Is there any other way to drive while listening to music?"

I manually roll down the driver's side window as she cranks hers down as well.

She reaches over and turns up the volume dial. That's more like it.

Smiling, I back the truck out of the parking lot.

"Where are we headed?" I ask her.

"To see Mr. Ray's wife, Sonjia." She smiles. "She's our first subject."

Olive navigates the way for the fifteen-minute drive. We are currently curving up the side of Jewel Mountain, which happens to be one of my favorite lookout spots in town. Surrounded by trees as we head around a narrow turn, Olive suddenly points to the left.

"There!" she blurts out, and I slam on the brakes. I see the small dirt road she's pointing to and take the turn.

"Man, they really live up here on their own!" I exclaim, heading slowly onto the rocky path.

"I know. Isn't it amazing?" she gushes. Her eyes sparkle as she inhales the fresh air deeply. "We're almost there. Just follow the road to the end. It's the only house around here so you can't miss it."

I nod and take in the nature around me; pine trees stretch as far as I can see. I turn the music off, so the only sounds left are my tires crunching over the crushed rocks and birds singing to each other. I see a small natural wooden cabin ahead and Olive seems giddy in her seat as we approach.

She claps her hands on her thighs. "You are just going to love Sonjia." She pulls some hair back that has blown in her face. "I hope you're hungry, because you won't be leaving until she feeds you. It's her love language."

"I can always eat."

I pull up in front of the cabin and take in the place. There are decorations everywhere: gnomes, little stone frogs, rocks painted in rainbow colors, wind chimes of assorted styles, and a porch swing with more pillows than space to sit on it. The wooden front door swings open suddenly, and a beautiful older woman with long dreadlocks wearing a floor length floral dress and lace cover-up steps out.

"Olive!" She holds out her arms and Olive hurries out of the truck to give her a hug.

I get out of the driver's side and approach the two of them. After finishing the hug, the woman looks over her shoulder at me.

"And you must be Hunter," she says warmly, as she walks around Olive, then pulls me into a hug also. "I'm Sonjia."

Olive's smile consumes her face. "I'm glad Mr. Ray filled you in on all the details."

Mrs. Sonjia pulls back from our hug, still holding onto my arms.

"That he did. He didn't tell me how handsome this young gentleman is, though." Her tan skin is covered in freckles that crinkle on her nose as she laughs. "A creative *and* easy on the eyes." She says it like a statement as she looks quizzically at Olive.

"Thank you." I clear my throat. "Your house is amazing, Mrs. Sonjia."

"It's special, isn't it?" She continues to smile. "Conner built it for me."

"Mr. Ray," Olive clues me in.

"That's incredible." I look around in awe. "I never even knew there were houses on this side of Jewel Mountain."

"We are the only ones," Mrs. Sonjia explains. "Follow me inside, I just finished baking a loaf."

Olive looks at me and smiles in an "I told you so" way, and I hold back a laugh.

Mrs. Sonjia guides us in through the front door of the cabin and the scent of freshly baked bread consumes the space.

"It smells amazing," Olive tells her.

"Thank you, I made a lavender and herb sourdough today."

She takes us to the kitchen and points to a natural wood table that is next to a huge window. "Sit," she commands.

We both comply and she slices the bread, then brings us each a plate. Mrs. Sonjia turns to the fridge and pulls out a little blue tray with butter and sits it in front of us as well.

She stares at both of us then, waiting expectantly. "Well, go on. Eat it while it's hot," she encourages.

Olive reaches out and cuts off a huge chunk of the butter with her knife. She drops the butter on top of her bread and then takes a bite without even spreading it.

I stare at her in shock.

She feels my eyes on her and freezes before she takes another bite. "What?"

I chuckle. "You *really* like butter. I've never seen someone put that much on toast in my life."

Olive shrugs. "Life's too short to not eat copious amounts of what you like."

"I think there's a little bread on your butter," I snort.

"Oh, be quiet!" She playfully shoves me. "*Eat.*"

Both women are staring at me now, so I lean forward and take a bite of the bread. It's crunchy on the outside, warm and soft on the inside, and has a savory kick of herbs at the end.

I smile up at Mrs. Sonjia. "This tastes incredible."

Olive nods next to me as she shovels more bread into her own mouth. "It's delicious," she agrees, her words almost unintelligible from the large bite she's chewing on. Then I watch her slice off another chunk of the butter and plop it onto my bread this time.

"Try it. Sonjia makes it."

I look up at Mrs. Sonjia in shock. "You make butter, too?"

"And honey," Olive adds. "Which is why we're here." She glances at the oven clock. "Speaking of, we have to get started because I need to get back to the bar before Tripp comes in."

I completely forgot the fact that I don't have unlimited time to spend with Olive today. I wish I did; our interactions feel so natural, like we have known each other for years.

I toss the piece of bread with the insane amount of butter into my mouth and give Olive a thumbs-up. The butter is delicious, she's right. But I'm not used to eating it in a layer thicker than icing on a cupcake. I swallow it quickly, apologizing to my arteries, and try to hold in a small cough.

Mrs. Sonjia hands me a glass of ice-cold water, then asks, "Where would you guys like to film?"

"Let's go to your porch! Is that fine with you, Hunter?" Olive's brown eyes grow wide as she anticipates my response.

"Sounds great. Let me run and get my camera bag from my truck." I excuse myself and jog out to my car so I can grab it out of the back seat.

As I head back inside, I hear Mrs. Sonjia speaking to Olive. "He is so cute. Is he your boyfriend?"

Olive lets out a small laugh. "Sonjia, no. We barely know each other. He's just helping me by making the video series for Whiskey's. That's it."

The way she says *that's it* sounds so final, like there is no room for anything else to happen.

I lean against the hallway wall as I continue to listen. I

know I shouldn't eavesdrop, but I can't help the temptation. I want to hear what Olive has to say about me.

Mrs. Sonjia continues, "Olive, you have to give someone a chance someday. Not all men are bad."

"I know. It's easy for you to say that when you have Mr. Ray." She sighs. "I've never found a man worth dating. The guys my age are horrible, and you know how my dad was...and then all my mom's boyfriends..." She trails off.

"You don't have to tell me, honey. I know he caused you indescribable pain and that you witnessed unhealthy relationships in your formative years. Just be open is all I'm saying. There is someone good out there for you. A guy with a golden heart, I just know it."

At that, I walk backwards and shut the front door firmly. I feel a twinge of guilt but also worry for Olive's sake. Who hurt her so badly that she doesn't trust men now and what pain did her father cause? I casually walk into the kitchen and their conversation silences quickly.

Olive gives me an overly bright smile, trying to compensate for the sudden awkward silence, and hops out of her chair.

"Ready?" she chirps.

I nod. "Of course. Lead the way."

Mrs. Sonjia opens the fridge and pours some iced tea into three mason jars. She hands us both one and takes a sip out of hers. Then she guides us through the living room and out onto a porch. It overlooks the town below; we are literally hanging over the side of the mountain.

"This view is awesome," I say softly, while taking in the picture-perfect scenery in front of us. Two small birds fly by together and swoop down to rest on a tree branch below.

Mrs. Sonjia sits down on a bench with a colorful quilt. "Do I look camera ready?" she jokes, touching her dreadlocks and smoothing down her long dress.

"You're perfect, *Mother Nature*." Olive smiles at her. This must be a nickname she has given her.

I chuckle. "You really do remind me of Mother Nature!" I open a zipper pocket of my bag and pull out my tripod. "I'm just going to set up the camera here." I unsnap each leg of the stand until it's a few feet high. "And I want you to talk to me like we are having a normal conversation. Don't worry about the camera at all. We are just two friends talking."

I have always found that the best footage is the stuff that is filmed organically—not overly composed or set up, but just showing everyday life. That's what people relate to and root for. The audience wants something real.

When I film skaters, I leave in a lot of the shots where they don't get the trick. The clips show how hard they work, so when they *do* land a trick, it's incredible. You celebrate with them as the viewer.

I twist my camera on the tripod stand and then press record. Olive grabs two stools from a porch table and drags them over for us. I thank her as she sits with me behind the camera.

Mrs. Sonjia stares at me. With the sun glowing down on her, she looks ethereal.

I begin to talk. "So, tell me, Mrs. Sonjia. What does Whiskey Jane's mean to you?"

Chapter 23

Olive

Three days later

I sit at the bar with Rick and press the video link that Hunter just sent me for approval. He wants to make sure I'm okay with everything before he posts it on his channel. Hunter asked for my phone number on the ride home from Sonjia's the other day. I gave it to him gladly, but then felt anxious after, worried he might get the wrong idea.

I bite my lip slightly as the screen loads. Hunter stopped by two days ago to film some more footage of the bar before we opened for the day. He spent an hour with Rob, interviewing him about Whiskey's and getting some more of the bar's history from him. By the time he left, Rob was grinning from ear to ear. Hunter seems to have that effect on everyone once he talks with them.

Unfortunately, he seems to have that effect on me, too. I haven't been able to stop thinking about him. Even though I just saw him a few days ago, it feels like it's been months.

Finally, the video starts to play. The screen is black, and I hear Rob's voice start talking about Whiskey Jane's. He talks about Seymour and Jane, his relationship with them, how they always treated him like family. The screen brightens and pans from the giant mountain view behind the bar to the front entrance of Whiskey Jane's. Then, as if the viewer is walking into the bar themselves, Hunter's hand reaches out from behind the camera and pushes the door open. When he enters, there's me behind the bar, dancing and singing along to Dolly.

Hunter's strong voice speaks over the video clip. "This local bar in my hometown is in danger of closing. It's a staple for people in this community and needs to be saved. Every time I come to Whiskey Jane's, I fall more in love with the bar. I have decided to bring you all along with me as I learn more about this local treasure and the community it has created."

The camera pans to the walls and Hunter's deep voice continues, "See the art on the walls? The love notes? The memories? This has all been created in the past forty years since the bar opened. Imagine the heartbreak for the community if the owner lost the bar. This is the owner's legacy and unfortunately, she has been very ill. I want to help the manager save the bar."

My cheeks flush as Hunter appears on the screen in a room. I'm assuming it's his bedroom. He talks to the camera like a natural, explaining his plan and that he created a funding page if viewers want to donate if they are moved by the cause. He pushes his hair out of his eyes and grins as he talks about picking the bumblebee picture first.

His smile is so endearing, I want to reach out and squeeze his face. No wonder he has so many subscribers; not only is he talented but he's so attractive. If I had to guess, half of them must be women who could care less about skateboarding.

Hunter continues to speak as the screen changes to the outside of the Rays' cabin. Suddenly, he stops talking and

121

there's no music in the clip either—just the beauty of the cabin and birds chirping as the camera pans over the scenery.

With the sound of birds still singing in the background, Sonjia appears on the screen, sitting on her porch bench. Hunter asks her the question, "So tell me, Mrs. Sonjia, what does Whiskey Jane's mean to you?"

Her face lights up instantly. "The bar means everything to me. It's where I met my best friend, Jane, and it's how I got my bees."

"Your bees?" Hunter asks from behind the camera.

"That's right," she responds. "One day, forty-six years ago, I was bringing my husband his lunch, which he always forgot"— Sonjia laughs while saying this—"to his store. As I pulled up, I saw a business was getting built across the street and there was a young man outside painting the building. I walked over and introduced myself.

"He said his name was Seymour and we talked for at least thirty minutes; he told me they were making the space into a bar. He then told me that I had to go inside and meet his wife, Jane, and have a beer. Seymour said that she would love me, and this first drink was on them because I was their first visitor.

"I walked in the building and found her wearing a pink spandex bodysuit up on a ladder to what I assumed was an attic space, cussing up a storm." Sonjia smiles as she recalls the story. "I cleared my throat and she popped her head down, saying, 'Oh shit, sorry. I didn't know anyone was in here with me. Pardon my mouth, but there are some damn bees in my brand-new attic.' She hopped down from the ladder and brushed off her hands on her bodysuit and then shook mine.

"I said, 'You must be Jane,' and she replied with, 'And you must be insane to walk into an unopened bar.' I explained to her how I had just met Seymour, and he sent me in telling me to meet her and have a beer. Jane continued to joke around with me, and I loved her feisty personality instantly. She was gorgeous." Sonjia tears up slightly. "She still is."

Sonjia sits quietly for a moment, thinking of her dear friend I'm sure, before clearing her throat and continuing. "Anyway, so Jane went behind the counter and poured me a beer from the tap and slid it towards me. I remember drinking it quite quickly due to the hot spring day.

"She asked me if I knew anything about bees. I didn't, but I popped my head up the ladder anyway to look. The hive was pretty small and was nestled between the brand-new wood beams. I don't know what it was, if I liked Jane so much and I wanted to help her, or if I was buzzed off the one beer." Sonjia lets out a long laugh and her eyes sparkle as she says, "But I took the bees."

"You took the bees?" Hunter asks, obviously shocked. My own laughter is heard from behind the camera. Picturing a slightly buzzed Sonjia taking a hive of bees home always cracks me up.

"I took the bees," she reiterates. "I took some tongs from the bar kitchen and lowered the hive into an empty liquor box that Jane had just emptied."

"You didn't get stung?" Hunter questions.

"Oh, I got stung a lot." Sonjia points to a small scar on her right arm. "Proof of the incident." She raises her eyebrows playfully. "But it was worth it. Jane kept questioning me, asking if I was sure what I was doing, and I assured her that the bees would be happy at my property since we have so many trees.

"I told her goodbye quickly and left with the buzzing box. I was halfway up the mountain in my car when I started to panic, having no idea what to actually do with them. When I got home, I sat the box outside our cabin by a tree and immediately left again. I decided that I needed to do some research at the library, so I headed there at once.

"When I finally came home five hours later, I was confident, feeling way better with the knowledge of how to care for the bees and a mission: I decided I was going to become a beekeeper."

The video then shows us standing with Sonjia next to six white bee boxes, as she explains how she gets the honey. She looks at the bees with so much love and compassion, then tells us how she and Mr. Ray were unable to have children, so the bees have always been her babies to care for.

"When people started writing on the walls after the bar opened, Jane told me to go leave my mark, so I drew the cartoon bee with the little inside joke that only Jane and I would understand: I came for a beer and left with bees." Sonjia's smile overtakes her face on the screen. "The day we met, Jane gave me a purpose and a friendship I desperately needed. I owe it to the bar. If not for that place, our paths never would have crossed."

Sonjia finishes talking. The clip of her sitting on the bench on her porch lingers for a few seconds and then goes black with a link to donate.

I sit still, overcome by what I just watched. "Wow," I whisper to myself.

Suddenly, I feel Rick's hand pat my back. "From what I heard, that was really great," he tells me.

I meet his eyes. "Jane would have loved that."

"No talking about her in past tense," Rick tells me. "She's still in there. Just give her time to recover from her cough."

I nod in response. I will not admit to him that I'm losing hope. Jane has been heavily sedated for a week now, and her breathing has not been improving. I visited her once and it was exceedingly difficult to see her in that condition.

I feel relieved that Hunter didn't mention Tripp at all in the video. I don't want to give any fuel to his hateful fire or give him a reason to try and shut our idea down.

I hear my phone chime and look down to a text from Hunter.

I'm nervous about what you will think, so please let me know as soon as you finish the video. I am sitting here in purgatory.

I laugh at the text and respond.

It's perfect. Post it.

Hunter sends back a thumbs-up within seconds.

One hour later I get another text from him.

I uploaded the video 42 minutes ago. It currently has 99,000 views and people have donated to the bar fund! Over $2,000 already!! This is really going to work, Olive!!!

I smile at the message and his optimism, wanting to believe it, too.

Chapter 24

Hunter

I look down at my phone, waiting to see if Olive has responded to the message I sent her, telling her the video is already doing well. A moment later she gives the message a heart and text bubbles appear, then go away. I wonder what she was about to say. I have been trying to think of any excuse to go up to the bar and see her again, while not wanting to come off as creepy.

Groaning, frustrated with myself and the thoughts swirling around in my head, I toss my phone on my bed and head downstairs. I walk past the kitchen to see if Dennis has shown up yet. It's been a week since he left me the note, and he hasn't returned yet, as far as I know. I peek in the guest room and see nothing but the stack of boxes I dropped off when I first retrieved them for him. Since he doesn't have a phone right now, to my knowledge, there's no way for me to contact him.

Most people would probably be concerned if a family member randomly disappeared for weeks at a time, but this is just Dennis's thing. He shows up when he needs something and abandons the situation when something better comes along. I'm just annoyed that I'm stuck with his belongings now. I guess his Ivy had the right idea when she brought up selling everything on Facebook Marketplace.

I head to my kitchen and grab some cleaner and a cloth from under the sink and take the steps down to the basement, deciding now is the perfect time to dust and shine my dad's collectibles. When my mind won't stop running, the only thing that makes me feel in control is cleaning. I have been known to manically clean my house after sad news. My house was always spotless after my dad got his cancer diagnosis.

Clicking on the basement light, I breathe a little easier, knowing it's just me down here. I don't have to perform or be who anyone else wants me to be. I can cry or yell and there's not a witness to laugh or judge me. Going over to my dad's record player in the corner, I select a vinyl disc from the shelf and wait for the song to start. The beginning beats of "Time of the Season" by The Zombies start and I close my eyes, remembering all the times I watched my parents dance in the kitchen together to this song as a child. This was their first dance song when they got married and my dad would always dip my mom at the end of it, her eyes sparkling with joy.

Feeling myself start to get choked up, I walk to the shelf and begin gently wiping down the old metal cars. I think about Olive then, wondering what her parents are like. Did she grow up in a home like mine? One filled with love and devotion? I think back to what Mrs. Sonjia said in her kitchen about her dad and wonder what it would take for Olive to let me in, to open up to me about her past.

The more I see her, the more I want to ask her out. She's all I can think about, but I also don't want to scare her off. I don't want her to feel pressured to say yes to me just because I'm helping raise money. My cycle of frustration and overthinking starts again, so I clean all sixteen cars on the shelf until they are pristine and shine like a trophy.

Deciding it's been long enough, and I'm now allowed to check my phone after I set a fake timer in my head for no reason, I click off the lights to the basement and run upstairs. I don't care how brave or manly a guy says he is, as soon as the lights are off in a basement, he is sprinting up those stairs. Anyone that claims differently is lying.

When I get back in my room, I sit on the bed and grab my phone, happy to see Olive has texted me back.

I get to pick the next quote we explore! I"ve already made my choice btw. Come by the bar Monday morning to film? Also, I will not let you in the door until you tell me your truck's name. So, get on that. You have homework, Curls. (Your new nickname —it's better than bar stool boy. I'm so nice, right?)

I laugh and reread the text five times. I really like her, and I'm screwed.

Chapter 25

Olive

Monday

I look in the bathroom mirror of the women's restroom one last time before I need to go greet Hunter. He just texted me that he's outside and I made sure to get here a little early to prep the bar in advance so I can have more time to film before we open for the day. I don't want to feel rushed this time.

I give myself a final pep talk. "Listen up, you beautiful, stubborn, funny, hot, cool bitch." I point at myself in the mirror. "No matter how cute his hair is today, no matter how many times he laughs at your jokes, no matter how much you want to lick his abs. You are not allowed to like Hunter! We have a mission to save the bar and you're not going to get distracted by a stunning specimen of a man who may or may not give you fanny flutters."

With that, I straighten my ugly work bow tie and walk out of the bathroom. I had a mini panic attack about what I should wear today and in the middle of my mental breakdown, I threw on my uniform. It's a walking chastity belt, which is what I need right now.

I hear three knocks on the main door and quickly walk forward to open it. Hunter's beautiful self is in the doorway, and he's staring at me with intensity.

"Old Fart," he says in a low, deep voice.

"Um, what?" I ask.

"That's the name of my truck," he says matter-of-factly, and points back towards it.

"*That's* the name you spent days working on?" I ask him, brows raised.

He holds up both hands, showing mock offense. "Whoa, whoa, whoa. This is *my* relationship with my car, remember. Only I know what name is worthy of it, and I choose Old Fart."

"Okay, if you say so. Old Fart it is." I smirk and surrender. "Come on in."

I scoot out of the way so he can enter, secretly checking him out from behind. Today he has on a short-sleeved blue henley with the top two buttons open, a black beanie, and tan pants. His curls pop out the bottom of his beanie and I have the urge to rip it off and tousle my hand through his hair.

I realize he has something behind his back when he quickly moves so I can't see it and then turns towards me.

"I have something for you." Hunter's eyes light up with mischief.

"You do?" I say with a hint of fear in my voice. I don't do well with presents or surprises; I just hate being put on the spot in general. That probably stems from my childhood, with my mom popping up with a new boyfriend every other week. That random guy would then toss a Barbie or a crappy candy bar in my direction to try and impress me so they could get in good with her.

"Close your eyes," Hunter says, stepping closer.

I reluctantly comply and I can feel his warmth as he stands right in front of me now.

"Put out your hands," he whispers, his voice rough and breath minty. I can feel goose bumps forming up my arms and I hope he doesn't notice.

I lay my hands out and feel something long and metal in them. It feels kind of like a knife. I open my eyes. *What the...*it *is* a knife.

"You got me a knife?" I ask.

His face is full of excitement. "Yeah! A butter knife!" he exclaims.

I awkwardly smile and laugh a little bit, unsure how to accept the gift. Then I see his face start to fall.

"I am just now realizing how creepy it is to give a woman a knife as a present. I literally just stood outside the bar, in the early morning, with a knife hidden behind my back to surprise you. My bad." He looks like a sad puppy trying to explain the gift to me. "I was at the thrift store yesterday and I saw this knife and it made me think of you because you love butter. When I saw it had flowers all down the sides and you have a flower tattoo, I knew I needed to get it for you." He runs his hand across his brow, obviously stressing now.

I feel my face warm at the mention of my tattoo. I look down at the silver knife and notice that it is beautifully etched with flowers. He noticed such a small detail about me after only being around me a handful of times. It's incredibly flattering, but I also don't want to give him the wrong impression. The gift shows he has been thinking about me and though I might like it, it's not something I should accept. Seeing him recoil with embarrassment snaps me out of my thoughts, though.

"This is so cool. I can't wait to enjoy a bucket of butter with this bad boy," I say, shaking the knife. "You're so thoughtful. I'm glad we are becoming friends. Thank you." I smile at him, trying to convince myself that it didn't feel like poison sliding off my tongue when I called him a *friend.*

He seems unsure by what I said, but plays it off quickly and gives me a small smirk in response. "Well, glad to know that gift made the *chopping block.*" Hunter raises his eyebrows and wiggles them at me as I groan at the awful dad joke.

"I think you should be called Old Fart, not the car, because that joke was horrible. What are you? Geriatric?"

"Getting up there. I turn thirty in a few months."

"Interesting." I look him up and down playfully. "I did see a few grey hairs last time you took your hat off."

His eyes twinkle as he laughs. "Well that's good, because I want to be a silver fox one day."

"Oh god. That's what Rick calls himself when he wears the fox mask at the bar."

"Sweet grandpa-vibes Rick?"

"Yeah, he was a real stud back in the day apparently. He wore bell-bottoms every day and was in a band back in the '60s."

"You're kidding!"

"Nope. Ask him for photos next time you see him, he will love you forever." I laugh.

His gaze lingers on my mouth, and I feel exposed, vulnerable under his glance. It seems like he notices me in a deeper way than just my appearance.

Turning away, I go and set the butter knife on the counter. "Alright, so you ready to get started?"

Hunter clears his throat. "You bet. Show me our next story."

"Follow me to the men's restroom," I tell him and lead the way.

He chuckles from behind me. "Oh. This should be good."

I walk into the men's bathroom to the wall by the sink and

point to the scribbled writing in blue marker next to the soap dispenser.

Last time I was at this bar, I got arrested. - Ted

Hunter reads where I am pointing and then looks up at me. "Sounds like an interesting one."

"I know. When I saw it the other day, I was so curious. Now I need to know what happened."

"You don't know the story?" he asks me.

"Nope! I never come into the men's bathroom other than to pop my head in at the end of a shift and make sure there aren't any drunk stragglers. Rob usually always stocks and cleans it; it's been that way ever since Seymour passed. He didn't want Jane to have to deal with the nasty men's room and it's just always stayed the same routine," I tell him, thankful. "*But* Tripp yelled at me, saying the bathroom needed toilet paper and more soap the other day before Rob was here so I went in and voila...I saw it." I make a chef's kiss motion with my hand. "Our next story for the series."

"Do you happen to know what Ted's last name could be? I feel like there are at least a hundred Teds in Clairesville."

"I don't, but don't you worry because I *did* talk with Johnny about it, and he *does* know the right Ted." I pull my phone out of my pocket and check the time. "Apparently, they are old friends, so he made a call for us. Ted is expecting us at his home in the next thirty minutes, so we better get going."

I smile at Hunter and hand him the address that Johnny scribbled down on a piece of paper for me.

"Look at you, quite the little journalist," he teases me in response.

"That's me!" I hold my phone under my chin as a pretend microphone, and joke, "If I lose my job at the bar, at least I will have a backup career."

He looks at me with a serious expression. "You won't lose the bar."

"Okay, okay." I nod and lead the way to walk out of the bathroom.

I rush to pick up my keys and Hunter grabs his equipment as I flick off the lights.

"Ready?" he asks.

"Yup!"

As he opens the bar door, I shout, "To the Old Fart!" and walk past him. Then I turn back to look at him and say, with an eyebrow raised, "You're right, it *is* a good name."

Chapter 26

Hunter

We drive through an old money neighborhood with matching brick houses one after another, like someone copied and pasted them on the land. All the lawns are perfectly manicured, not a single weed to be seen. My old diesel truck sticks out like a sore thumb on this upper-class street.

"So, you thrift shop?" Olive asks from the passenger seat.

"Yeah." I glance over at her. "My dad, uh, passed away last year." I stammer and pause for a second, hating that the words are true. "We used to go thrift shopping together. He had a huge vintage model car collection that I now have so I want to keep the shelf growing. Thrift stores are always a good place to find them."

Olive reaches over and touches my right hand, which rests on my thigh. "I'm sorry about your dad."

I'm taken aback by her physical gesture of sympathy and just want to grab on to her hand and hold it. When she moves it away a moment later, my own hand feels cold and empty.

"It's okay," I tell her. "I mean, it's not *okay*, but it's not going

135

to change. I feel the saddest for my mom, who lost not only her husband but also her best friend. My dad was her everything."

"That must be so hard for her. But that's also beautiful to hear, that they were so connected," Olive explains. "Marriages where the couple actually continues to like each other are rare. In my opinion at least." She laughs a little when she says it, but I can tell there is more meaning behind her statement.

"Yeah, they were meant for each other." I think over if I should say anything and then decide to pry a little. "What are your parents like?"

I see her shrink into herself. I regret saying anything immediately. As if I'm saved by the bell, my phone alerts me that we have reached our destination.

Olive looks out the window to her right as I turn into the driveway of a giant brick house with white pillars.

"Wow," she breathes out.

"This place is insane," I say. The house must be at least three stories tall.

"Alright, well I'm officially intimidated." She looks at me anxiously. "What if this guy is a dick?"

"Are you judging someone by the size of their house?" I joke.

"Yes! I am!" She widens her eyes at me. "This place looks like it has a butler named James."

"Well, good thing you're dressed like a butler then," I tease, and she stares down at her work uniform. "You guys will get along great."

"This uniform is horrible, I know. I swear Tripp just makes me wear it to piss me off."

My gaze lingers on her. "You make the uniform look good. Really good." I rub at my facial hair and continue, "I'm still anxiously awaiting the first time I get to meet Tripp."

"Thank you." She lowers her eyes at the compliment. "Also,

trust me, you don't want to meet him." She makes a horrified face. "He's my sleep paralysis demon."

I throw my head back, laughter bursting out of me. I never know what Olive is going to say next and I love it. I lean closer towards her and say, "Alright, listen. I'll ring the doorbell. You can hide behind me till we make sure this guy doesn't bite. We don't need you having two sleep demons."

"Deal." She flips her dark hair over her shoulder and gets out of the truck.

I grab my equipment bag from the back seat and meet her in front of the large white door. Olive vibrates nervously next to me as I click twice on the heavy brass lion-shaped door knocker.

Not even five seconds later, an elderly man wearing a black coat with a white shirt underneath opens the door. "Hello, I'm Benjamin. Mr. Purngast is waiting for you in the study, follow me."

Olive gives me a *you've got to be f-ing kidding me* look and I hold in a laugh at the fact that he actually does have a butler.

We follow him through the fanciest entry room I have ever seen. This house is all white marble and there is a giant crystal chandelier above our heads. This place looks clean enough to eat off the floor. Our footsteps echo as we walk. I wonder how someone of this status ended up in Whiskey's and how he is friends with Johnny, quirks and all.

Benjamin knocks twice on a set of double doors, and I hear a Southern drawl respond, "Enter."

He opens the doors and moves to the side, where a man behind a giant mahogany desk stands to greet us. I almost sigh with relief when I see Ted. Instead of an uppity rich socialite coming towards us, it's a small, old man dressed like he raided Adam Sandler's closet. He has a wide smile that stretches across his face, pulling a giant caterpillar mustache with it. He looks like a cartoon in the best way.

"You must be Olive and Hunter. Ted Purngast," he announces with his gruff Southern twang as he enthusiastically shakes Olive's hands in introduction. When he does, her whole body moves from his aggressive happy shake, and I stifle another laugh. He turns to me next and does the same, my arm vibrating with his strength. For such a small guy, he's really got some power in that grip.

Olive is grinning now. "Thank you so much for meeting with us, Mr. Purngast. I'm excited you are willing to tell us your story."

"Please call me Ted," he explains. "Anything for my friend Johnny."

"How do you know Johnny?" Olive chuckles.

"He is quite the character, huh?" Ted says. Olive nods and he continues, "We grew up together actually, in the Sunny Brights Trailer Park right by the bottom of Jewel Mountain."

"No way! I lived there, too, as a kid!" She lights up. "Johnny and I talk about it all the time. I'm sure they were a lot nicer when you were kids though."

Hearing this bit of information about her past, I mentally write it down on my Olive List. I want to absorb every piece of information she gives crumbs of.

Ted snorts in response. "You would be surprised. I spent years with a bucket next to my bed growing up because there was a giant hole in our ceiling."

Olive nods her head in agreement and jokes, "That sounds about right. 'Welcome to Sunny Brights, where every trailer comes with duct tape and a prayer that your place won't blow away.' Man, they were the worst. So how did you end up here then? Sorry if that's too forward, but this place is *incredible*."

"Well, that's part of my story, actually. Would you like to get your camera before I start?"

I nod quickly and begin assembling my Sony. After clicking on my lens, I turn and let them both know I'm ready. They each sit on a white couch across from each other.

Scooting next to Olive's side across from Ted, I press record and give him a thumbs up.

"The year was 1981 and I was a homeless alcoholic..."

Olive and I shoot each other a look, knowing we have just struck gold.

Chapter 27

Olive

As soon as Mr. Purngast started talking about growing up in the trailer park, I felt an instant connection to him. There is something about knowing what upbringing someone had that makes you feel safe around them. I spent over half my childhood living in Sunny Brights and as far as I know, my mom still lives there. The hurt of knowing she is so close to where I live and work, but couldn't care less about maintaining a relationship with me, makes me feel sick every time I drive by. Her boyfriend of the month has always been her only priority.

Hunter holds up the camera and sits next to me and I feel comfort in his warmth, as Mr. Purngast begins to tell us his story.

"The year was 1981 and I was a homeless alcoholic."

I glance at Hunter and his dark eyes meet mine, holding the same expression. Interest.

"I had been living on the streets for a while. Bumming money and cigarettes off anyone who would throw them my way. I had no purpose or direction. I wanted to be a writer when I was a kid, but I didn't even finish high school, and I had no family that gave a shit. My parents were both alcoholics—my mom met an early grave from liver failure, and my dad was an angry drunk.

"I was thirty-two the first time I walked into Whiskey Jane's. Obviously, I knew the bar was there—alcoholics can always find a drink, but it was cheaper to get beer at the gas station. Also, I didn't want to talk to anyone. I was in a bad place." He points to his head and chuckles. "Mentally...and physically. I had not had a shower in weeks, usually just rinsing my clothes in the sink of a public bathroom. My hair was long and red, and my beard almost touched my chest. I looked like a warlock; that's actually the nickname Jane gave me.

"One day I decided to go in; I'm not sure why. When I first went in, I remember seeing Jane behind the bar. She was beautiful and vivacious. Her voice was so commanding and strong. She was everything I wasn't ready for.

"I stumbled up to the bar and asked for a beer. She took one look at me and said, 'No.' I was about to get belligerent, ready to tell her off for her instant judgment of me based on my appearance, when she continued, 'How about some coffee and a meal instead? On me.'

"My stomach was eating itself; I was starving. I hadn't had a real meal in a long time, but I wanted one thing and that was booze, so I told her, 'No, I want a drink.' But still she refused and tried to reason with me to have some food. I got angry and started to get nasty.

"As we were going back and forth, I didn't notice a man walk up next to me. Then, I heard my name. 'Ted? Is that you, bud?' Whipping my head around I saw Johnny standing there, in his dirty work clothes—he worked in construction at the time. Yes, he still had on his iconic top hat; he would wear it over his hard hat.

"I was so embarrassed to have someone from my past recognize me in that condition. When we were young, everyone in the trailer park used to call us brothers because we looked so much alike. I pushed past him and tried to make it out to the street when Johnny grabbed my arm. He was stronger than I was. I looked at him in the face and snarled, 'Get your fucking hand off me,' and shoved him. Johnny let go of me." Mr. Purngast runs his hand over his face, in obvious shame. "I deeply regret the way I acted back then; my brain was warped."

I lean in, encouraging him to continue. "It's okay. Then what happened?"

"I walked out the front door and sat on the sidewalk near the entrance. Johnny came out and sat next to me. 'You see that lady in there?' he asked me. 'She's one of the nicest people in the world and now that she has met you, she won't stop trying to help you. So, you're going to go inside, have a meal, and then tell her thank you and apologize to her for raising your voice.' He stood back up and walked inside then. I felt like a child that had just been scolded.

"I heard the door open a few minutes later and Jane sat a plate next to me, said nothing, and walked back inside. I looked at a triple stacked club sandwich, with a pickle and chips on the side. My mouth watered at the food, so I dug in.

"After I was done, I grabbed the napkin from under the plate to wipe off my hands when I noticed something was written on it: *Please come inside, I have some clothes you can have. Jane.* I looked down at my shirt, the red now faded to a dull pink from the sun, holes in multiple spots, and thought, *why not, sure.*

"I stood up, plate in hand, and pulled the door open. Jane acted like she didn't notice me walking in, not wanting to spook the metaphorical bear. I sat the empty plate, crumbs and all completely gone, on the counter and gruffly said, 'Thank you, ma'am.'

"At that, I heard Johnny release his breath next to me in relief. 'Call me Jane, sugar,' she said. She smiled at me and then reached underneath the bar. 'These are some of my husband's clothes he keeps here in case he gets dirty fixing up stuff. You take them.' She slid the box towards me, and I started to decline when I saw how many items it was, but she cut me off. 'Now, you take them. I don't want to hear any fuss.' I thanked her again and started walking back towards the door when she called out from behind me. 'Come see me here once a day, Warlock. I will feed you.'

"I was so confused." Mr. Purngast laughs, recalling, "I had no idea what a warlock was. I thought she was calling me some mean name for homeless people. I nodded my head, though, and left the bar again, starting to walk towards the main street, when Johnny drove up next to me in his car. He told me to get in and he would take me to his place to have a shower. I said no, but he insisted, so I went with him.

"He took me to his place and helped fix me up. Cut my hair, trimmed my beard, gave me a deodorant stick and toothbrush. He told me I could even stay at his house if I wanted, he just had to get back to work. I told him thanks for the help, but I left at the same time as him. Johnny said he hoped I would take Mrs. Jane up on her offer and I said I would.

"From that day on, I would go up to the bar once a day, and Jane would feed me. She wouldn't bring up that I was drunk. I always was. She just gave me food and listened to me talk. Judgment free.

"Her husband, Seymour, met me after my first few meals

there. His presence was instantly friendly and welcoming. He was just as great as Jane.

"After months of free meals there, I started drinking less. I had something to look forward to. I got excited every day to go visit them, not about the thought of drinking, which was a new feeling for me. One day I asked Jane what a warlock was, and she laughed while explaining that it was a man that could perform magic, a wizard. I felt dumb for not knowing. 'But I guess you don't look like a warlock anymore,' she told me, looking over my appearance, which had improved significantly in the past few months. I told her I wanted to keep the nickname anyway.

"Johnny and I bonded again, too, from the times I would see him at the bar; he's the person that told me I should write again. He said he remembered all the stories I would scribble down as a child and that he always loved to read them. Seymour overheard the conversation and walked to the office and came back with two pens and a notebook for me. So I started to write, probably absolute gibberish, but the bar inspired me with the art and quotes all over its walls.

"Over the next six months, I wrote a whole book about a kid that becomes a baseball player. Every time I came to the bar, Jane would take the notebook out from under the counter and hand it to me—our routine. I kept the notebook at the bar so it didn't get messed up, since I was still homeless. Johnny offered for me to come stay with him multiple times, but I was too proud for that. I refused to take more help than I was already getting.

"I was almost done writing the novel when I went into the bar one day and saw Jane in tears behind the counter. She couldn't even look at me. Seymour had his hand on her shoulder, consoling her. He met my eyes and solemnly told me that a pipe had burst under the bar counter, and it ruined my notebook. My months of work, gone, just like that. I was so upset when they told me that I just backed out of the bar and ran. I heard Jane crying out from behind me apologizing, saying it was her fault for putting the notebook there, but I didn't stop. I thought that book was my ticket out of my current situation.

"I did the only thing I knew that would comfort me and got hammered. I got so drunk that the next part of the story is patchy in parts," Mr. Purngast explains. "But somehow in my angry stupor, I ended up at the bar and smashed one of the back windows with a rock. This event is what fills me with the most shame so buckle up." He looks down at his hands. "I robbed them. I went into the bar and stole all the money out of their office. I blamed what had happened to my book on them and I wanted them to pay for it. I took at least fifteen thousand dollars, which back then in the early eighties was a ton of money.

"I ran out of there as fast as I could and bought more alcohol, continuing my bender. I don't know what happened to most of the money. I probably dropped it somewhere, honestly. It was all gone within a few hours.

"The next morning, I was still very drunk. I walked into the bar expecting to get my free meal, feeling no shame whatsoever. What I didn't expect was for Johnny to be standing there with Seymour, talking with a police officer. They all turned towards me, and I tried to run but was stopped at once by the officer. I was in no condition to fight off the police. I could barely stand up straight. I was arrested and spent the next few years in jail.

"I was filled with so much anger at first but then I realized that they actually saved my life. I was forced to rehabilitate myself in jail, where I sat in a cell all day, which caused me to start writing again out of boredom. I scrapped the horrible baseball story and ended up writing the story that changed my life. The Winter Warlock series."

145

Hunter and I both interrupt him at once.

"You wrote that series?" I ask in absolute shock.

"Those are your books?" Hunter questions at the same time.

Mr. Purngast laughs. "Yes, that was me. I use a pen name, Freddie Finnely, just so I can stay in the shadows. I never wanted the fame, I just wanted to write, and once I was finally sober, I could."

I am physically shaking; the Winter Warlock series is the biggest young adult book series to have ever been written. I have read every single book and I'm sure Hunter has, too. It was a childhood staple, no matter who you were.

"So, the name of the book," Hunter continues, "is from Jane?"

"Yes." Mr. Purngast smiles vibrantly, his mustache tickling his nose. He almost looks like a human version of the Lorax. "It was from Jane, her nickname for me. The series was almost like my tribute to her and Seymour."

Tears fill my eyes as I whisper, "Wow." This has turned out to be one of the most incredible stories I have ever heard, and I had no idea. Jane did so many impactful things for people before I ever met her. She has never been one to boast but I can't believe she never told me this story.

I swipe away a tear as Mr. Purngast chuckles and hands me a tissue. "Don't cry, honey, my story has a happy ending."

"I just can't believe that I'm sitting here with you and had no idea. I have all of your books on my shelf at home. We live in the same town as a legend," I exclaim to Hunter.

He smiles next to me and agrees. "Your books really are incredible, sir."

Mr. Purngast nods his thanks. "So as you can see, the bar and Jane mean a lot to me. I was so sad when I heard Seymour passed. I was traveling for the release of my sixth book, so I was unable to attend the funeral, but I sent my condolences to her. I want to help Jane any way I can now."

He points to the camera. "Can you put that down for a second, son?"

Hunter complies and once he sets it down on the coffee table, Mr. Purngast continues talking. "I want to donate five hundred thousand dollars to the fund for saving the bar."

At that I don't remember anything else, I just attack him with a hug, crying profusely.

Chapter 28

Hunter

After talking to Mr. Purngast for a little while longer, Olive realizes the time and needs to leave so she can get back to the bar. Once we get to the truck, I am still in shock, unable to process everything that just occurred. I can feel the energy vibrating from Olive, too, her own excitement palpable. I slide into the driver's seat and her eyes are wide when she slams the passenger door next to me.

"Wow!" she gushes. "Can you believe that?"

I shake my head and chuckle. "That was not how I expected our morning to go." Meeting one of the greatest authors of many generations, here in Clairesville...

"I have every book he has ever written!" Olive continues, pushing her dark hair away from her face. "I used to read the books as a kid when I lived at the trailer park, dreaming of another world, not knowing that *the author also lived in that trailer park as a child!*" Her voice is a shriek now, sending me into a full-on laugh.

Then she bounces towards me and engulfs me in a tight hug. It catches me by surprise and takes my breath away

148

momentarily. I don't want it to end. I squeeze her in my arms, resting the edge of my chin on her shoulder for a moment, her scent of roses stronger than before. How desperately I want to cup her face in my hands and kiss her, but she told me this morning I was a *friend*. The friendzone, ouch. It did sting, but I will also take friendship if that's all she wants. I just want to be near her and make her day a little better.

When she finally backs out of the hug, she looks at me, still grinning. "Thank you. If it wasn't for us making the video series, I never would have found that out."

I smile back, "Hey, all I'm doing is filming. The stories are doing all the heavy lifting. Jane really sounds amazing."

"She is." Olive bites the inside of her cheek and I can see emotion swirling in her eyes. "I wish you could meet her—the her who basically raised me. It's just different now; sometimes she doesn't even know herself."

I clear my throat. "I was wondering if you wanted to film one of the episodes talking about your relationship with her. We don't have to put her on camera. I don't want to take advantage of her in a vulnerable state for views or anything. Her character speaks for itself through these stories, but I want you to talk about her. Your relationship is the one that matters the most to me. If you're comfortable with it, of course."

"I would love that," Olive quietly says and looks out the window.

I roll down my window and then she also rolls down hers as I back the truck up. I hand her my phone. "Choose from my playlist."

She touches her heart in mock honor. "This is escalating quickly. First you give me a gift, now I get to go through your phone," she teases me.

I look at her out of the corner of my eye and say, "Eight-seven-three-four," before glancing back to the road.

"What?" she asks.

"That's my password. Use my phone whenever you want. I'm not someone with anything to hide."

With one eyebrow raised she says, "My best friend would love you. You're like every girl who has ever been cheated on's wet dream."

I chuckle and ask, "Have you been cheated on?"

She is momentarily distracted while she punches in the code and begins looking through my music. Realizing the question is probably not one she wants to answer, I'm about to tell her that she doesn't have to when she responds.

"Nope! I don't date." Olive snorts. "No relationship equals no cheating and lying. Problem solved."

I'm wondering who did a number on her to make her think every relationship is like that when I hear a song start playing. "Right Down the Line" by Gerry Rafferty surrounds us, the notes to the intro smooth and provocative.

I meet Olive's eyes. "I love this song."

"Same."

She lifts her hands in the warm breeze and sways them, singing along to the words as I head out onto the main road.

The song ends while we sit at a red light and I quietly say, "You know, not all guys are like that."

"What?" she asks.

"Not all guys are bad in relationships; not all guys are cheaters or liars," I respond, louder this time.

"Of course not," she tells me. "Seymour and Jane, Mr. Ray and Mrs. Sonjia, Rob and Missy; there are good relationship guys out there, they are just all old or married."

I stare at her for a long moment, wanting to tell her, *Me, Olive, me. I'm faithful and I like you.* I'm too shy, though, to try and cross that boundary she has set between us.

"Green!" she exclaims, pointing to the light and snapping me out of my thoughts.

I turn back towards the wheel, cursing myself for not speaking up.

"Let's play a game." She claps her hands together.

"Okay, sure," I respond.

She jumps right in. "Would you rather have bug eyes or a monkey's ass."

I throw my head back, laughing. "What does that even mean?"

"Like a million little lenses together that give you the crazy wide vision, bug eyes. Or a butt that sticks out to attract your mate, like a baboon."

"I think only the female baboons have that," I tell her.

She shrugs her shoulders. "Okay, so you're hypothetically a woman, too."

"Okay, I guess the butt, then."

"Oh, of course. Such a *male* response." She rolls her eyes playfully.

"I couldn't handle having that type of vision; my mind would explode from trying to process so much," I defend my response. "Also, you can judge someone's Would You Rather answer, it's universally known. So, give me a nice butt."

Olive holds her hands up. "Okay, okay. I guess you are right. The ass it is, then."

"Speaking of ass," I say, as we pull into the bar parking lot, "I think your boss is here." I point at a stuffy-looking guy in a polo, leaving out the front of the bar. He aggressively walks over to a silver car that I assume is his.

Olive groans seeing him. "We aren't even open yet. Why is he here? Hopefully he's leaving."

We watch him grab something out of his passenger seat, a file folder, and then stand by his car, like he's waiting.

I park in a spot next to her purple car and she grabs her stuff, then turns to me. "Thanks again for this morning, I had a blast."

"Me, too." I smile at her. "I will edit the footage later and send it to you."

She slides out of the car. "I can't wait to see it. Everyone is going to lose their minds after seeing Mr. Purngast. He is literally so secretive, no one knows details about Freddie Finnely. Who knew Whiskey's would be the thing to reveal his identity?"

"People will be lining up now to view the men's bathroom wall," I joke, knowing it's probably true, though.

"Olive," I hear the man bark out from behind her.

"Yes, Tripp?" she responds, still looking at me.

"I need to talk to you. Come to my office, now." He sneers. "Quit flirting in the parking lot and do your job."

I make eye contact with him, the furthest thing from a smile on my face. He has no right to talk to her that way and I would love to give him my two cents.

Olive gives me an apologetic look. "Gotta go," she says quickly, and starts to walk away.

I continue to stare at this Tripp guy, his gaze never leaving mine. I can't wait till she can take the bar from his grubby hands. He finally breaks our staredown, and turns to walk towards the bar, following Olive. One day I hope to give him what he deserves, but not while he owns the bar. I will play nice for her. For now.

Chapter 29

Olive

O nce I get inside, I silently curse Tripp. If I didn't have to play nice for the bar's sake, I would have cussed him out vividly already. I feel like I am going to be up against a mountain by trying to get him to sell it to me instead of the investors. The B&B guy has come by nonstop, and I heard Mr. Cronline discussing with Tripp that there's no need for him to fix up the place because it will be a "tear down" anyway. He just wants the land. I feel sick inside knowing that if he buys and demolishes the place, it won't only be me without a job, but also Rob. I know they rely on the extra income Missy makes bartending, too. They've been trying to save up money in hopes that they can start a family soon.

I unlock the office door for the first time today and look around to see that Tripp has removed all the photos off the lined walls. Where there used to be photos of Jane and me laughing during a karaoke night, singing Abba together on stage, or Jane and Seymour behind the bar, there are now blank spaces. There's not a single photograph left.

I hear Tripp walk up behind me, and I turn around, demanding, "Where are the pictures?"

"Huh?" he questions, boredom evident in his response.

"The pictures that used to be on the wall." I point to the blank spaces. He knows exactly what I'm talking about; he's just playing coy.

He stares at me and takes a long sip of his coffee, enjoying that I'm riled up by this. "Oh, I took them down. They were dusty, and it was bad for my allergies. I kept sneezing while I was trying to work and it was distracting me. They are in the dumpster if you want to fish for them."

"How could you throw those away? Your mom loved those photos." I step closer to him. "Are you so unhappy with yourself that you want to make everyone else miserable, too?" My voice raises and I can't bite my tongue anymore. "You had no right, Tripp." I push past him and grab a pair of disposable gloves from the prep station before I walk out the back kitchen door.

I hear him calling after me that "we need to have a talk," but that can wait. My blood is boiling. Only Tripp can take one of the best mornings of my life and destroy my mood in seconds. I know that I shouldn't let him get to me, but a person can only take so much crap before they explode. He knew exactly what he was doing when he took down the memories that I shared with his mother. It was a big screw you to me, a power move.

I make it to the large green dumpster out back and cringe as I take a peek inside. The trash hasn't been picked up in almost a week, so it's full. The stench is overpowering. I slide the gloves on and pull my weight up over the side of the dumpster. I assume he must have just tossed the pictures in here this morning before I got back, because the photos were on the wall when I left last night.

I spot one small photo of Seymour in a wooden frame and lean over to grab it. Successfully retrieving it, I hold it under my arm and begin to search for the next one. I find two photos of Jane and me under a bag of sour trash, the frames sinking down between the crevices of the bags.

After spending fifteen more minutes rifling around the top piles of garbage, I realize if I want to find the rest, I'm going to have to go further into the dumpster. I crawl out so I can gently lay the three frames I found on the ground and then get back into the mounds of trash. I whimper as I push through the bags. Old coffee grounds and rotting leftover ham slide in between my shoes and after minutes of gagging, I realize I can't do this anymore. I'm covered in trash and sweat is dripping down my back at this point. I climb out, defeated, and apologize to Jane in my head for the fact that I couldn't find the rest of her photos.

Pushing open the back kitchen door, I see Tripp leaning out from the office in the desk chair. "How did it go?" He stifles a laugh.

I hold up the three frames I found and don't make eye contact. "I'm going home to shower; I'll be back before the lunch crowd."

"Yeah, good idea, do that. You smell horrible." He sneers as I walk past.

Before I get to the door he adds, "Oh, I forgot to mention, I saved some of the pictures. They are in a box in the attic."

At that, I continue to walk out of the bar quickly, pretending I didn't hear a word. He doesn't deserve the satisfaction of a response.

Chapter 30

Hunter

By the time I get back home, I still have a smile on my face. As soon as I get inside, I begin uploading today's footage on my computer. Seeing Olive so excited this morning just makes me want to finish editing the video as quickly as possible. I need another excuse to film with her and see her again. She is so effortlessly fun to be around, and I find myself craving her attention. I really want to spend time with her other than us just working together on the series. Friends hang out, right? I'm nervous about taking that leap, though; she is obviously very resistant when it comes to trusting men. That honestly just makes me want to prove myself more to her.

I lie down on my bed and scroll through my unread texts. It can get overwhelming sometimes, the number of messages I get every day from people wanting me to film them. Skaters constantly begging me to come to a park and record them, or a brand asking me to shoot sponsored content for their social media. Last year I started putting my phone on *do not disturb* most days, for my sanity. I only look at my phone when I feel ready to respond to people, instead of forgetting the messages and never getting back to them. I scroll through a few and answer the questions or decline offers. I see a message from Eddie towards the bottom of the list and tap it.

Wanna go to the lake tomorrow? Invite your girl. We want to get to know her, and we are all bringing some people, so don't worry, shy guy, it won't be weird.

Yes, I want to go to the lake, and absolutely, I want to hang out with Olive. I text Eddie back letting him know I will be there. I work up the courage to text Olive. I know it's a long shot that she can come on such short notice, but I decide to ask her anyway.

Hey, Olive, a couple of my buddies are getting together as a group to go to Onilley Lake tomorrow. Do you want to come with us? I can give you a ride so you don't have to worry about driving there. Sorry about the short notice.

A few minutes later, I get a response.

Hello, Curls, I am currently covered in trash juice and sweat. Nothing sounds better to me than a day off at the lake. Let me see if Missy might be able to cover for me.

Trash juice? I text her back. *Everything okay since I left the bar?*

It's over an hour before she responds.

Sorry to leave you hanging. Long story, but I'm back at work now. Missy said she can cover. Yay!

Hell yeah, I am so excited that she wants to come.

I hope everything is okay, I send and then add, *That's great to hear. I will pick you up outside your place at 9 am if that's okay with you? I'm going to grab some food to bring, too. What do you want?*

Her response chirps on my phone seconds later.

Perfect! I want beef jerky, a Dr. Pepper, and cashews.

I chuckle to myself—the perfect road trip snacks. I meant

that I was going to go to the grocery store and get an actual meal to bring for us, but I will grab those for her, as well.

You've got it. I'm going to finish editing everything tonight, so it will be done before we leave in the morning.

Olive texts me back an hour later.

That's great! Sorry I can't talk anymore; Tripp has been on even more of a tear than usual today.

I wish I knew what he said since he told her they had to talk this morning.

My door nudges open and I see Dog shimmy in, then leap on top of my bed. I pull her into my arms and nuzzle her to my neck. The bell on her collar lightly jingles and she meows. I realize she wants her food, so I get up. As I head downstairs with her in my arms, I daydream about tomorrow.

Chapter 31

Olive

The next morning, I look out my window anxiously waiting for Hunter's arrival. I was taken by surprise when he texted me yesterday, inviting me to come with him and some friends to the lake today. I've never been before; Onilley Lake is out of town and Ivy has a huge fear of water, so there was no point in me going alone.

I've changed swimsuits twice already, feeling insecure about showing too much skin, but then getting angry with myself for caring about showing skin in front of other people. It's not like I'm going on a date or anything, so I'm not sure why I feel so nervous. I end up settling for a cherry red bikini and I tie a silky cheetah-print sash in my hair. I top it off with my cat-eye red sunglasses and I look straight out of the 1950s.

I see Hunter's truck pulling in and notice he's a few minutes earlier than our agreed time. I continue to spy on him as he sits in his truck for a moment, pops something in his mouth, and then gets out. Jumping back from my window so he doesn't see me watching him, I stand behind the door, waiting for the knock. Not even thirty seconds later, I hear three thuds against the door. I take a deep breath to shake out the nerves before releasing it as I pull the door open. Just like that, the breath is swept out of me again. Hunter is wearing a blue tank top, black board shorts, and a light blue snapback. His exposed arms are tan and toned.

He smiles, his eyes crinkling in greeting. "Hey, stranger," he says warmly. "I love your outfit, very Wendy Peffercorn!"

I look down at my outfit and laugh. "I guess you're right!"

"You ready to go?" he asks.

"So ready."

He reaches out and takes my bag from my hand. "I'll carry this for you."

I thank him and lock my front door before we head down to his truck. Hunter opens the passenger door for me again, and I murmur my thanks. I'm not used to chivalry, and I don't know what to think of it. Is he always like this with women or is he trying to hit on me? I don't want to give him the wrong impression or hurt his feelings.

I might get butterflies in my stomach when I'm around him, but I refuse to think of it as anything other than nerves. I can admit to myself that he's gorgeous, but won't allow myself any other possibilities.

When I slide into the seat, he jogs around to the driver's side and sits down next to me. After he turns on the truck, he smiles at me. That vibrant twinkle is always in his deep brown eyes.

"I got you something," he tells me.

"Oh god, is it another knife?" I tease him.

Hunter chuckles. "Hey! You told me you liked it, but no, it's not a knife. Close your eyes."

I shut my eyes and hear him reach into the back seat of the truck, then something heavy is plopped onto my lap.

"Open!" he exclaims.

I comply, and when I see what's in my lap I can't hold back my laughter. It's a basket with the biggest bag of beef jerky I've ever seen, a liter of Dr. Pepper, and four tubs of cashews.

"I didn't want you to starve while we are at the lake," he jokes, shrugging his shoulders.

"You really are *something*. Always bearing gifts," I tell him. At the comment his cheeks flush. "Thank you," I continue, and place the basket between my legs on the truck floor.

He connects his phone and turns on the song "Baby It's You" by Smith.

"Love this one," I gush. "I think we like the same kind of music!"

His gaze lingers on me. "Yeah, I think so, too. That's so important."

I laugh. "Is it?"

Hunter clears his throat. "Yeah, for road trips, I mean. Imagine having to ride in the car with someone for a long time and you hated their music."

"True," I agree with him. "Imagine if I only wanted to listen to 'Baby Shark' on repeat."

Hunter pretends to shiver and glances at me. "Nightmare fuel."

I laugh. Before long, I'm singing along to the lyrics of the song and he surprisingly joins in. His voice is deep and rough, but we are having so much fun in this moment together. I belt out the chorus and he smacks his hands against his steering wheel to the beat. Once the song ends, we chuckle together and fall into comfortable silence.

After heading down a few roads, Hunter suddenly grabs at his pockets, searching for something. "Shit."

"What?" I ask him.

"I think I forgot my wallet at home. Do you mind if we go grab it?"

"Of course not. Let's go. I want to see where the genius works on his videos...in his evil lair?" I joke.

"Get ready to be disappointed, then. It's just in my bedroom."

As if any woman would be disappointed going to his bedroom, I think to myself, and then shove the intrusive thought away like the horny mosquito it is.

"I live on the other side of Clairesville, so I apologize in advance. It's going to take us even longer to get to Onilley now," he tells me.

"No problem." I shrug. "I'm just happy to have a day off work and away from Tripp."

"Yeah, I was going to ask you, what happened yesterday?" He pushes a curl out of his eyes.

I tell him the story about Tripp and the pictures, having to go through the full dumpster. Then to top it off, the fact that he was messing with me, having kept half the photos in the attic. When I finally got back to the bar, I found out the reason that he called me to the office in the first place. Tripp had me sign a form for being late to work last week and told me if I'm tardy two more times, he's going to fire me. By the end of the recap, Hunter's face is full of anger and shock.

"What the hell is wrong with that guy?"

"I have no idea," I respond. "I wish he would just get some karma. Even if I raise the money, he could still be a dick and decide to sell it to someone else instead, just to spite me. Which is why I must act like nothing he does bothers me, even though it eats me alive inside."

"I know how much Whiskey Jane's and *Jane* mean to you. Everything will work out. Don't worry," he responds, his voice sure and strong.

"What makes you so sure of that?" I ask him, not feeling the same confidence in the current situation.

He bites his bottom lip for a second and shakes his head. "Honestly, I'm not sure why but I just know it will work out. I know that you will get the bar." He meets my eyes. "I'm positive."

The sincerity in his expression fills me with a peace that I haven't experienced in a long time. The last person to make me feel this safe was Jane. I reach for his hand, overcome by the moment and squeeze it. "Thank you," I whisper. "I needed that."

He nods and when I pull my hand away, we sit listening to music for the rest of the ride. After a while, he turns the truck onto a winding road with trees that create a canopy above our heads. I love when trees connect like a bridge, it's one of my favorite things. I start to notice the cottage-style houses on the street, and I lean a little closer to the window for a better view.

"Almost there," Hunter tells me, and we pass two more houses before pulling in a driveway. I stare at the coolest A-frame house I've ever seen. It has a large, vibrant garden wrapping around the front of it.

"This is your *house*?" I ask, in awe.

"Yes, it is," he says, putting the truck in park. "Do you like it?"

"*Like* it?" I sound shrill. "This place is the coolest house I've ever seen!"

Hunter chuckles. "You haven't even seen the inside."

"Yeah, I'm sure it's a real dump inside," I say sarcastically.

We both get out of the truck, and he leads the way to his front door. I walk slowly behind him, taking in the flowers, searching for petunias, Jane's favorite. It's become a habit of mine over the years. Whenever I see plants, I search for them, like it's a little token of her.

Hunter notices me lingering and glances back at me from the door. "Do you want to pick some?"

"No, thanks. I was just looking to see if you had any petunias."

He smiles. "Yeah, I do actually." He walks over, showing me two bushes of bright pink and purple ones hidden behind a few other plants.

I grin. "Cool, thank you for showing me."

"Are they your favorite flower?" he asks.

"Jane's," I respond. "I just have this silly thing I do where I look for them wherever I go, for her."

"That's really nice," he says in a deep voice. "It's important to remember the things about people we love. To keep their favorite things around, even when they no longer are."

I can tell he's thinking of his dad at this moment, not just Jane.

I nod my head in agreement as he continues to talk in a low, calming voice. "Come on, I'll give you a tour of my house."

We walk back towards the front door, this time keeping the same pace next to each other. His front door has a wooden frame with stained glass in the center. Just when I thought this place couldn't be any cooler, it has details like this to make it even more unique. I run my hand over the door.

"Hunter, you've got some good taste."

He grins. "Well, I can't take the credit for this place, it was already incredible. Which is why I had to buy it when I saw it was for sale. I didn't want to change a single thing; I wanted to keep all the charm."

"Thank god," I tell him. "I'm so over people buying beautiful old houses just to change everything about them. It's a huge pet peeve of mine."

"Right!" Hunter exclaims. "If you want a simple, modern house, find a simple modern house. Don't change the old, cool ones."

"Let people like us appreciate them," I add.

"Exactly." He pushes the front door open.

I'm not prepared for what I see when I walk inside the doorway. The interior opens straight to a front room with a large, vaulted ceiling. A unique '70s style prism glass chandelier dangles down and the opposite side has a giant window overlooking trees in the backyard.

"I like how you acted amazed when you went to the Rays' house, when you come back to this place every day. It's equally, if not more, incredible."

Hunter chuckles. "Their place is amazing. Of course, I like my house, too. I even dreamed of living here as a child."

"I would have, too, if I knew this place existed," I agree.

"I actually grew up down the street, so driving by it a few times a day really cemented it into my brain. I had a goal to work towards."

"Does your family still live down the street?"

"Just my mom," he says. "I was an only child."

"Me, too."

"Did you like it?" he asks me.

"Heck no," I respond. "I was so lonely growing up, all I wanted was a sibling. I used to pray at night for one. But now as an adult, I'm glad I never had one. I wouldn't want another child subjected to the stuff that I was growing up."

Hunter looks concerned by what I said, and I try to quickly brush off what I just shared with him. "So, give me this tour!"

He breaks our eye contact and begins to lead me through the house. Every room is clean and simplistically decorated. There isn't an item out of place.

We get to the kitchen and there's all blue cabinetry and a small wooden dinner table. I walk along the side of the table and rub my hands over the wood. Then I notice a room off to the right of the kitchen. "What's that?" I ask him.

"That's the guest room; my cousin is staying there. He's

been gone for a little while, though, so I'm basically just holding his stuff."

I shake my head. "Cool, cool."

"Yeah, I guess," he murmurs, as I hear a little jingle noise. "That's Dog."

"Dog?" I ask, confused. "Does your dog not have a name?"

"Dog is a cat named Dog." He beams as a small black cat comes around the corner.

"Oh my god." I drop to my knees when I see it and the cat comes towards me. "Dog." I laugh. "Okay, how did that name come about?"

"After my dad passed, I went to the shelter to get a dog and instead I came back with this little lady. She wouldn't stop meowing when I walked past, so I asked if I could hold her and as soon as she was in my arms, it was over for me. I had to adopt her. Later that day, my mom stopped by with a dog collar, a bed, and dog toys she had bought prematurely when I told her I was adopting one. I felt so bad when she showed up with everything because she made the effort, which she hadn't been doing much at that time, after my dad passed. I saw her face fall when she realized I didn't have a dog, so in the moment I quickly said, 'It's fine, Mom! It's Dog!' And that was it, the name just stuck."

"I love that," I tell him. "Dog is a perfect name for this cutie."

I coo at the cat as I stroke her back. She gives me one last second of her time and then saunters off to another room. I start to get up off the floor as Hunter reaches out his hand to help me. Déjà vu from when this happened before flashes through my mind and I internally cringe. I can tell Hunter is recalling the moment, too, as he helps me up.

"Sorry about brushing you off before when you tried to help me up that night at the bar. I was so embarrassed," I say, my words drifting off into the space between us.

"Are you kidding me?" he responds. "You had nothing to be ashamed of. I made an ass out of myself and hurt you at the same time. I still think about it every night before I fall asleep."

I laugh. "So, you think about me in bed?"

Oh my god. Why did I even just say that? A manhole can swallow me up now. Beam me up, aliens.

Hunter bites at his bottom lip, seeming unsure how to respond. His familiar shy blush blooms across his cheeks.

I quickly say, "Kidding!"

He tucks his hands into his pockets. "On that note, follow me to my room." He raises an eyebrow playfully and we head upstairs. At least he didn't make it awkward. I'm getting way too comfortable with him.

Chapter 32

Hunter

Olive follows me upstairs to my room and I think about the joke she just made about me thinking about her in bed. If only she knew how much I actually think about her. Every time something happens to me, I think, *I wish Olive was here.* I know it's wrong, it's a complete overstep. She's not mine to have, but damn I wish she was.

Olive asks me a question and it snaps me out of my thoughts. "Did you decorate this place yourself?"

"Yeah, I got a lot of the stuff from thrift stores or furniture stores out of town. I had a lot of fun finding stuff for the house."

"I would love to do something like that."

"Your place isn't decorated how you like?"

I push open my bedroom door and she follows me into the room. She awkwardly stands against the wall, so I motion to my desk chair for her to sit while I search for my wallet. Olive slides into the black swivel chair and continues to talk.

"It is to some extent," she responds. "My place is tiny, though, so I can't do much. Also, there's this thing called *money.*" She laughs as she says it, really emphasizing the word. "The bar doesn't bring in customers like it used to. It's hard for me to run it basically alone now and there's not a budget to hire on more staff. The karaoke nights are usually our big money makers each month; they always turn a crowd."

"I was going to ask you when the next one is. I want to film some of it for the series."

"Next Thursday." Olive smiles at me. "And this time you don't even have to wear a mask."

"Are you messing with me, so I'm subjected to another *task?*"

"No, I swear." She giggles. "This time it's animal print night. Like a safari theme, so I better see a badass printed shirt."

"I actually do have one of those," I say with a grin, as I walk to my closet to retrieve it. I dig through and find the cheetah print button-up that Eddie's twin sister, Leena, got me for my twenty-first birthday. I still haven't worn it. I turn around and show it to Olive.

"That's perfect!" She claps her hands together. "You can come to the bar a little bit early that night if you want to film some of the quiet before the storm."

"I am always down to spend more time at the bar," I tell her, hanging the shirt back in my closet.

I dig through a few drawers, wondering where my wallet could be, before I remember the last time I had it in my hand was when I was in the kitchen this morning.

"I think I know where my wallet is." I feel like an absolute idiot. "It's downstairs."

Olive stands and motions for me to lead the way out of the room. I head down the steps back to the kitchen and open the fridge. Sure enough, my wallet sits on the top shelf, right next to the milk.

"How did that happen?" Olive laughs, peering from behind me.

"I had some drinks in my one hand and my wallet in the other this morning when I was getting stuff out of the fridge. I was in kind of a rush to get out the door, so I guess I tossed my wallet in as I pulled the drinks out." I glance at her, grinning slightly. "Honestly, I don't know."

I run my hand over my eyes. "Alright, let's go."

Once we get on the road, I start to feel nervous. Knowing that my friends can be a lot to handle, I hope they don't scare her away. Don't get me wrong, they are all nice, but they can be intense. Wes has no filter; he will ask anyone anything without thinking twice. Eddie is a straight shooter; he sees right through people's intentions. I just know they are going to grill her with questions and then probably try to make her do a beer bong five minutes later.

I texted them in advance this morning, asking them to take it easy on her. Wes just sent me back a wink and Eddie gave the text a thumbs-up. Whatever those responses mean, they do not instill confidence.

I turn to Olive. "I want to apologize in advance for whatever my friends do today."

She gives me a funny face. "Are you kidding me? I work at a bar; I can literally handle it all. I'm not afraid of a couple drunk bros."

"Is that what we are? *Bros?*" I laugh. "I think we are more like distinguished gentlemen. I don't even watch sports."

She stares at me. "You're kidding me, right? Wes actually looks like the definition of a bro. He had short shorts and a lacrosse jersey on when you came into the bar for the first time."

I throw my head back and laugh at that, realizing he did look like a total bro. "He might dress like one sometimes, but he's not. Except, well, he does sleep with a lot of women so maybe that is bro behavior."

Olive raises an eyebrow. "Exactly."

"Well, you got me there." I'm smiling from ear to ear. "We are just a bunch of bro degenerates."

"I knew it." She smirks as we pull up to the lake entrance.

She grabs one of the bags of beef jerky from the truck floor and rips it open. "Why does beef jerky taste so good, but smell like a bag of farts?" she asks, eyes wide.

Laughter consumes me again. Everything she says is always something I don't expect to come out of her mouth.

"I think it's just from the spices or dehydration process or something?" I respond.

"I don't know, but man, it's good. Just bad for everybody around you while you eat it."

"I can handle it; you can eat a bag of farts around me any day."

She holds her hand to her heart. "That's the sweetest thing anyone has ever said to me," she says playfully. Then, she shoves a piece in her mouth.

I continue to smile as we turn around the right side of the lake, pulling up to a rocky area where I see Eddie and Wes already set up with a small group. Eddie turns from their game of football, hearing my truck, and waves. I wave back and throw the truck in park.

I turn to Olive just as she leans in and whispers, "Do I spy a few *bros* playing football?"

I slide even closer to her, our faces just inches apart. "You're right. The bros are bro-ing."

I hear her breath hitch as I stay close, keeping our eye contact. She looks down at my mouth, her gaze lingering. I'm not going to be the one to break this moment of intimacy first.

Suddenly, she pulls back as if remembering herself and exclaims, "Great! Let's go! Introduce me to the group."

Then, she pops out of the passenger seat and shuts her door. I blow out my own breath and adjust my hat, knowing that my feelings for her are intensifying and there's nothing I can do now to stop them. The train left the station the first second I laid eyes on her.

Chapter 33

Olive

To say I rushed out of the truck would be an understatement. I practically jumped out of my seat when I realized how close we just were to kissing. I constantly catch myself letting my guard down around Hunter, which terrifies me. He gets out of the driver's side and gives me a quick, inquisitive look before heading to the bed of his truck. I meet him around the back and grab a pop-up chair, slinging it over my shoulder.

"It's fine, I can carry that," he tells me as he reaches for it.

I pull back gently. "You know, I'm not some fragile little bird; I can carry stuff. I carry kegs at work."

"I know that," he tells me, "I just want to help if I'm here."

Before I can respond, I see his two best friends, Wes and Eddie, walk up towards us. Wes gives me a huge smile, his blond hair shining like silk in the brutal sunlight. "Hey, Fruity O's!"

I groan. "Oh god, is that nickname going to stick?"

Eddie chuckles. "Wes is all about nicknames. You got off easy."

"Oh yeah?" I raise an eyebrow. "Well, let's hear these other nicknames."

Eddie points to himself. "Bologna." Then he points to Hunter. "Hot Dog."

"I'm noticing a food theme." I look at Wes.

"Well, Eddie used to have a bologna sandwich every single day for lunch growing up."

"And you?" I turn to Hunter and ask him.

Hunter deadpans. "I ate too many hotdogs at his ninth birthday and threw up all over the place."

"And how many hot dogs was that?"

"Six," Eddie, Wes, and Hunter all say in unison.

"Hmmm, so five is the perfect number of hotdogs, then." I playfully tap my index finger to my mouth. "Good to know."

"Mind you, I was nine years old. I could eat way more now," Hunter points out.

"Did you know every hot dog you eat takes thirty-six minutes off your life?" Eddie adds.

Wes groans. "Don't mind him. Eddie is our professional party pooper. Mr. Intellectual Health Nut," he says in an uppity British accent.

"Okay, I'm not even British? Also, sorry for caring about what I fuel my body with. My body is a temple."

A beautiful tall girl with braids walks up behind Eddie, smacking his back. "'My body is a temple,'" she mocks while making air quotes. Then she walks past Eddie and gives Hunter a hug.

"Hey! I haven't seen you in forever." She squeezes him tight and then grabs onto his shoulders as she pulls away.

"Hey, Leena! Yeah, it's been ages." He smiles kindly at her. "This is Olive." He turns, motioning to me.

Her face lights up as she looks at me. "I didn't know you

had a girlfriend, Hunter! And she's *gorgeous.*" She walks towards me. "Is it okay if I hug you? I'm a hugger."

She pulls me into her arms before I can even tell her *it's fine* as I hear Hunter say, "She's not my girlfriend, just a good friend."

For some reason, it sounds like there is disappointment in his voice as he says it.

"Oh, of course I put my foot in my mouth the second I meet someone new. I'm sorry for assuming!" she says to me, apology in her eyes. "Hunter just never brings girls around to hang out with the group, so I was overexcited." She laughs. "We need more females! Anyway, I'm Leena, Eddie's twin sister."

"It's totally fine!" I smile at her. "And it's great to meet you, Leena."

"Follow me, I'll introduce you to everyone!" she chirps as she leads me towards a group that's gathered on a grassy area near the water. Her bouncy, vibrant energy reminds me so much of Ivy.

When we get over to the group of people, Leena introduces me and then begins naming everyone off quickly. "This is my roommate, Alice." A pale girl with green hair leans forward from her chair and shakes my hand.

"My boyfriend, Parker."

A short, red-haired guy stands. "It's nice to meet you, Olive."

I love that Leena is taller than her boyfriend; there's something so attractive about a man that isn't intimidated by a taller woman.

"Parker's younger sister, Ysabel."

A small girl with matching red hair smiles up from her towel and waves. "Ezra." She points to a large guy with shaggy brown hair, currently holding the football, running away from another guy with long dark hair. "Donovan," she says, pointing to the long-haired guy. "Skater friends of the guys."

Leena yells out to them while standing next to me, startling me. "Come meet Olive!"

The guys stop their game and run over. As they jog towards us, it might as well be slow motion. Their bodies are shimmering with sweat in the light. I feel like I'm watching something intimate and seductive. Both men are heavily tattooed and jacked. I snap out of my trance when I realize one of them just said something to me—the Ezra guy.

"I love your shades," he repeats, pointing towards my head, where they are currently resting in my hair. I reach up and touch them.

"Oh, thanks! One of my regulars at work gave them to me last year for my birthday."

"Very cool." He nods. "I'm Ezra." He reaches out his arm and the tattoo of an eagle on his pec moves as he does. Did it just get ten degrees hotter outside? I shake it and then the other guy holds out his hand with a serious expression.

"Donovan," his deep voice murmurs. Who knew they made them like this at the skate park? I've got to let Ivy know.

I hear someone clear their throat from behind me and turn to see Hunter standing nearby.

"I brought some sandwiches and fruit if you're hungry." He holds up a tan wicker basket with a half-smile playing on his lips.

"You made me a picnic?" I ask, unable to contain my grin.

He shrugs. "I just thought we would get hungry."

"You're speaking my language."

"Well, come, sit, eat," he tells me and motions to a large teal blanket on the grass. "After lunch we are going to take Donovan's boat out. Have you ever been water skiing?"

"He has a boat?" I follow him over to a blanket and sit next to him.

"Yeah, the guys both live on the other side of the lake." He points towards the right of the water. "They are cousins and run a fishing charter together. They have *multiple* boats. But we are just going on a smaller one today." He motions towards an at least thirty-foot boat sitting by the dock.

"Oh yes, their tiny little boat," I say sarcastically. "How sad that they didn't bring their yacht. I'm deeply offended."

Hunter laughs. "That does sound pretty ridiculous, huh?" He reaches into the basket and pulls out two sandwiches. "PB&J or peanut butter and banana?"

"Oooooo," I respond. "Definitely peanut butter and banana. Got to get my potassium up before a long day of falling on my ass in the water."

"You don't have to water ski if you don't want to." Hunter hands me the sandwich. "They also brought a tube."

"I'm gonna be honest with you," I tell him, "I've never been on a boat."

"You're kidding!" He leans in towards me, eyes wide. "Never?"

"Nope, trailer park kid doesn't scream knowing a lot of people with boats," I joke.

Hunter's eyes glow. "Your first time on a boat, you're going to love it!" He takes a giant bite out of the PB&J in his hand.

"I'm a little nervous." I pull my sunglasses over my eyes to hide the vulnerability behind them. "I'm not a great swimmer; I was never taught growing up so I kind of sink like a rock. I didn't really think this through before agreeing to come to the lake."

"Don't worry, they have life preservers on the boat, and I will stay next to you the whole time if you want." He stares at me with such sincerity. "I would never let anything happen to you. You're safe with me."

Those words ping off my brain and soak into my chest, my heart suddenly feeling like it's expanding. I don't know how he does it, but he tells me exactly what I need to hear in this moment. He knows what I need to feel safe and secure.

The warm sensation continues to flow through me as I finish my sandwich, and we eat the fruit he brought. Hunter talks to me about his childhood with all the guys. Then, how he met Donovan and Ezra. "They were the wild kids at the skate park growing up," he recalls, laughing. I listen to his stories and feel myself enamored with him as he lights up a little more with each memory.

Leena and Alice come over, pulling me out of my trance.

"Ready to go?" Leena asks, grinning as she pulls her braids back into a ponytail.

Hunter glances my way, his expression unsure, waiting to see if I want to go on the boat.

"Yup!" I say to her, feeling more confident with him at my side.

I stand up and adjust my bikini bottoms as the rest of the group begins to walk down to the dock. Ezra is already on the boat, turning on the engine.

I stand next to Ysabel as everyone starts to get on board.

"Have you ever been tubing, Olive?" She smiles, freckles covering her fair cheeks. She looks like a real-life Strawberry Shortcake doll.

I shake my head. "No, I haven't. Is it fun?"

"It's a blast, ride with me when we go."

"Okay." I smile at her. Hunter stands on my left, and I feel braver by the second.

I climb up onto the boat and take a seat on a long, padded bench behind the wheel next to Wes and Alice. The boat engine vibrates under us, and I let out a breath as Donovan unties us from the dock before hopping on the back.

We ride around the lake for ten minutes and I'm starting to enjoy myself when Ezra lets off the gas and asks, "Okay, who's skiing first?"

"Me!" Wes hops up.

"Could have called that one," Eddie teases.

"Oh, shut up," Wes responds. "Everyone watch and learn." He stands and rips off his shorts, revealing a bright red Speedo underneath.

Eddie groans and Hunter says, "What the—"

Wes cuts him off. "Don't be jealous. This is what peak male sexuality looks like." He walks towards a life jacket and clips it on, then turns to Donovan who hands him the skis.

I look at Hunter across from me and mouth, *"Bro,"* raising my eyebrows.

He throws his head back, laughing in that uncontrollable way he does, the laughter charging out of him, full speed. Everyone else looks at him confused as he explains, "Just thought of something funny from earlier."

Wes jumps off, skis on his feet, and Donovan tosses him the handles attached to the back of the boat. We begin to pull away, slowly. Wes adjusts himself in the water and gives Ezra a thumbs up, signaling he's ready to go. With the go ahead, Ezra gases the engine and we take off quickly, my hair whipping at my face. Leena lets out a squeal as she slides into Parker from the sudden movement and he wraps his arms around her, steadying her.

Once he sees Wes is up on the water, Donovan lets go of the back railing that he was gripping onto when we took off. He doesn't even seem phased by our quick speed as he walks through the center of where we sit. He stops next to Ezra and connects his phone to a speaker next to the steering wheel. The song "Cowboys from Hell" by Pantera begins blasting, echoing over the lake. Wes is still up on the skis, riding the wake behind us, and I lean my head back, laughing as the music and wind overtake me.

The warm sun beats down on my face and I feel free and happy in this moment. Like nothing can get to me. The only thing I'm thinking about is how weightless I feel as we glide over the water.

I bring my head back down after a few minutes and meet Hunter's eyes. He is staring at me with an intensity I haven't seen before, and I bravely hold his gaze instead of shying away like I did earlier. A soft smile plays on his lips, and I bite at the inside of my cheek. This moment feels magical and there is nowhere else I'd rather be.

He is the first to break eye contact this time when Leena leans over to him and asks him a question. I can't hear what he responds but he nods his head at her and quickly glances at me again. I look out past him at the water, like I didn't notice the interaction, but I'm actually dying inside to know what she said to him.

All of a sudden I hear Donovan shout for Ezra to cut the engine and I see that Wes is floating in the water.

"Man down!" Parker shouts and I'm worried that Wes is injured until I notice he has a big smile on his face as he lays on his back, the gentle waves from the boat rocking him.

Ezra steers the boat carefully to Wes's side.

"I'm tired! My arms are burning like pepper on a pimple. Pull me in, man," he says as he swims over to the handle and grabs back on. Donovan begins to pull the rope back in towards the boat, his muscles flexing vividly, and I bite back a laugh as I can see Alice practically drooling, staring at him.

Wes pulls his body up onto the boat's flat back and unclips the skis.

"Hot Dog, you're next," Wes commands.

"Someone else can go if they want," Hunter replies casually.

"Oh please," Eddie says, rolling his eyes. "We all know you're itching to get out there."

"Okay, fine. I'll go." Hunter chuckles, then looks at me. "You cool?"

I nod quickly and hold my hands up, shooing him. "Go, go!"

"Alright, be right back." He smiles, his curls loose and wild from the boat.

He puts on a life vest and straps himself into the skis, the same way as Wes. Then, Hunter jumps off the back into the blue water and gets in position to take off.

Leena leans forward towards me, a hint of mischief in her eyes. "You're in for a treat."

"Wha—" I start to ask her, but then we blast off again, and I instantly find out what she's talking about. Hunter is immediately up and begins hopping the wake behind the boat. Then he switches, and does it one handed, casually pushing his hair back like it's nothing. A confident smile is on his lips as he waves to me and I wave back like some fan girl, practically giddy.

He shouts for the whole lake to hear, "This one's for you, Olive!" and then proceeds to flip, over and over and over again, on the wake.

And at that, the water unfortunately isn't the only thing that's wet around here anymore.

Chapter 34

Hunter

By the time I'm done skiing, I'm out of breath and my muscles ache from holding onto the handle so tightly, but I couldn't be happier. I tread in the water, waiting for Donovan to pull me back in, and hope that Olive was fine on the boat. When I pull my body up onto the back of the boat, I see her smiling ear to ear. Good. Her fair skin is starting to turn red, so I need to remember to grab the sunscreen out of my truck when we get back to shore. I unclick from the skis and take the towel that Parker tosses to me.

"Thanks, man," I tell him.

"You killed it out there," Parker says. "I think you've chosen the wrong career."

I laugh. "Nah, I'll stick to being behind the camera and filming other people." I shake my hair in the towel and slide down next to Olive as Alice moves to the side to make room for me.

"That was impressive." Olive nudges my shoulder playfully with her own. "Who knew you could walk on water?"

Alice cuts in, "You should see him skate; he's just as good at that, too."

"Wow, look at you, quite the overachiever." Olive raises an eyebrow. "Is there anything you can't do, Curls?"

I think to myself, *Yeah, make you mine,* as I grin and respond, "Plenty. I can't play an instrument to save my life or even draw a straight line."

"Yeah, he's bad with his hands," Wes teases.

"I doubt that," Olive rebuts and I turn to her in shock as she continues, "He has very steady hands when he films."

"Ha! I thought you were going to say you knew *firsthand.*" Eddie winks at her.

Instead of shrinking back at what he said, Olive states firmly, "No. We're just friends. Right, Hunter?" She turns to face me.

"Right," I respond, trying to muster as much enthusiasm as I can while I can feel Wes and Eddie's *yeah, right* stares penetrating through my skin.

Ezra asks, "You guys ready to get the tube out?"

Ysabel jumps up. "Yes!" she says, grabbing Olive's hand, pulling her up as well. "We are going together first."

I stand, hearing that, and grab a woman's life jacket. "You'll need this. Here let me help you."

"Thanks." Olive nods her head and walks in front of me, holding her arms out.

I slide the jacket over her arms, and she pops them through the holes, then I click the buckles, making sure they are tight and secure to her. She looks up to me when I finish. I can see she's anxious—her big doe eyes always show her every emotion.

I lean in and whisper in her right ear, "You okay?"

Her warm breath tickles me as she reaches on her tippy toes to respond back, "I'm scared. What if I get eaten by a shark?"

I chuckle as I say, "Don't worry, it's a lake in the middle of Tennessee. Shark free." I squeeze her shoulders. "I have an idea. How about together we lean into something that scares us today? Instead of shying away, we commit and do it."

"Okay. Deal. But if I do this, you must do yours later. What is it?" She looks at me, curious.

"I'll tell you later, just focus on your mission right now." I smile down at her and nudge my head towards the back of the boat where the tube is now attached.

Ysabel plops onto the giant yellow tube. "Come on, girl!"

After one final look at me, Olive turns and grins at her. "Coming!"

I watch her sit next to Ysabel, who grabs both of her hands and says something to her that causes Olive to smile in response and scoot closer to Ysabel.

Donovan gently pushes their tube off into the water and they float back behind the boat. "We're ready!" Ysabel screams and Ezra takes off.

Instant screaming comes from the girls, as they hold on for dear life. Both of them are laughing and squealing together hysterically as they hit the wake. I wish I had my camera right now to film this moment. Olive has had an undercurrent of stress around her since I met her—who can blame her with what's going on with Jane and the bar. But right now, she looks alive and carefree. I take a mental picture, so I never lose this moment, promising myself that this must be enough for me, getting to see her like this, but not having her.

By the time we get back to the lake shore hours later, the sun is starting to go down.

Chapter 35

Olive

The ride home from Onilley Lake is peaceful and relaxing. Hunter and I fall into an easy conversation, joking and comparing interests. I find out he hates mayo and loves the movie *Pride and Prejudice*, which I can't get over. He explains how he used to watch it with his mother when he was little and ended up loving it; it became his comfort movie. I chuckle to myself thinking about Hunter in all his masculine glory, sitting alone in his room, watching Mr. Darcy confess his love to Elizabeth.

By the time he drops me at my house, I feel like I have learned so much about him today. It's not until I get inside that I realize, I never asked him what his part of the deal we made was. I wonder what would scare him—he seems so confident and sure of his actions. He may be more reserved than his friends, but I like that about him. He doesn't try to put on a persona or peacock around in front of other people. He just is who he is.

I send him a quick text.

Okay, you cheated. What were you supposed to do today that scared you? I never found out.

I hop in the shower while I wait for his response, wincing at how burnt my skin is. Hunter brought me some sunscreen but by the time we got back on land, it was too late—the damage was done to my cherry red back. It's my own fault for not being prepared, knowing my fair skin can't handle the sun for more than an hour without burning to a crisp.

I replay every moment of the day in my head, smiling every time I think about the group's playful banter and how welcoming everyone was. I don't usually hang out with anyone but Ivy. I'm always with her or working so it was nice to meet some new girls today.

Leena and Alice were like yin and yang—Leena bright and cheery, while Alice rarely showed emotion. Ysabel even asked for my phone number before I left, which made me excited. She works for a local interior designer and told me she spends most of her time going from stores to galleries looking for clients and would love some company. I quickly agreed; any excuse to go shopping without having to spend my money sounds great to me.

By the time I finally exit the shower and wrap a towel around my body, I realize it's been over thirty minutes, and I have two texts sitting on my phone from Hunter.

I'm trying to convince myself that it doesn't scare the crap out of me that I might never know what it feels like to kiss your lips.

I gasp. Then I read the other message, sent just a few minutes ago.

I scared you. Forget I said any of that, please. I will see you on Monday to film.

I walk over to my bed and sit on the edge of it in my towel. I keep reading over his first message again. I can't even lie to myself and say I'm not tempted to know what his lips taste like. What I feel for him is lust, though, nothing else, and it's not worth it to sleep with him and ruin the friendship we have formed. At least, that's the story I'm sticking with; if I tell myself that enough, maybe I will believe it.

I text him back thanking him for today and saying that I will see him Monday, completely ignoring his other text. I don't need anything else to worry about right now and I need to prioritize visiting Jane. Knowing I most likely have only a few months left with her causes my throat to constrict. I promise myself that I'm going to see her tomorrow morning before work and then get ready for bed.

Chapter 36

Olive

One week later

The past few days have been a whirlwind. Hunter and I filmed another episode for the series, and he already posted it. I was worried when we met up on Monday that things would be awkward after the text he sent me, but he acted completely normal. He didn't bring it up once and that was a huge relief for me.

This time Hunter picked something off a wall for our video, and it was easy to find the woman because she put her first and last name under her writing.

It said: *Today's my 21st birthday! - Hannah Glesby, 2003.* Once we tracked down Hannah, who lived only a few miles from the bar in a residential neighborhood, she was happy to tell her tale. Hannah is now a stay-at-home mother of four, married to a plumber named Ron. She laughed as she told us about how her friends handed her shots all night at Whiskey Jane's and she ended up throwing up out the window of her best friend's car the whole ride home. Hannah said it was still one of the best nights of her life and she'd danced on top of the bar while screaming Shania Twain. By the time Hunter finished filming her story, we were both smiling and laughing along with her.

Since Mr. Purngast's video was uploaded last week, there has been a ton of attention on the series. Comments began pouring in, saying funny things like "I've never wanted to see a men's bathroom so badly," or "Currently planning my trip to Clairesville so I can eat a sandwich on the sidewalk like Freddie Finnely."

The internet went insane learning about the past of this beloved author. Everyone was calling him an inspiration for sharing his history of addiction and overcoming so many struggles to come out on top.

Thanks to that interview and Mr. Purngast's generous donation, we have now raised over $750,000 for the bar. That doesn't even include the money the videos are generating from being monetized. Hunter said the balance is around $11,000 right now so I am growing increasingly hopeful that we will hit our goal.

I set down the bar glass that I'm currently drying and walk towards the front door, peeking outside for Tripp's car in the parking lot, knowing he will be here any moment. He usually comes in early on karaoke nights because he doesn't want to stick around for the *chaos* at night—his words. He has been nicer to me the past two days and I've been shocked by his change in behavior, but I will take what I can get.

I'm relieved to see that his car isn't here yet and I walk over to pick some music on the jukebox. I pick "White Room" by Cream and turn around at the same time the bar door jingles open.

"Hey, Olive Oil," Rick says as he walks towards the counter and pulls out the chair he always sits in.

"Hey, Rick. Coffee?"

He nods and takes his daily newspaper from under his arm. "Of course."

I go behind the bar and pour him a fresh, hot cup of coffee in a mug, then slide it towards him. He acknowledges it and thanks me, barely glancing up. His usual smile is nowhere to be seen and that worries me.

"What's wrong?" I ask him, cutting to the chase. There's no room for bullshit when we have known each other for ten years.

"I just visited Jane." He meets my eyes and sighs. "It's not looking good."

"I know," I quietly respond.

When I visited her last week and yesterday, she was completely out of it, not even acknowledging my presence. I just sat beside her and squeezed her hand the whole time while she blankly stared at the TV. Jane no longer recognizes me, and her cough continues to wreck her lungs. I can hear her wheeze as she draws each breath, and it doesn't seem like having an oxygen tank is even helping her at this point.

I hate seeing her in this type of pain. She is so confused, no longer caring about anything or wanting to eat. I tried to lift some broth to her mouth when I visited yesterday, but she just shook her head *no* and pushed it away. I feel selfish for wanting her to hold on, to live, so I don't have to lose her. I'm just not ready to let go. I need her.

Rick reaches out and takes my hand, seeing that I'm deep in thought. "She was the best thing about this bar, I always said."

I nod my head, agreeing with him as he continues, "That is until I met you. You are just like her. Strong. I know she would be so proud of you and everything you are trying to do to save the bar, if she knew."

Hearing those words, a dam releases inside of me and tears flow down my face.

I squeeze his hand back. "Thank you."

Tripp walks through the door then, spoiling our moment. "Geez, who died?" he snorts when he sees the tears streaming down my cheeks. Rick stares at him, a stern expression across his brow, as I turn away and wipe at my face quickly, hiding my emotion.

"Is everything prepped for tonight?" Tripp asks me as he shuffles through some papers.

"Yes," I curtly respond. Like I don't know what I'm doing after running this place for years alone. I've handled hundreds of karaoke nights at this point; I could practically get everything ready in my sleep.

"Good, good," Tripp says as he still doesn't even look up from the papers.

I notice some earwax on the edge of his ear canal and want to gag. He looks up at me then and I break eye contact with his ear, plastering a fake smile on my face. He nods at me once and walks through the kitchen door, towards the office. I turn to Rick once he walks off and roll my eyes. Rick shakes his head, sharing my feelings.

The rest of the day goes by quickly and before I know it, it's 8 P.M. I hurry to the women's bathroom so I can throw on some mauve lipstick and change into my animal print outfit. I brought the tiger print orange dress that I usually wear for this theme. It hugs my body but also has stretch, so I can still move easily behind the bar.

Hunter is coming by tonight to film. He's also bringing Eddie, who wanted a redemption after he didn't get to do karaoke on his birthday. I told Hunter that Eddie can have the first song of the night, and he gladly relayed the message. They should be coming in the door any minute now.

I'm starting to feel a little nervous. Lust, *just* lust. I have been thinking about his text nonstop since he sent it, the curiosity getting the best of me. Maybe if I did kiss Hunter, I could get him out of my head. If he's a bad kisser, then that will instantly handle the problem. If he's a good kisser, I will dissociate until we finish filming the series.

I leave the bathroom and walk behind the bar, pouring myself a generous shot of tequila and quickly downing it.

"Whoa," I hear Rob say from the kitchen window behind me. "Everything good?"

"Perfect." I turn and plaster a forced smile in his direction as I smooth down my dress. "Just a little jittery about tonight."

"Since when does karaoke make you nervous?"

I hear the bell chime behind me; Rob's eyes meet someone entering the bar.

"Oh. Now I see." He smiles and looks back at me with a wink.

I turn around to see Hunter and Eddie strolling towards me. They look like two Calvin Klein models. I glance over my shoulder so I can shut Rob down about whatever he is assuming, but he is no longer in the window. I scoff and then walk up to the bar counter.

"What will it be, gentlemen?" I grin and motion to the liquor bottles as they slide onto the bar stools in front of me. Hunter has on the cheetah shirt from his closet and Eddie is wearing a silky zebra print shirt that clings to his pecs underneath. I don't know how either of these guys are single.

Eddie speaks up first. "Four shots of gin and some Limp Bizkit, please."

"In the mood to 'Break Stuff'?" I joke, naming the band's most popular song.

"Yeah, I am actually," he responds. "One of the guys that

helped me develop my app stole my concept and is now making an AI app with the same intent."

"What?" I ask, sliding the shots towards them both. "How can he do that?"

Eddie shrugs. "I will be asking my lawyer the same thing in the morning."

Hunter claps him on the back with one hand. "It will be okay, man. Don't worry."

Eddie shakes his head and throws back his first shot as Hunter continues to calm him down.

His constant reassurance and care for other people makes my heart beat quicker. Hunter is so attentive to everyone around him. He always knows what to say to make someone feel at ease and I wonder if that trait is something he's always carried. I think of him as a shy kid, being more intuitive than everyone else. Always sitting back and observing everything around him before he spoke. I can imagine Hunter being the childhood friend that you could turn to if your parents got divorced or you flunked a class. I wonder if he would have wanted to be friends with me back in the day. When I was living in a trailer park, basically raising myself, he was living a completely different life in a nice area, with loving parents.

Hunter waves his hand in front of my face and chuckles. I realize he has been talking to me this whole time, as I was deep in my thoughts.

"Sorry!" I laugh sheepishly. "I've been zoning out a ton today. What did you say?"

"It's okay." He blows a curl out of his eyes. "I was asking if it's okay for me to start filming some shots?"

"Yeah, of course." I give a thumbs-up. "Go right on ahead."

"Thanks." He half smiles and looks at me like he wants to say something else.

"What?" I ask him.

Hunter's eyes sparkle with mischief as he raises an eyebrow. "In a non-creepy, just friends way, you look beautiful tonight." His gaze lingers on me for a moment before he taps his hand against the bar top once, and then walks off to set up his equipment.

It's at that moment that I decide, I'm going to kiss him tonight. Lust wins.

Chapter 37

Hunter

Two hours later, I stop recording, set my camera down on the bar, and glance up at Olive. She is watching some of the bar regulars sing a drunken rendition of "Freak on a Leash" by Korn and it's horrible. Like, ears bleeding horrible. That doesn't even matter, though, because the women are having a blast and it's entertaining to watch. Both of them must be in their mid-40s and they look like they needed a night off from parenting. The women are really letting loose as they scream, "Go!" into each other's faces. Rick, who is sitting to my right, jumps at their sudden yelling, and it makes me chuckle.

"Not a Korn fan?" I ask him.

"I'll stick to The Rolling Stones and Nat King Cole," he tells me.

"Where's Johnny at? I haven't seen him the past few times I've been here."

"He's been visiting his daughter in Arizona; she just had a baby so he's on grandpa duty now."

I'm taken aback to hear that Johnny has a daughter. "No way! I had no clue he has a daughter."

"Yeah, he keeps his personal life private from most people. I know he comes off as a jokester, but he can be a serious guy, too."

I wonder about Johnny's past then, knowing there must be a lot more to the guy other than his playful quirks and usually inappropriate jokes. I got a little peek into the man under the character when Mr. Purngast talked about how he tried to help him, showing what a good friend Johnny was to him.

Suddenly, I see a draft beer slide in front of me and look up to see Olive smiling.

"I thought you would need some liquid courage." She has a slight smirk on her lips and a hint of naughtiness in her eyes. "Because you're up next." She motions towards the stage.

I look over at the current drunken singers and quickly shake my head.

"No, no, no." I turn to her, my eyes widening. "I don't sing."

"Everyone sings," she tells me, and crosses her arms. "Also, you sang in the car with me."

"Yes, I know I *can* sing, but I usually choose not to. Especially in a bar full of people."

She leans over the bar, and I quickly try to divert my eyes from the sudden cleavage on display in front of me.

"Do something that scares you tonight," she teases. "If I can go tubing when I can barely swim, you can sing for a room of drunk people."

I run a hand across my face, thinking it over. "I'm warning you. I'm a terrible singer."

"So?" Olive smiles. "The worse the singing, the better the karaoke. I love when someone has the confidence to get up on that stage knowing they aren't a vocalist. It takes balls." She gives me a look, challenging me.

Hearing that, I have to do it now. I want to impress her, so I stand up. She raises an eyebrow, obviously happy with herself, so I decide to reach for her hand across the bar.

"Fine, but you're doing it with me."

She bites the inside of her cheek. A moment goes by before she looks at my awaiting hand and finally places hers in it. The contact is like a jolt of electricity, always.

"Okay," she concedes. "Let's go, Curls."

"I'll watch your equipment," a half slurring Eddie yells from a booth where he is currently chatting with the nice cougar that Wes gave a lap dance to.

"Great," I murmur. "I'm sure you will, Eddie."

"Come on, it's just one song." Olive laughs and pulls my arm, guiding me towards the stage.

"What song do you want to sing?" I ask her.

"Do you know 'Lonely Day' by System of a Down?"

"Yes, actually." I snort. "That's Eddie's favorite band which means I have heard almost every song weekly for the past twenty years of friendship."

"Perfect, because that's what I want to sing." She steps on the stage with me and leans forward to set up the song on the karaoke machine.

As it starts playing, I see Eddie's head pop up from the booth and he lets out a "whoop!" in excitement. Olive hands me a microphone and I can feel my hand start to sweat with nerves when I see multiple eyes staring at me from the crowd. I clear my throat, and she winks at me. She reaches out and gives my free hand a squeeze in comfort. The lyrics start and we both awkwardly begin singing them.

After the first minute of the song, we grow more comfortable, and our voices get louder, more confident. A few people watching us start to sway, and someone even holds up a lighter. Olive is loving this, I can tell; she's smiling from ear to ear and

197

giggling. I decide that this is my moment to make a grand gesture. To show her I will put myself out there for her, even if it makes me uncomfortable.

I channel my inner Gomez Addams and take her hand, dramatically bowing towards her as I sing. Her eyes grow even bigger than normal as I maintain eye contact with her and bring my lips close to her hand. Then, I gently kiss the top of it, my lips barely making contact. I hear her gasp softly, and someone cheers in the audience, but Olive doesn't break eye contact with me for a second. She has completely stopped singing as I continue to serenade her. Horribly. I know every word to the song without looking, so at least that's a win to make up for my terrible singing.

As I stand up again from my bowed position in front of her, I draw her closer to me. We are less than an inch apart now, the only distance between us our microphones.

I continue to sing while we both hold intense eye contact with each other. I perform the last few slow lyrics of the song and when it ends, she's still staring at me. I'm about to break our eye contact and start laughing when she grabs both sides of my face and pulls me in. It takes me completely by surprise as she begins to kiss me deeply.

I fucking love karaoke.

Chapter 38

Olive

The second I put my lips on Hunter's, I know I'm screwed. This isn't just lust; I like him. I *really* like him.

His strong arms reach around me and grip the back of my hair as he continues to kiss me. He pulls me even closer, like he's trying to show me every last drop of passion that consumes him in this moment. I can't help moaning into his mouth and wrapping my own arms around the back of his head.

I never want this moment to end. The environment around us has completely faded away. I feel like I'm on my own private little island with him, not standing on the stage of the bar. I feel unimaginably safe and secure in his muscular arms. The feeling consumes me and almost makes me want to cry. I have longed to have this, deep down; I've dreamed of this type of intimacy with a man.

But admitting this to myself scares the crap out of me. I think of my mother and how she constantly threw everything away for her boyfriends. The negative thoughts begin to consume me, and it only gets worse as I start to think of all the horrible relationships that I've nursed Ivy back from. The intrusive thoughts take over and cause me to pull back from our kissing. I look up at Hunter. He looks flushed and thrilled until he sees my expression.

"I'm sorry," I say to him, and his expression turns to hurt and confusion as I back away from him slowly, and then run off the stage.

The audience that was cheering and celebrating us a moment ago goes silent. Some people turn back to their conversations and the room begins to fill with chatter again. I'm grateful for them, the regulars, trying to make it less awkward.

I burst through the kitchen door and walk over to the office, where I lean against the wall and breathe heavily. I hear someone come up behind me and know it's Rob.

"I need to go home," I tell him, feeling nauseous as I can't slow my breathing.

"Okay, okay. Try to calm down." He rests his large, rough hand on my back, as I continue to hyperventilate.

"Fuck," I cry out, and slide down to the tile floor. I bury my face in my hands. "I just ruined everything."

Rob sits down next to me. "The kiss?" he asks quietly.

I groan through my hands, refusing to meet his eyes. "Yeah. I can tell that Hunter likes me. I like him, too, but not in the same way," I lie to myself and Rob. "I got caught up in the moment and I wanted to kiss him. So, I did."

"It seemed like you enjoyed yourself on stage." Rob nudges my shoulder, and I pull back from my hands to look up at him. He has an eyebrow raised and a playful smirk on his face.

"Yeah, but now I just led him on, like an idiot."

"You wouldn't date him?"

I shake my head. "I can't handle that. I'm not in a good headspace."

"I get that," Rob says. "But let me just play devil's advocate and ask you when you would ever say you are in a good head-space to meet someone?" I glare at him. "I'm always going to shoot it to you straight, you know that. You're like a little sister to me so I will call you on your bullshit when I think it's bull-shit. In my opinion, you will always make an excuse, even if the right guy walks into your life. You need to stop running away."

I am hurt by what he says to me, but what makes me even more angry is that I know he's right. I'm angry at myself more than anything.

"I can't listen to this right now," I tell him, knowing I'm deflecting from the truth. I stand back up and adjust my dress.

Rob nods his head. "Okay, fine. I won't press anymore. Just know I love you and I only want the best for you. I tell you this because I want you to share your life with someone that brings it value. Life is better with someone that gets you and stands by you through everything. Missy is my lighthouse in a storm. I want you to find your lighthouse."

I shuffle anxiously on my feet. "I hear you, but I need to get back to work," I tell him, wiping under my eyes quickly.

He looks satisfied at the fact that I'm at least staying here. I turn away from Rob and head back out the kitchen door, ready to talk to Hunter. I need to tell him that I made a mistake kissing him. That I value his friendship and don't want to lose the bond we have created.

I know he won't stop doing the video series, even if he's upset with me right now. I don't have to worry about that because I know Hunter is a man of honor. Once he commits to something, he sticks to it, and he would never want the bar to get sold and taken away from everyone that loves it.

When I look around, my shoulders fall. Hunter and Eddie are no longer here.

"If you're looking for him, he left," Rick says from his stool.

"Shit."

I jog out of the bar to see if his car is still in the parking lot, but he's gone. I just want to be able to explain myself to him. Looking up at the stars lining the dark night sky, I wish I could be anywhere but here. I feel stuck in my life right now, like everyone else is in control of my fate with Tripp, the puppet master, pulling my strings.

I need Hunter, that I know.

I pull out my phone and start writing him a text.

Hunter, please let me call you after my shift. I need to talk to you.

By the time I close the bar hours later and clean up after my shift ends, my phone still sits without a reply. I feel like I've lost one of the only people that has ever made me feel secure in my life.

Chapter 39

Hunter

I pull up to Eddie's house and park the truck on the cement driveway. He is quite drunk, but even in his intoxicated state, he can tell I'm gutted right now. He shoots me a look laced with sympathy, and I put my hand up before he can say anything.

"Please. I just want to process the night. I'm tired, man," I tell him. "I'll text you in the morning."

"No problem," he responds and pushes open the passenger door. He's drunkenly swaying as he steps out of the truck.

"You need help to the door?" I ask Eddie.

"No—" he starts to say, and then bends over and vomits on his driveway.

I lean my head back against the headrest, not wanting to deal with this right now, but I'm not leaving him alone in this condition, either. Eddie is stressed about his app and made some poor drinking decisions tonight. I shut off my engine and get out of my truck.

"Give me your keys," I tell him as he stands up and wipes the back of his hand against his mouth.

"I feel better." He smiles and hands me the keys.

"Okay, come on." I chuckle and take them from him before leading him to the door.

Once I'm inside Eddie's house, I slowly help him get to his room. I look around and find a small trashcan to set next to his bed. He gives me a thumbs-up and then passes out, asleep within minutes.

"I'm going to sleep on your floor, tonight," I tell an almost silent room, only the sound of Eddie's snoring answers me.

I kick off my shoes and remove my cheetah shirt. Then, I head out to his hallway so I can find a pillow and blanket. I see a checkered decorative pillow tossed in the corner of the living room and scoop it up. I check both closets and find no blankets, so I settle for a cream throw blanket that his mom placed on the back of his couch. She decorated most of his place; Eddie couldn't care less about the house. The only important thing to him in this place is the technology down in his basement office.

Heading back to Eddie's room, I situate the pillow on the ground and lie on the carpet floor, glad that it's plush.

I stare up at his ceiling and think about Olive. Kissing her for the first time was like a dream. Her lips were soft and supple, and her kiss felt like an electric shock. I was addicted from the first touch of her lips to mine, never wanting it to end.

When she pulled back from the kiss, I expected her to match my expression. She seemed so into it, and she was, after all, the one that made the first move. So, when I looked into her eyes and saw absolute horror, I felt my heart crack a little. Did I make up her moaning into my mouth? Did I create the connection at that moment in my head to convince myself that she was into me, too?

I feel hopeless right now because I know I will never be the same after kissing Olive. She gave me a high that I will spend the rest of my life trying to recreate. My body just responds to her in a way I have never felt before.

After she ran off the stage, I was so embarrassed. Not because it felt like some form of rejection in front of an audience, but because she seemed terrified of me after that kiss. It seemed like she couldn't stand to be around me for another second. So, she fled.

Eddie met my eyes from his seat and motioned towards the door, trying to help me save face. I didn't even want to leave. I wanted to go back to the kitchen and talk to her so I could try to understand what was going through that gorgeous head of hers. But then I saw Eddie start to sway into a table and push some chairs over, trying to hold himself up, and I knew I needed to get him home.

I am always trying to help everyone else and make sure they are okay. But I'm not sure if I'm okay.

Chapter 40

Olive

It's 9 A.M. and I still haven't gotten a text back from Hunter. Trying to occupy myself until work, I walk down to Ivy's apartment. When she opens the door, she has her hair pulled up into a crazy, messy bun, with strands falling all around her face. She puffs out a gust of air, trying to move a strand from her eyeline. Her shirt is covered with pit sweat and she has eyeliner smeared under her eyes. She looks like an absolute wild woman.

"I need to talk to you," she says.

Oh god.

"Pregnant?" I ask.

"Nope."

"Got back together with Dennis?"

"*Hell* no!"

I give her a disbelieving look. "Oh yeah, because that's so far-fetched."

"Come in." She grabs my arm and pulls me in, then walks me over to her couch. "You're going to want to sit down for this."

My heart starts beating quickly, wondering what's going on. "You're scaring me," I tell her as I take a seat on her purple suede couch. I pull a pillow over my lap—a coping mechanism.

Ivy sits next to me and takes a deep breath. "I'm moving to Atlanta."

"*What*?!" I jump up out of my spot.

She looks up at me from the couch. "I applied and had an interview to work at a high-end bridal boutique that I've been stalking for years on social media, and I got the job."

"You're kidding me!" I say.

Ivy shakes her head. "I didn't think I would actually get the job. The shop is super exclusive and expensive, but I did a Zoom interview, and they offered me the job on the spot. I didn't even think about it; I knew I wanted to do it."

She has always been the more impulsive of the two of us, never backing away from a new experience. I admire her for it most of the time, but it's also what has led her into so many unhealthy relationships that move too quickly.

"I can't believe this," I tell her.

"I know," she whispers back.

"I'm happy for you." I force a small smile, and she gives me a *yeah right* look. "Seriously, I am. I'm just surprised, that's all. I didn't even know you were looking for a new job."

"Yeah, I'm sorry for not saying anything. I just didn't want to mention that I was applying places until I knew for sure what I was doing. I know you've been dealing with so much already; I didn't want it worrying you. My life just feels stagnant right now and honestly, I want to start over somewhere new."

I listen to her as she describes the new bridal boutique in Atlanta and scrolls through their Instagram, listing off the designers to me. Her excitement is so palpable that I try to bury my feelings of self-pity and celebrate Ivy's accomplishment. I know I will be devastated once she leaves. I barely have Jane anymore, my maternal figure, and now I'm losing the only best friend I've ever had. I don't even realize I'm in a trance while she talks until Ivy sets her phone down and takes both my hands.

"I have kind of a crazy idea."

I wait for her to keep talking.

"If, for some reason, and I preface this by saying I really hope this doesn't happen," she quickly adds, "but if for some reason you're not able to buy the bar from Tripp, I want you to move to Atlanta with me."

I pull my hands back from hers. "I'm not leaving Clairesville. This is my home, and the bar isn't going anywhere. We're raising the money; we've almost hit the goal."

"I know." Ivy nods, agreeing with me. Then, more gently she adds, "I'm just saying. If it doesn't work out, consider starting over with me. Just think about it."

"Okay," I tell her. "I will consider it. When do you move?"

"September first."

"That's in two weeks!"

"Yup. I've been going through my shit all morning. I'm trying to purge most of my closet. I'm going to be a classy broad now," Ivy jokes. "I get to wear heels every shift. Actually, it's *required*."

"Your poor feet," I tell her.

"I know. Good thing I can soak them in all the money I'll be raking in," she jokes. I laugh and then we hold eye contact, our faces turning sentimental. Knowing each other's thoughts so well, I can see that she feels as torn up at the thought of leaving me, as I do of losing her.

"I'm really going to miss you," I say.

"I will visit you all the time. I promise. I will only be nine hours away. That's basically one audiobook of a drive."

"Okay and I will visit you, too, if I can ever get Barney to be reliable." I roll my eyes and Ivy snorts.

"I would love to see Barney take Atlanta; she deserves a joy ride."

"I will just need to have AAA on standby. She's one drive away from exploding."

"Our girl would never. She would possibly die a dramatic death in the middle of traffic so everyone would have to stare at her as they angrily passed, though. Barney would love the attention."

"Who else am I going to talk to like this?" I sigh.

"I will just be a phone call away," she tells me.

I nod as she sits up quickly. "I've been so wrapped up in figuring out what I'm doing recently that I completely forgot to ask you how it's going with the video series!"

I start to tell her about everything Hunter and I have filmed recently, feeling myself smile as I think about the adventures we have been on so far.

"What's his YouTube channel?" Ivy asks, pulling her phone out of her back pocket. "I can't believe I haven't watched any of them yet. Sorry, I've been a horrible friend."

"It's fine, I get it, you've got your own stuff going on." I laugh and tell her his channel name.

I scoot closer to her as she clicks the first video, the one that features Rob's voice and shows the bar. Then it's the clips of Sonjia and her bees. Ivy says "aww" as it continues to play. Finally, it cuts to the final moments of the video. It's Hunter sitting in his room, explaining the purpose of the video series. Suddenly, Ivy drops her phone like it's on fire.

"What the fuck!" she says and picks it back up, blinking like she can't believe her eyes.

"What?" I ask her. She's freaking out.

"That is *Dennis's cousin!*" She looks at me wide-eyed and points an accusing finger at the phone.

"*What!*" I shriek. "Hunter? There's no way."

"One hundred percent it is. He came and got Dennis's stuff after I kicked him out."

"Dennis must be living with him," I say, putting the puzzle pieces together. When Hunter said he had a family member staying in the guest room, it was Dennis. I feel sick suddenly, thinking of someone sweet like Hunter letting someone as vile as Dennis live with him. Is he like his cousin? Dennis told Ivy everything she wanted to hear in the beginning, treated her like a queen, only to end up a lying, cheating dick. Is Hunter like that? He seems so different to me. He made me feel safe; he *still* makes me feel safe. I feel so confused and overwhelmed. Last night weighs even heavier on my mind. I need to talk to Hunter. Now.

"Ivy. I've gotta go," I tell her and quickly get up. I walk out the door and head to my car without even saying goodbye. I'm not going to let myself chicken out of this. I'm going to his house to talk to him.

Chapter 41

Hunter

After barely sleeping on Eddie's floor last night, my neck is stiff, and my mood is even lower. I decide I'm going to head home so I can work out and shower, knowing that will improve my mood. I walk back inside from Eddie's porch where I was taking in the sunrise and drinking some espresso from his fancy machine and head to his room. Eddie is still out like a light, snoring like a foghorn, face-down on his pillow. I shake his shoulder, and he stirs lightly but continues to sleep.

"Eddie," I say.

Nothing.

I shake his shoulder again and say louder, "Eddie, I'm going to head out."

"Huh?" His head shoots up and he looks confused as hell until he makes eye contact with me. "Shit, man, alright." Then, he flops his head back down and is asleep again.

I search around his room for my phone, but then I realize I never had it last night in the house. I must have left it in the car. I grab my truck keys and walk out of his place, turning his bottom lock before I shut the door. I have my cheetah print shirt slung over my shoulder and I toss it into the passenger seat once I'm seated. I refuse to put it back on when it reeks of alcohol and sweat at this point. I want to wash off last night. Not the kiss but everything else.

I find my phone stuck between the driver's seat and the floorboard and pick it up so I can turn on music. The first thing I see when I click on the screen is a text from Olive.

Hunter, please let me call you after my shift. I need to talk to you.

I tap my empty hand on the steering wheel, deciding if I want to call her right now or not. I conclude that I need to get myself right first. I will call her after my workout and shower. My mind will be clearer then.

I swipe the text away and open my playlist. Clicking on the happiest song I can find, "Mr. Blue Sky" by Electric Light Orchestra fills my car. I'm going to trick myself into being happy right now. My mom used to tell me even if you don't feel like smiling, sometimes forcing a grin can improve your mood. I've learned it's true. I plant a stupid smile on my face and bob my head to the music, manually rolling down the windows as I pull out of Eddie's neighborhood.

By the time I get out on the main road, my music is blasting and I'm yelling the lyrics like a madman. It's not until I stop at a red light and the song ends that I realize there are two women smiling and laughing in the car to my right. My cheeks flush with embarrassment.

"Don't stop for our sake, cutie," the driver of the car says, leaning out of her window. She has curly black hair and a nose ring; she also looks to be around my age. I would usually be attracted to her. Years ago, I might have even tried to get her number if I was feeling brave. But right now, I don't want to deal with this at all. I just want to get home, and the only girl I want to look at is Olive.

"Sorry," I tell her, feeling weird knowing I'm shirtless and unsure how else to respond. Is this what women deal with daily? Thankfully, the light turns green and I keep driving. I peek at my rearview mirror, and luckily, the women turn down a side road before the next red light.

Ten minutes later, I turn onto my street, and I'm taken aback when I see a car outside my house. I'm even more shocked when I get closer and see it's Olive's bright purple car. I see her leaning against the hood. If she didn't instantly make eye contact with me, I might have tried to drive away before she noticed, but that's not my luck. I wish I looked put together right now, or at least had taken a shower before seeing her. The last thing I expected was to see her at my place, waiting on me.

As I pull my car in, she stands from her leaning position on her car and heads towards me. I shut off the engine and get out. She looks over my body, shirtless, and my hair, wild. I push a few strands back, feeling scrutinized under her gaze.

"Long night?" She raises an eyebrow.

"Just stayed with Eddie; he was sick last night."

Olive nods. "I texted you last night. I wanted to talk to you about...everything." She looks down at the ground and pushes a small rock around with the front of her sneaker.

"Yeah, sorry." I slide my hands into my pockets. "I didn't have my phone on me last night. Left it in the car."

Olive nods again, still not meeting my eyes. I'm beginning to grow exasperated from my lack of sleep and her inability to tell me what's going on.

"So, what did you want to talk about?" I ask.

"Can we go inside?" She finally looks up at me. She shows worry and a little bit of hope in her expression.

"Okay, sure," I respond, my rough exterior softening.

I unlock the front door and lead her into the house. She shifts on her feet uncomfortably behind me, so I go and sit down on my sofa, motioning for her to take the cushion next to me.

She does and then she takes a deep breath. Her floral scent makes me want to reach out and take her in my arms. I notice her shaking slightly and rest my hand on her back in concern.

"Are you okay?" I ask her and she meets my eyes. Her own are lined with tears, and she shakes her head no. "Tell me what's going on," I say in a low voice.

"Everything is a mess right now. Literally everything. I ruined our friendship by kissing you. I just found out my best friend is moving. Jane is dying, and Tripp's selling the bar. How much can one person handle? I feel like I'm breaking."

At that confession, tears begin to stream down her face, and I reach out and wipe them away. "Please don't cry," I tell her.

"And you're also related to Dennis!" she continues, blubbering out and pointing an accusatory finger at me.

"Wait, what?" I visibly shrink back. "You know Dennis?"

"Yes!" she continues to exclaim. "He's my best friend Ivy's horrible ex."

I stare at her in shock and confusion. "Ivy is your best friend?"

"Yes! And now she's moving, and I'm convinced that the main reason for it is so she can get away from him." She continues to cry, her eyes spilling with tears. It breaks my heart to see her crumbling like this. I never even thought to mention that I retrieved Dennis's boxes from the apartment below hers.

Before I can ask her another question, like summoning the devil, Dennis bursts in through my front door and shouts, "Hey, shitbag! I'm back!"

Chapter 42

Olive

I'm a sobbing mess on Hunter's couch when my archenemy walks through the front door. I *hate* Dennis, and I know he can't stand me, either. Ivy learned to keep her relationship completely separate from her friendship with me because we couldn't get along. I tried to at first, for her sake, but it was pointless. He treated her horribly in front of me and I couldn't sit by and witness the mistreatment, so I was always calling him out on his crap, which he hated.

"Olive!" Dennis shouts, shock on his face. "You know Cuz?"

I look over at Hunter as he says, "I've been holding your crap here for a while, man. Where have you been?" His expression is annoyed, which brings me a little bit of happiness, knowing that he isn't welcoming Dennis with open arms.

"I went to Vegas with some of the boys. *Wild time*," he responds, his eyes wide, strung out.

"Okay, well a heads-up would have been nice. I was getting to the point where I was going to sell your stuff. I'm not a storage facility," Hunter tells him. "You need to grow up."

215

My head bounces back and forth from one guy to the other as they continue to argue. Feeling uncomfortable and like I would rather be anywhere else in the world than in the presence of Dennis right now, I stand and mumble that I'm going to the bathroom.

"Down the hall to the right," Hunter tells me, kindness in his eyes. I can almost read an apology in them for his cousin showing up.

Once I find the bathroom, I splash chilly water on my face and stare at myself in the mirror. My eyes are swollen and puffy from tears, my cheeks flushed. Dennis probably loves seeing me like this. His ex's "evil" best friend in obvious distress.

I stare at myself for a second longer, cursing myself silently for coming here this morning. What was I thinking? That I would show up at his door and cry in Hunter's lap, then somehow everything would work out? I feel pathetic for leaning on him like this. I don't even know why I continue to spill my guts out to him. It's a level of vulnerability that I can't seem to hide when he's nearby. He brings out a different side of me, a soft and intimate one.

Realizing I've been in here awhile, I click off the light and head back into the hall, where I hear Hunter and Dennis still arguing. This time, it's about me.

"Don't talk about her like that," Hunter commands. His tone is full of aggression.

"I'm just telling you, she's a huge bitch. She ruined my relationship," Dennis throws back.

"The only person that ruined your relationship is *you*," Hunter snaps.

I peer around the corner to see Hunter standing in front of Dennis now, his face laced with fury. The argument grows more tense by the second. Dennis is tall but Hunter still towers over him.

"I'm just trying to warn you, man." Dennis lifts his arms, shrugging. "No pussy is worth the mouth on that bitch."

At that, Hunter punches him in the face, *hard.* I let out an uncontrollable gasp as Dennis wobbles backwards. He stumbles into the wall and wipes the back of his hand against his bloody nose and mouth. When Dennis sees red smeared across his hand, he laughs and almost looks manic. I realize he is definitely on something right now, and I know whatever it is, it's not legal.

"Dude, I didn't think you had it in you. *Shy little Hunter* has some power behind his punch."

Hunter ignores this as he leans towards Dennis. Jabbing a finger into his chest, he says so quietly I almost can't hear, "Get your shit and leave *now*. I don't want to see you until you get your life together. You have ten minutes to get everything out before I throw your belongings on the lawn."

The venom in his voice causes Dennis to stop laughing and he almost looks fearful. Hunter backs away as Dennis quickly pushes around him and begins walking towards the hallway.

When he sees me standing there, he sneers as blood drips from his face to his shirt. "Congratulations, Olive. He must really like you. I've never seen him like that."

I hurry past him before he can say anything else to me.

When I make eye contact with Hunter, he shakes out his hand and clenches his knuckles. "I'm so sorry about that," he says.

I look down at his hand and walk towards him quickly. "Are you okay?"

"Yeah, I'm fine." He also looks down towards his fingers and then meets my eyes. His own are piercing and sincere. "If you heard anything he said, please ignore the comments. Dennis is a mess. The whole family knows it."

I nod my head and look down at the wood floor. "It's okay. I know I can be a bitch; I was one to you last night." My throat feels tight with the confession.

"No, it's not okay." Hunter gently touches my chin and lifts my head so my eyes meet his once more. "No one should ever speak about you that way. Do you understand me?"

I dip my head in response as his hand still rests on my face. I feel myself lean into his touch. "I hate that Tripp talks down to you and that I can't do anything about it right now. I won't allow one of my family members to disrespect you. That's something I *can* control."

I listen in silence as he continues, "I understand now why you left last night; you got swept up in the moment. It's my fault for wanting you when you made it clear you only see me as a friend."

As he says the words, I feel a bitter taste in my mouth. The lies I keep telling myself are beginning to swirl around inside me like a disease. I shake my head as he continues to make excuses for my actions.

"No, no," I tell him, cutting him off. "I wanted to kiss you last night. I made the move." I take a deep breath as his eyes stare into mine with such intensity that I want to confess my deepest thoughts. "Hunter, I do like you. I like you, too."

Hearing those words, his dark eyes illuminate and his expression grows hopeful.

I stammer, "But I can't date you right now. Maybe one day, but not while I'm trying to figure everything out with my life."

He reaches out and takes my hand as I continue, "It wouldn't be fair to you, for us to be together when I have so many things to deal with right now. I can't even get my emotions in check, so I can't be a partner to someone." I breathe deeply. "If you want to wait for when I'm ready to be with you, then great. But if you don't, I understand that, too. I've always told myself that if I ever chose to be in a relationship, I was going to go in as my best self. I'm never going to date someone to provide myself shelter, like my mother, or because I can't handle being alone..." I look down the hallway and then whisper, "Like Ivy has done. I need to stand on my two feet securely before I can be with you."

Hunter absorbs everything I'm telling him. "Okay. I'll wait," he says matter-of-factly. Like it's that simple.

"I understand if you find someone else in the meantime. I can't tell you how long it will take me to be ready."

He draws me into his arms and looks down at me, a small smile playing on his lips.

"Olive, don't you understand? I would wait a lifetime for you. You're incredible. I want *you*."

I sink into his arms at those words, holding him tight. The connection between us consumes me. His arms wrap around me even tighter, and I bury my head in his chest. I inhale deeply and he laughs. "You might not want to do that. I haven't showered."

I laugh, too. "I don't mind. I just like you," I tell him softly.

It feels so good to finally admit it to myself. I feel like a weight has been lifted off my shoulders, now that he knows my true feelings. With everything on the table, I don't have to worry about hurting him because the ball is now in his court. He can choose to wait or move on if he finds someone else. Would it wreck me if he did? Yes, but it wouldn't be fair to not give him a choice. I want him to be happy, and I have dealt with heartbreak my whole life—maybe not from boys I've dated, but from my parents. I can handle not being chosen by someone I care for. I always find a way to stay strong.

Suddenly, the door slams behind us while I'm still in Hunter's embrace, and I realize Dennis just walked out the front door.

We both pull apart and look towards the sound. "Don't

worry, he won't be staying here anymore. I'm done making excuses for him," Hunter tells me.

At that I release a wide, relieved smile. "That's the best news I've heard all day."

Chapter 43

Hunter

The past four weeks with Olive have been incredible. Time feels like it's flying by. Now that we have laid everything out on the table, there's a level of comfort and intimacy between us that feels even more natural. Knowing that she likes me back, that I'm not alone in my feelings, has made my heart full. I feel myself falling in love with her and know that I'm so lucky to have her in my life. I will wait forever if I must for her to be ready to be with me.

We have filmed two more episodes of the series recently, and every single episode has made the bar fund grow. We have almost hit our goal of a million dollars. I know Olive realizes that this means she will have to ask Tripp if he will sell the bar to her soon and it's making her anxious. I might have to threaten the guy if he doesn't sell it to her. I can't watch Whiskey's get taken from her.

Today we are meeting at the bar to have lunch and then film. She has the day off since Missy is working and I'm excited to have some uninterrupted time with her. I pull up to her apartment complex, preparing to get out of my truck, when I see her burst out her front door, all smiles, as she waves to me. I chuckle and wave enthusiastically back to her. She bounces down the concrete steps to the ground floor and my breath escapes as it always does when I take her in. Olive has her hair pulled back into a high ponytail that swishes when she walks and puts her long, swanlike neck on display. She is wearing a simple white tank that shows off a sliver of her stomach, and a pair of jeans. She always looks so effortlessly beautiful.

"Hey, stranger." She smiles as she walks up.

I step around to the passenger side of the truck and pull open the door for her, motioning to the seat. "Your chariot awaits, princess."

She rolls her eyes. "Princess?" she snorts.

"Too much?" I chuckle. "How about 'doll'?"

"How about no nicknames for me, *Curls*." She playfully tussles my hair as she shuffles past me into her seat.

"Not into nicknames?" I lean against the side of my truck, looking down at her.

She wrinkles her nose. "No, I always feel like they are condescending most of the time. I only like 'baby' or my own name."

I throw my head back and laugh. "Condescending?" I smile. "Okay. *Baby* it is."

"I love when you do that." She smiles up at me.

"What?"

"Throw your head back when you laugh; it just bursts out of you. It's contagious and it makes me happy."

I didn't realize that she notices these minute details about me. I lean forward and kiss her on the forehead. Her eyes close and I hear her breathing hitch slightly. We both have decided it's best to not be fully intimate with each other until she's ready to be in a relationship, but I am glad I still get to show her some affection. These small intimacies feel almost more sensual, like we are really appreciating each other as our connection increases.

I draw back from her forehead and playfully pretend to tussle her hair like she did to me. Olive giggles as I close her door and walk back around, smiling to myself like an idiot. This is the happiest I've been since losing my father; I didn't know it was possible for me to feel this amount of joy again.

Soon we arrive outside the bar. I hear her let out a sigh of relief when she sees that Tripp's car isn't in the parking lot.

"Looks like today will be a good day," I tell her.

"You read my mind."

We get out of our seats simultaneously and shut our doors. I walk to the back of my truck and pull something out.

"I have something for you. Well, not technically for *you*, but...here," I say as I pull out the basket with a lid that was sitting in my truck bed.

"Thank you?" Olive questions as I hand her the basket.

"Open it."

When she does, she gasps. She stares down at a basket full of petunias from my garden. "For Jane," I tell her.

Olive shakes her head and looks back up at me. "You're amazing," she whispers.

I chuckle, as she continues, "No, I'm serious. You're perfect. You always know what I need and how to make me smile."

I feel my skin flush at the compliment, but also know I'm sweating. The intense sun causes a bead of sweat to drip down my neck. "I would do anything for you," I tell her. "Seriously. But can we please go inside because I'm sweating like a pig out here."

She places the basket back in my truck bed, then grabs my right arm and leads me towards the door. By the time we get to the bar entrance we are holding hands, and I clasp hers tighter as we walk in.

The first person I see when we walk in is Johnny and his eyes widen when he sees our connected hands. He begins to slow clap, dramatically.

"I never thought I'd see the day. Olive has a boyfriend. And it's barstool boy, I'll be damned."

"Oh god, stop that. Don't make it weird," Olive scoffs at Johnny. "Also, we are taking it slow, so please, no pressure. We aren't in a relationship."

"Oh, friends with benefits. Got it." He turns towards me and winks.

"Gross." Olive groans as a woman I assume is Missy comes from the kitchen and smiles at us. She is petite, with straight brown hair and a sweet, mousey appearance.

She looks like she would be softspoken or reserved, so I'm surprised when she shouts out, "Hey, guys!"

"Hey, Missy!" Olive responds joyfully. "This is Hunter."

"Ahhhh, the camera man." She reaches out and shakes my hand, giving me a toothy, knowing grin.

"That's me," I say, chuckling.

"You're too pretty to be behind the camera," Missy says to me, giving me a once-over.

"Hey! I heard that!" Rob's voice booms from behind the kitchen window.

"Don't you worry, Robert," Missy teases him. "You have my heart. I'm not swayed by a young, beautiful man with a full head of hair."

Rob grunts and peeks out the side of the window, eyeing me suspiciously. She winks at me and turns towards Rob, swatting him away. "Back to work, sweetcakes." Then she reaches under the counter, grabs her pad of paper, and pulls a pen out from behind her ear. "So, what will it be for lunch?"

Olive orders us some burgers and fries and then we sit at a back table in the corner. When our burgers come, we both dig in at once. The meal is exactly what bar food should be: a greasy, savory burger and crisp, hot fries. I swear we inhale the food in minutes, barely acknowledging each other until our plates are empty. Once we're finished, we look at each other and burst into laughter.

"I was hungry." I grin, pushing my plate away.

"Me too," she says, wiping her mouth with a napkin, then tossing it on top of her own plate. She looks at me inquisitively, a smile playing on her lips. I'm ready to talk about our next video and I can tell she is, too.

Olive clasps her hands. "So," she says and leans closer towards me.

"So," I respond and do the same. "Have you chosen your next subject for the series, *Olive?*"

"Why yes, *Curls.*" She smiles. "I have."

Holding up her index finger she continues, "Actually, it's the reason why I chose this table." She stands and pushes her chair sideways, away from the wall, and squats down. She motions for me to come over. I get up from my seat to see what she's looking at, and squat next to her, leaning against the table.

On the wall, about two inches under where the table covered my view, there is a heart in black marker with writing scribbled inside it.

The words I read take my breath away.

AR & FR

JUST MARRIED

7-14-1990

225

Nicole Mikell

TIME OF THE SEASON

"I know, isn't it so cute?" Olive turns towards me, gushing. "I want to know their love story."

"I know their story," I tell her, stammering. I can barely believe my eyes as I say, "It's my parents."

Chapter 44

Olive

I stare at Hunter in shock; my mouth is currently hanging open. "Your parents?"

Hunter pushes his hair back, obviously surprised by this discovery, as well. His eyes widen as he continues to look at the heart drawn on the wall.

"How do you know for sure?" I ask.

"I know it's them," he responds breathlessly as his dark eyes meet mine. "My mom's name is Amy and my dad's name is Frank, our last name is Rowe. That's their anniversary date." He pulls at the collar of his T-shirt as if it's choking him suddenly.

"This is insane," I tell him in a soft voice. I point to the text then. "'Time of the Season' like the song?"

"Yeah. It was my parents' first dance song."

"I looked those lyrics up when I first noticed the heart on the wall years ago. It's been one of my favorite songs ever since. This is crazy," I tell him, shaking my head. It feels like him coming into the bar that first night was almost like fate. Who

227

knew his parents' own history was on the walls of Whiskey Jane's?

"I guess I should ask my mom if we can come over to film..." He half chuckles and puts his hands behind his neck, stretching. "Unbelievable," he whispers to himself.

A minute later he goes outside to call his mom, and I continue to crouch by the wall, running my fingers over the textured lines of his parents' script. For years I have sat right by this spot, wishing I could absorb this couple's story, and I always wondered how their lives turned out. The bar door jingles and I look behind my shoulder to see Hunter sauntering back in the bar, a bright smile on his face.

I grab the dishes from our table as he walks up and takes one of them out of my hand.

"We are good to go. My mom's ready and excited to meet you."

I lead him back towards the kitchen. "Geez, this is a lot of pressure. I didn't think I would be meeting your mother so soon," I joke, but deep down, I mean it. I want his mom to like me.

"My mom will love you," he says as he pushes the kitchen door open for me. I thank him and take his dish back. "Staff only. Tripp's rule. Be right back."

I head over to the sink across from the grill where Rob currently stands and begin washing our two plates. I can feel his eyes on my back and ignore it until I finish drying the dishes and place them on the rack. "Yes?" I ask, turning around.

"What are you doing, Olive?"

"What?"

"You're leading the poor kid on; he really likes you. I can tell."

"I like him, too." I shrug. "We are just taking it slow."

"I feel like you're going to end up breaking his heart," Rob continues, a serious look on his face. "He seems really invested in you and I actually like the guy."

"I thought you were supposed to be on my side about things." I raise an eyebrow.

"I am on your side. I'll always stand by you, but I will also give you a reality check when you need it. Stop messing around and either be with him or let him move on. I don't know if there will ever be a day where you will wake up and think you're ready to be with him. I think you're making excuses because you don't want to get hurt by him. I say stop lying to yourself and go for it. You know Jane would tell you to get your head on straight if she was here. Be *brave*, Olive."

I feel like Rob just exposed all the hidden parts of my mind. Yes, I am scared, and he's right, I don't know if I will ever wake up and decide it's the right time for Hunter and me.

I bite the inside of my cheek as Rob continues, "I'm not trying to make you sad; I want to see you happy. I want you to wake up and realize there's a great guy waiting for you out there."

I snort. "Wow, I didn't realize you guys were so close."

Rob shrugs nonchalantly. "We text sometimes."

"Oh, is that it?" I tease, but I'm happy to hear that they have a friendship blooming. Rob really is a brother to me.

Missy pokes her head through the kitchen window, obviously eavesdropping from the other side. "They have a bromance," she chirps.

I shake my head hearing that, my smile growing. "How sweet," I say, drying off my hands with a nearby towel. "Alright, I'm leaving. See you tomorrow."

Rob nods. "See ya."

I push through the door and wave goodbye to Missy and Johnny at the bar.

"Go enjoy your day off." Missy smiles.

"It's like you're obsessed with us," Johnny jokes. "Even on your day off, you want to bask in my beauty."

"Yeah, right. We are leaving," I say as Hunter walks up behind me. I point at Johnny. "You better tell me about your new granddaughter tomorrow. I haven't seen you in weeks!"

His face lights up. "Oh, don't worry, I will be talking your ears off for hours tomorrow."

I feel Hunter squeeze my shoulders and I lean into his touch, without even meaning to.

"I will be expecting an update, too, a detailed one," Johnny jokes as he looks at Hunter's hands on me.

"Yeah, okay." I roll my eyes playfully. "We're out of here."

Hunter kindly tells everyone goodbye and strides to the front door, opening it for me before I can touch it.

After a leisurely ride in the truck, our conversation flowing easily, Hunter drives past his house and within a minute, we pull up to his childhood home. It's a small, traditional-style home that's a cream color, and has a large awning over the front porch with small yellow flowers in planters hanging from it.

"Man, you weren't kidding. You really did grow up right near your current home."

"Yup. Drove by it every day, dreaming about it being mine someday."

"This place is so cute," I tell him cheerily as we get out of the truck. He grabs his equipment from the back seat, then leads me towards the navy-blue front door and knocks.

Seconds later a woman with dark curls, just like Hunter's, and large, wire-framed glasses opens the front door. She looks effortlessly artsy and cool, wearing some paint-splattered overalls, and has colorful tattoos lining her arms. *This is who I want to be in my 60s*, I think to myself.

"Hi!" she exclaims and pulls both of us into a hug at the same time. Together we let out an "oof" noise as she grips us in a bear hug. She smells like patchouli and cinnamon. It's a stark contrast to my own mother's rare hugs that smelled like cigarettes and some cheap perfume that gave me a headache.

I almost don't want the hug to end as she pulls back and Hunter looks at me. "I'm sorry. My mom's a hugger."

"I'm just so excited to meet you," she exclaims. "Hunter has never brought a girl home! Can you believe it? He's such a cutie." She leans over and messes with his hair playfully, exactly like I always do, tussling the curls. "Well, at least I think so, but maybe I'm biased because I'm his mom." She smiles at me, her glasses raising as her cheeks lift.

"I wish you would have told me the project you've been working on together, Hunter," she continues. "I would have told you all about our story!" She turns to me then. "I had no idea! He is such a private person."

"All the videos are on my channel, Mom." He chuckles.

"I'm sorry, son. I love you, but there's only so much skateboarding I can watch. I had no idea you were doing something this different, though! I watched a few videos after you called me and had tears in my eyes. *Freddie Finnely?* I couldn't believe it."

"I know!" I gush, meeting her enthusiasm. "I still feel like it was a dream meeting him!"

"Come on in and you can tell me all about it!" She backs up from the doorway so we can pass her and then shuts the door behind us.

The inside of Hunter's childhood home is warm and inviting. The walls are lined with photographs and floral paintings.

"Are you an artist?" I ask his mom.

"Oh just for fun." She laughs. "Keeps me busy these days."

I look at a painting near me, intricate jewel-toned flowers swirling around the canvas. "These are really beautiful," I tell her. "I would love for you to paint something for the bar," I add quietly, knowing that could only happen if I save it.

"My mom's being modest," Hunter chimes in. "She's painted murals on the side of my elementary school and lots of other spots in town. She is super talented."

"That's so cool!" I light up. "Better idea. I want a mural on the outside of the bar."

"Deal." His mom smiles. "That will be my gift to you *when* you save the bar," she responds kindly. She leads us down a hallway. "Come to the sunroom, I made some snacks."

We get to brightly lit, small room filled with eclectic chairs and a wooden table in the center. On the table there is hummus and pita bread on a platter, and some veggies sliced in a bowl.

"Mom we just ate," Hunter says. "I told you that." He laughs as his mom brushes the comment away and helps herself to the veggies and hummus.

She then plops onto an oversized green chair and opens her arms. "I'm ready for my close-up."

Chapter 45

Hunter

I turn on my camera and pan it around the room I spent so many warm days coloring and reading in as a child. Olive sits next to me in a yellow, cube-shaped chair as I hit record.

"So, Mom, tell me about how you and dad ended up at Whiskey Jane's."

My mom pulls her legs up in front of her, sitting in a criss-cross position, and holds her ankles with her hands.

"Well, you never knew this, but Grandma Gretta and Grandpa Ed didn't used to like me very much." She laughs as she mentions my dad's parents. "I was the crazy, artsy girl with tattoos, and your father was strait-laced, on the track to attend law school. They thought I was corrupting him with my ideals." She smiles. "We were madly in love, though; nothing was going to change that.

"We had a whirlwind love and within two months of meeting, we got engaged. Everyone thought we were crazy, and we were—crazy for each other—and we knew it was meant to be. One day we were lying out by a community pool, trying to decide how we would afford a wedding. Frank was still in school, and I was waitressing, so funds were low. His parents already told us they would not contribute to the wedding and if we got married, they would stop paying for his school. My own parents had passed away years before in a car accident," my mom says solemnly.

I can feel Olive on the edge of her seat as she breathlessly says, "So what did you do?" I know she relates to the lack of support that my mom is talking about.

My mom grins at her. "Well, Frank leaned over to me from his pool chair and said, 'Let's elope.' I was totally on board—I love spontaneous stuff, Hunter can tell you."

I snort from behind the camera. "Yeah, one time I came home from school and my mom decided we were going to drive to Memphis to get some barbecue, six hours away. We pulled up to the restaurant ten minutes after they closed and ended up eating McDonalds in the car. Another time, she got her motorcycle license on a random Tuesday." I turn to Olive. "My mom doesn't even have a motorcycle."

At that, Olive laughs. "I'm inspired," she tells my mom, her eyes sparkling with admiration. "I wish I was that carefree."

My mom waves her hands. "Oh, sweetie! You can be! Just stop giving a fuck." She covers her mouth, looking at me and cringes. "Sorry I cursed in your video."

"It's fine." I grin, knowing I can censor it, or edit it, so the video can still be monetized. "Let's get the story back on track."

"Okay! So, we decided to tie the knot on our own. That day. We went back to my apartment and showered and then I dug through my closet for something special to wear. I found the purple flowy dress I wore on our first date and slipped it on. Your dad wore a striped shirt from the trunk of his car and his board shorts. He looked so handsome." She stares off into the distance, deep in thought.

"We found a small chapel near my place and knocked on the door. A younger man came to the door, a napkin hanging from his shirt, and a newspaper under his arm. He was the pastor, and we'd interrupted his sandwich. Frank told him we wanted to get married *right now* and the man told us no; we would have to schedule in advance for a wedding. We begged him and told him our situation. He must have taken pity on us, seeing the love in our eyes. Twenty minutes and fifty dollars later, we were married. Obviously, we had to get a marriage license afterwards." Mom laughs. "That was just logistics, though. We figured it out.

"After we were married, we went back to my apartment and put together a picnic to eat on Jewel Mountain to watch the sunset. It was one of our favorite things to do. We watched the sun go down and then made love under the stars when it was finally dark," she says dreamily. I try to pretend like I didn't hear my mom talk about her sex life with my father.

"We drove back down the mountain a little while later and decided we wanted to get a drink somewhere to celebrate. It was our first time going into the world as a married couple and Frank said this deserved a toast. We passed Whiskey Jane's frequently when we were headed up the mountain, but had never been in. That night we decided to go. The bar was packed when we pulled up. We grabbed a table towards the back of the bar, so we had a little privacy.

"After I took a seat, Frank went up to order us some drinks. We had a few beers, and Frank was starting to have a rapport with the bartender after an hour or so. He was very smiley and when he found out that we were just married, he shouted for his wife to come over. She was standing at the other end of the bar, chatting with some customers, and we hadn't met her yet.

"I remember his wife having a commanding, warm presence. She had on a deep blue dress, and her hair was thrown up in a messy bun with large sparkly earrings. I thought the woman was effortlessly gorgeous. When she found out that we were just married, she walked around the bar and gave me a huge hug. I was a complete stranger to her, but she treated me like a best friend that night, celebrating our marriage with me. She asked us if we had a first dance and we both told her no, which she said was *unacceptable*. She shouted out to the guests telling everyone to 'clear the floor, move the tables,' and that we were going to have our first dance.

"Everyone instantly complied." Mom chuckles. "Within a minute, the floor was cleared of all people and tables, and the woman motioned for us to go stand in the circle. She selected a song on the jukebox for us. It was the song 'Time of the Season' by The Zombies." My mouth drops hearing my mother say this. How many times through the years have I heard about their first dance, never knowing the story behind it? Never knowing this bar that I have been filming in for months now created a magical moment for my newlywed parents.

My mom continues talking, her voice rising with emotion. "After the song ended, the man handed us a marker and the woman told us to go write our big day on the wall, since it deserved to be memorialized. There were already multiple areas covered with writing, so we decided to put it on the wall where we first sat, not wanting to forget the table where we had our first toast as a married couple. Your dad sang the song in my ear as I wrote our initials in a heart and the date. I decided to write the name of the song, too." My mom softly sings the lyrics to herself. I feel Olive shaking slightly next to me. I know it's because my mom is talking about Jane and Seymour, and she doesn't even realize it.

"And that's our story with the bar." Mom smiles, clapping her hands together. "The end." She holds her eyes with the camera, a twinkle in them, as I click the button to stop recording and set the camera on a chair to my left.

"Did you ever go back?" Olive asks her quietly.

"Not together. We had Hunter shortly after and our days of going out at night ended. Not that we were party animals anyway." Mom laughs. "But I went back once alone, a month after Hunter's father passed. I sat at our table, buried my face in my hands, and cried. The woman from the night we got married was actually there. She took a seat next to me and asked me if I was all right. I'm not sure if she recognized me, but I told her how I had just lost Frank, and she told me how she'd lost her husband, too. She took my hand in hers, and we sat there in silence together for an hour. Two widows in our grief." Mom is quiet then.

Olive breaks the silence. "That was Jane. You must have caught her on a good day, while she was still working in the bar."

Olive then explains her relationship with Jane to my mother. My mom reaches out her hand from across the table. "I have something for you. Sit tight." She leaves the room. I have no idea what my mom is going to get, and when she comes back in the room with a large canvas turned away from us, I'm confused.

"I want you to have this," my mom says to Olive, spinning the canvas. I hear Olive gasp when she sees the painting.

"It's Jane." She puts a hand up to her mouth, her shock evident.

The painting is gorgeous, with shades of blues and purples swirling in the background, a portrait of a woman in the center with a blue dress and blonde hair up. I realize that it must be how Jane looked the night my parents were married.

"I painted her when I was pregnant with Hunter. I was unable to do much because I was on bed rest, but I couldn't get her image out of my head. She was beautiful to me, ethereal and strong. Everything I wanted Hunter to see in me as a mother. I've had this sitting in the back of my closet for years, unable to part with it, but also not knowing what to do with it."

My mom hands the canvas to Olive, who shakes her head. "I can't accept this. It's yours."

"No, honey. I want you to have it. Fate must have brought us together so I could give this to you."

Olive holds the painting close. "Thank you." She looks up at my mother with admiration. "I will treasure this."

"Alright, enough of the heavy shit," my mom jokes. "Who wants to smoke some weed?"

That's my mom.

Chapter 46

Olive

wo days later, I wake up to the call that I've been anxiously dreading. One of Jane's favorite nurses, Jojo, at the memory care facility, tells me that she recommends me coming to visit Jane *today*. I know what this call means; she's telling me that this might be Jane's last day. I planned to visit her tomorrow on my day off, but I know the urgency of seeing her today. She has not been eating for a while now and no longer wants to even take a sip of water. Her body is failing her.

I tell the nurse that I will be there within the hour and thank her for letting me know. Since I am not family, I know she took a risk by telling me this information, but everyone there knows how close Jane and I are.

I stand up to get dressed and stare blankly at my closet. What do you wear to possibly say goodbye to someone? I throw on a sparkly top with a butterfly on it that she gave me for my birthday a few years ago. The shirt is much more her than me; I never knew where I would wear it. Jane would always buy me shirts she found at the store in the juniors' section. I think she knew I didn't have a mother that cared enough to buy me fun, girlie things as a child, and she never had a daughter of her own. She was always trying to make up for the time in our lives before we knew each other.

So today I will wear the top for her. I throw on some jeans with it, and look at myself in the mirror. I glance down and make eye contact with the painting Hunter's mom gave me. It currently rests in the corner of my room. After looking at the canvas in the mirror, I walk over to my jewelry box and find the biggest dangling earrings I own and put them on. For her.

My stomach rumbles, so I eat a quick bowl of cereal in the kitchen. I'm almost done when I hear my phone ring again. I hold my breath as I check the caller ID and feel relief when I see it's Hunter.

"Hey," I answer.

"Good morning, beautiful," He sounds cheery on the other side of the call, and I can't even fake match his enthusiasm as he continues talking. "I was going to see if you wanted to grab breakfast before work."

"I am actually about to go visit Jane." I clear my throat. "She's not doing well; a nurse at Hills Pointe called me a few minutes ago."

I hear Hunter breathe deeply on the other side. "I'm sorry to hear that. Is there anything I can do to help you today? Would you like me to come?"

I think this over momentarily and I realize, yes, I would like him to come. I feel so safe with Hunter next to me. He's almost become like a security blanket unintentionally. But I also don't want to ask him to come—knowing he lost his father, this would be heavy for him. I feel like I need to do this alone, that I need time to say goodbye to Jane. *Be brave, Olive,* I tell myself.

"No, it's okay," I say to Hunter quietly.

He seems concerned but says, "Okay, text me after if you want to talk. I'm here."

"Thank you," I tell him and hang up shortly after. I grab the basket of petunias that Hunter brought me from next to my front door, and feel my hands start to shake.

Knowing I can't put this visit off any longer, I head to see Jane. When I arrive, there are only two cars in the parking lot. It's still early and I know most of the residents will just be starting their day. I'm thankful for this because I don't feel like small talk right now. No one is sitting at the front desk yet, so I head straight to Jane's room.

When I get to her room, I see the nurses have moved her into a hospital-style bed towards the corner of the room. She is asleep, snoring lightly, and I quietly set the basket of flowers on the floor nearby. Then I take a seat on the side of her bed.

I look at her for a moment—her body looks even smaller in the bed than usual. She can't weigh more than eighty pounds now. I'm not sure when the last time she actually ate a meal was. The nurses and I tried everything to get her to eat this past month, but she just continued to say, "I'm tired, I'm not hungry."

Taking a shuddering breath, I reach out for her hand. It's warm and quaking slightly. I run my thumb over the top of her wrinkled hand, aged with years of a beautiful life lived, and start to think about my best moments with her. I decide to tell them aloud to her, hoping maybe she will feel comfort from my voice while she sleeps.

"You know, Jane, you have always been the most generous person I've ever met," I rasp out, emotion taking hold of me already. "I remember every time I would give you a compliment about something you were wearing, you would say, 'You like it, baby? It's yours!' in your Southern accent and then try to give me the item the next time I saw you." I softly laugh to myself.

"I remember how many times you dragged me onto the stage of the bar to do karaoke with you when I was young and awkward. I remember looking over at you in awe, constantly. Seeing someone that had suffered the pain of losing her husband, her best friend, and still getting up every day with a smile. Doing what you had to do for the bar. You didn't care what anyone thought of you, and I admire that so much. I want to be like you. Thank you for always taking care of me like I was your daughter. I hope I made you proud."

At this, I break into violent tears, my vision blurring as they soak my face. My whole body shakes as I continue to talk. "I met a boy I like, and I wish you could have met him. He even gave me petunias to bring for you. He's basically perfect." I laugh through my tears, and I grab a flower out of the basket and place it next to Jane. She stirs lightly, and I see her blink her eyes open.

"Good morning, sleepy head." I smile at her, brushing the tears away from my face quickly, wanting her to see my smile, not my tears, if this is our last time together.

She doesn't say anything but gives me a small smile back. Her breathing is heavy and I can tell it pains her.

"I know you are tired, Jane," I tell her and brush my hand over her white hair. "It's okay for you to be with Seymour now. I'm sure he's looking down at you, getting ready to give you a big hug."

Jane opens her mouth and quietly whispers out a weak, "Seymour."

"Yes. He's going to be so happy to see you." I fight back the quiver in my voice, struggling through tears. I continue to brush my hand over her hair softly.

Jane nods her head once and closes her eyes again. Her exhaustion is clear, and I watch as she drifts back to sleep. Then, I reach forward, take her hand again, and squeeze it tight. We sit there in silence for at least an hour while I weep. I don't think I have the strength to get up and leave her, to say goodbye. Knowing I need to be strong, though, I lean in and hug her. I hold her frail body for a minute and then pull back to kiss her on the forehead.

"I'm going to leave these flowers here for you," I tell her. "How about next to the window?" I pick up the basket, placing them on a small table by the window. "You're going to love these when you wake up."

I force myself to keep talking, swallowing down the pain of what I'm about to say. "Alright, well I'm going to head out now. I need to go get ready for work." I chuckle and try to keep my voice light, not wanting there to be sadness in the room, even as it consumes me internally. "I promise I'll take care of the bar for you." I head towards the door and breathe deeply. I turn back to face Jane, and I say the thing I've always wanted to tell her. I bite the inside of my cheek and then say with the only strength I have left in my body at this moment, "*I love you, Mom.* I'll see you again."

Chapter 47

Hunter

I'm sitting outside of the memory care facility in my truck, which is currently parked next to Olive's purple car. I tap my fingers against the steering wheel, anxious and questioning my decision to come here in the first place. Olive sounded so upset and scared on the phone this morning. I know she was trying to hide it from me but after getting off the call, I couldn't just leave it be; I needed to be here for her.

I've been sitting out here for a little over an hour. I just feel so much compassion for her, deep in my bones. I know the feeling of knowing your time is coming to an end with someone you love deeply and not being able to stop it. I think back on my last months with my father. He was so weak and fragile. A shell of the man he was before. I think about the story my mom told us, about him loving her more than anything else. Putting his love for her above his parents' opinions. I feel that way about Olive, I think. I would put her above anything else.

I feel butterflies in my stomach as I realize...I love her.

I see a woman with dark hair hunched in on herself walk out

of the front door of Hills Pointe and realize it's Olive. I quickly get out of the truck and close my door. She still has her head down, walking almost dazedly, when I meet her on the sidewalk. She finally looks up and when she does, her expression crumbles.

"Hunter," she says breathlessly, and then throws herself into my arms as she begins to sob. Her whole body shakes violently as the emotion grips her. Her breathing is fast and uncontrolled.

I hold her tight in my arms, relieved she is at least accepting my comfort and presence here. I gently stroke her hair as her cries turn into silent sobs.

I console her softly. "I'm here, Olive. I've got you. You're my girl."

"I feel like I didn't take enough time to see her these past years. I could have told her I loved her more; I could have thanked her while she still understood. I could have shown her the love that Tripp never did. I want to go back in time, to tell her what she means to me." She confesses all her thoughts, and her tears soak my shirt as I silently listen.

We stand like this for a while until the only thing left is her hiccups, an aftermath of the tears.

"Would you like me to give you a ride to work? I can bring you back to your car later?" I ask her in a low voice.

"No, it's okay," She looks up at me with red-rimmed eyes. The hurt in them makes me want to kiss her deeply, to try to remove some of the pain in her heart.

I tuck her dark hair behind an ear. "What time do you have to be there?"

"Eleven-thirty." Olive sniffles.

I pull my phone out of my back pocket and check the time:

10:45. "Would you like to come sit in my truck with me for a few minutes, then?"

She nods her head yes and clasps my hand weakly as I lead her to the passenger side. She slumps into the seat, and I gently shut the door, then run around to my side. Once we are in the truck, I take a deep breath. "I want to tell you about my dad, if that's okay?"

She looks over at me and gives me a whisper of a response. "Yes. I would like to hear more about him."

I fidget with my steering wheel, knowing the vulnerability of what I'm about to share with her is deeper than anything I've told her before.

"I'll start by telling you, my dad and I didn't have a perfect relationship when I was growing up. I spent many years as a teenager arguing with him over the stupidest things, like having a curfew or getting in trouble for drinking. I was always seeing what I could do to push the boundaries with him; I was kind of a punk kid. I didn't want to listen to any authority, even when it was someone who loved me as deeply as he did.

"My dad was the strict parent, at least compared to my mom. She was always a free spirit." I chuckle. "I told him I hated him many times during fights when I was young and he would just look at me and tell me in response, '*That's okay, son, because I will love you enough for the both of us while you're mad at me.*'

"I wish so deeply I could change my teenage years and the way I treated him. As an adult, I tried to do everything I could to make up for those years where I was a shit to him. I spent every moment that I wasn't working with him once he was diagnosed with cancer. The guilt still consumed me, though. The time I didn't appreciate that I had with him, when he was healthy.

"I bought this truck because of guilt," I tell her, motioning around us. "Because it was always his dream to restore an old car with me. It was his hobby, and I wanted to get that connection with him that I had missed out on before. I wanted to apologize for the stress I caused him when I was young, but for some reason you always just think you will have more time with someone, so I never said it to him. I couldn't get the words out, even during his last moments.

"I was weak. I have let it haunt me ever since. You don't expect your dad to die when you're a young man in your twenties. You think your parents will always be there. The time you have never feels like enough. Which is why I can't even begin to comprehend the absolute heartbreak you must feel right now. You didn't have that nurturing parent growing up, and you finally found it in Jane. She gave you what your mom and dad never could. You have had way less time with her than I ever had with my dad and that makes me so angry for you. You don't deserve any of this. Jane doesn't deserve any of this."

I take a deep breath and hold both her hands in mine. "I'm not going to lie to you and tell you that things will be easy. It's not easy to lose someone you love deeply. You're going to feel lost and angry without her. All I can ask of you is please don't shut me out. I know Ivy is moving this weekend, so lean on me. I will help you get through this. I will be your strength when you have none. My friends forced me to get up and keep living when the loss of my dad consumed me. I felt angry with them at the time. I wanted to lay around and do nothing. I almost felt like if I wasn't suffering, my dad wouldn't think I loved him enough. Now I know that's not true; my dad would want me happy, always. I know Jane would want the same for you.

"Look at how many people she picked up and helped in the stories we've heard. She wouldn't want you in pain for a minute; she would want you to *live*. Let me be your strength, lean on me when you miss her. I will come and be with you; all I ask is that you open your door and let me. Don't shut me out."

I sit next to her in silence after I've finished talking. She is looking out the window, deep in thought. I'm not even sure if she has been listening, but she finally turns to me and says, "Okay, Hunter."

I lean over and kiss her cheek. "Olive, you mean the world to me."

I know this isn't the right time to tell her I love her.

She nods and pulls back. "I've got to go to work now." She begins to open the passenger door and adds, "Thank you for being here for me." Her eyes are red-rimmed and empty at this point. I'm so worried about her. She's been hurt by so many people before; I know her control tactic is to shut down emotionally.

"Of course. I'm here, always," I say.

Olive gets out of the car and starts to walk to her own vehicle.

"Will you please text or call me later?" I call after her.

She turns back towards me quickly. "Yes," she says, and then gets in her car and drives away.

I text Olive later that afternoon to check on her and get worried when I still haven't heard anything after an hour. By nightfall, I grow even more concerned, so I drive past the bar to see if she's still at work. The lights are off...not good.

I anxiously park at The Mart across the street and walk in to see Mr. Ray behind the counter. He gives me a sad small smile in greeting. I look at him and ask the question, my voice like gravel, because I already know the answer. "Jane?"

Mr. Ray looks down at this lap and shakes his head sadly. "Gone."

I rush out of the store, knowing I need to get to Olive.

Chapter 48

Olive

Two weeks later

I feel like I have been living in a blur recently, going through the motions every day but feeling nothing. I am completely numb to everything around me. The bar was closed for a few days after Jane's passing. I couldn't bring myself to work and Tripp surprisingly didn't bother me or Rob about going in.

We had a small funeral for Jane last Tuesday morning. She was laid to rest next to Seymour, just like she wanted. Tripp was there, but left as soon as the memorial was over. He didn't acknowledge anyone. Hunter stood next to me the whole time. As I watched her coffin lower into the earth, his hand kept me from collapsing. But still, I felt nothing.

Hunter has visited me every single day since the moment he found out that she passed away, just like he said he would. I kept my promise to him, letting him be here for me, knowing he is trying to help me. That doesn't change how broken I am inside, though. I can't describe this type of loss. I don't want to eat and I spend every moment that I'm not working asleep. Hunter doesn't say anything; he just brings me a meal each day and hangs out on the couch while I sleep. I can tell that he is worried about me.

Two days ago, Hunter told me that we reached the million-dollar goal so I can now buy the bar. I felt nothing when he told me. I know I should be thanking him, but I just can't seem to voice it. I need to talk to Tripp, but I've been trying to get my head on straight before I approach him. I feel so much anger towards him; it's the only emotion I can muster right now. I also know that isn't going to help convince him to sell Whiskey's to me. So, I need to be rational and handle the conversation in a professional manner. Today I will do it. I can't wait any longer, knowing he is going under contract any day now with B&B Investments.

I force myself to get out of my bed and shower. Basic care has become a chore for me at this point. I struggle to want to even brush my teeth. Jane would never want this for me, I know, but I just can't snap out of it. The nights are the worst, sitting alone with my thoughts. At least at work I'm kept busy, and my mind is constantly occupied. Except every time I see a customer give me that sad *you poor thing* look, I feel myself shut down a little bit more.

When I finish my shower, I throw on my hideous work uniform and brush my wet hair into a ponytail. I grab my keys and open the front door. A note falls from the crack of my door-frame and floats to the ground. I pick it up and read it.

Good morning, beautiful,

I am going to bring you some lunch later.

I left you a CD under your mat. Cheesy? I know.

But I wanted to make you a playlist that made me think of you.

I bend down and lift my rattan mat and sure enough there

is a CD in a case underneath it. I haven't listened to a CD since I was in high school. Ivy and I used to burn them for each other for our car rides to school. Curiosity gets the best of me as I lock my front door and head down the stairs.

I glance at Ivy's old place as I pass and miss her presence. She delayed her move for a few extra days after Jane passed away but couldn't stay any longer than that. Her new job at the bridal salon was waiting for her. She told me she would say *screw it* to the job and stay for me, but I told her to go. She can't put her life on hold for my sake. I want her to be happy and to get away from here. She deserves to find what she's looking for.

I walk to my car and sink down in the driver's seat. I'm grateful my old car still has a CD player as I slide the disk into the stereo. A slow beat starts, and I turn over the plastic case where I see Hunter has written each song name in Sharpie on the outside. The first song is "With Me" by Sum 41, and I listen to the lyrics as I back my car out of the parking spot. I've heard this song many times, but never with the context of someone dedicating it to me.

I feel like a bitch suddenly; Hunter has done everything that he can to help me since he's met me, and I have nothing to give him. This makes me feel angry and I hate it. Why can't he just let me suffer? Why does he keep showing up? He won't let me be miserable, which is how I *should* feel after losing someone that I love more than anything.

I grow angrier as I click to the next song and then the next. Each song pours his heart out to me, and I feel the shell I have built around myself, the hardened exterior I've created these past few weeks, cracking. I slam my hand into the power button on my stereo, clicking the music off. I can't handle this right now. I need to stay numb while I talk to Tripp, so whatever answer he gives will just bounce off me.

When I get to Whiskey's, the first few hours of my shift are easy. Just a few regulars and Rob are here. No Tripp in sight. I glance at the clock and see it's close to 1:30 P.M. and I know Hunter will be dropping food to me soon. He waits till the lunch crowd is done because he wants to make sure I actually eat what he brings me. That I don't use being busy as an excuse to not feed myself. I can tell I've lost weight recently—my uniform hangs on me in a way it didn't before—but food tastes like dirt when I force myself to eat. The death diet.

Five minutes later, Hunter walks through the entrance and holds up a bag from Smiley Sushi. Of course he picked up my favorite food. He had to drive at least thirty minutes to grab it, too. I give him a small wave as he strolls over, smiling wide, like he does every time he sees me.

"Hey, Olive, hope you're in the mood for cheeseburgers," he jokes as he hands the paper bag to me. I open it up, deeply inhaling the scent of miso soup and tempura rolls. My mouth waters and I decide I will have a few bites. I look back up at Hunter and tell him a faint *thank you*. The relief on his face when I take a bite makes me feel even worse inside. Why does he care so much about me? Why can't he just leave me like everyone else?

"I don't want to put pressure on you, but have you talked to Tripp yet?" he asks me quietly.

I shake my head in response. "No, I'm going to today, though."

"It will be okay," he tells me, his never-ending optimism that things will just work out a harsh contrast to my own mind.

Hunter fills the rest of the time together with stories while I eat. He tells me about Eddie hiring a lawyer to deal with the app issues, about his mom getting asked to paint a mural at a local park, and about how Wes is going to start a band, apparently.

I smile listening to the stories, but I know it doesn't reach my eyes. I am just going through the motions, doing the things the old me would have done. Deep inside, I know that girl is gone.

When I finish eating, Hunter gives me a hug and says good-bye, telling me he will stop by before work tomorrow so we can get coffee.

I nod my head. "Okay."

He smiles at me one last time before leaving.

I know that if this conversation doesn't go the way I want it to with Tripp, I will be busy packing tomorrow.

Chapter 49

Hunter

I woke up this morning feeling strange. I didn't feel anxious or sad, just kind of like something ominous is coming. I even spent an extra thirty minutes working out to try and shake off the bad feeling, but still it remains.

The past few weeks I've done everything I can think of to help Olive. I hope each time I see her that a little bit of healing will show through. That there will be a hint of the woman she was before still in there. But I think I've lost her. She seems completely shut off from me; she never tries to touch me or look at me. She glances at me, but her stare goes right through me. I can tell her mind is always far away.

I hear a tap on my window and look up to see Mrs. Sonjia Ray knocking on it. She smiles brightly as I roll down the window.

"I thought that was you!" she greets me warmly. Her outfit is colorful with long and flowy layers; she looks like a woodland fairy or Mother Nature, like Olive said.

"Hi, Mrs. Ray." I grin back.

"Sonjia," she corrects me, still smiling.

I nod my head. "You've got it." I then remember that Jane was her best friend. I meet her eyes and add, "I'm so sorry about Jane."

Mrs. Sonjia looks off at the mountains past me. "Yes, well, I'm lucky to have had a friend like her. Losing her doesn't take away the many magical years we had. She was a real gem."

I look at my steering wheel and rub my finger over the stitching, not sure what else to say.

"How is Olive?" Mrs. Sonjia asks. "I'm here to visit her."

"She's struggling, I can tell." I feel like there's a frog in my throat. "She will be happy to see you, though."

"I brought her some butter." Mrs. Sonjia pulls a large mason jar full of fresh butter out of her bag and winks at me.

"Well, if anything can make her feel better, your butter will." I chuckle.

"How are *you* doing, Hunter?"

"I'm great," I quickly say, my go-to people-pleasing response.

She stares deeply at me. I feel like she's reading my mind. "Tell me the truth, it's okay. I see a sadness in your eyes, too."

I blow out a breath. "I'm really worried about Olive and honestly, I'm worried about losing her. I feel her trying to cut me out of her life." I look down at my lap as I confess. "I need her."

"You love her," she says in understanding.

"Very much."

"Tell her."

"I don't think it's the right time," I respond. "She's dealing with so much."

"There's never a wrong time for love," Mrs. Sonjia tells me. "You were put in her life for a reason; I just know it."

"Thank you," I say quietly.

She holds out her hand to me. I reach across my car

window and take it. Her wrinkled hand is comforting. She squeezes mine. "You have a good heart, Hunter. Your dad would be proud of you."

I draw my hand back at the statement, shocked by what she just said. I'm suddenly wondering if Mrs. Sonjia is psychic, when she laughs warmly. "Olive and I talk. She mentions you a lot more than you realize." She winks at me. "Tell her."

This push of confidence from Mrs. Sonjia is what I needed to make up my mind. Next time I see Olive, I will put my heart on the line.

Chapter 50

Olive

I t's almost closing and I'm cleaning some bar glasses when Tripp finally walks in. He heads straight to the office without even glancing my way. I'm surprised to see him here since it's after midnight. I make eye contact with Rick across the bar, and he nods his head to me as if to say, *it's time.*

Rick and Rob have been trying to psych me up all day for this conversation. Rob has already left for the night and Rick now cashes out with me quickly; he's the only customer left in the bar. I say my goodbyes to him as he walks out. Then, I set down the glass I'm drying, smooth down my hair, and inhale a deep breath.

"Okay," I say to myself and push through the kitchen door.

Tripp has the office door shut when I approach, so I knock.

"Come in," he murmurs from the other side. I open the door and when he sees me, he looks annoyed. "What?"

"I was, um, I was wondering if I could talk to you about something?" I stumble over my words as I uncomfortably stand before him.

"Okay, I only have a few minutes. I'm just getting something off the computer for tomorrow morning for B&B Investments," he tells me as he turns back towards the computer screen.

I walk in another step and stand awkwardly in the doorway. "That's actually what I wanted to talk to you about."

Tripp turns in his chair to face me, looking disinterested. "Okay?"

Well, here goes nothing. "I want you to sell the bar to me instead of Mr. Cronline," I blurt out. "I have the money, and you know your mom would rather me run the bar instead of it getting torn down. I know you hate this place, but I love it—"

Tripp holds up his hand to stop me. "You have two million dollars laying around?"

Two million?

"Wait, what? No...I raised a million dollars, like you said it was selling for."

Tripp lets out a cackle of a laugh. "Oh, Olive, no, sweetie. That was before. There's been a lot of interest in this property." He crosses his arms smugly. "Especially since people found out this place gave Freddie Finnely the inspiration for his books. Thanks for that info, it's really helping the sale. Developers are saying this land is basically historic now. Who wouldn't want to claim they live where the most famous YA author wrote?"

I can't even believe what I'm hearing. "Wait, you knew I was trying to raise the money for the bar?"

"Of course." He sneers. "People talk. I saw the info about Freddie Finnely on the news, for god's sake. I started watching your little videos with your boyfriend after. I know what you've been doing this whole time; I honestly should fire you for filming at *my* bar without my consent." He gives me a once-over. "There will be no need for that, though. I am going under contract with B&B Investments tomorrow morning at nine A.M. In thirty days, you will be jobless."

My lungs feel like I can't even get air. I'm completely speechless. I stand still as a statue as he continues to mock me.

"I'm honestly surprised you worked up the nerve to even ask me for the bar. I've been waiting." An evil smile pulls from his lips. "It's cute that you thought you could do it."

"Fuck you, Tripp," I say with venom in my voice, and storm out of the office. "I quit."

I throw my apron on the bar counter and breathe heavily as I grab my stuff. I can't stand another second in this place knowing it is going to be torn down in less than a month. I feel like I'm suffocating as I push through the front door and am blinded by rain.

"Shit," I say as I run to my car. I'm dripping wet by the time I unlock it and get in the driver's seat. I put my keys in the ignition and try to start my car, but nothing happens. I try again. I hear nothing but my car clicking. My battery must be dead. I smack my hands on my steering wheel in frustration and scream out, "Right *now*? Are you *kidding* me?"

I run around to my trunk so I can grab my jump box and realize it's not there when I open it. I took it out last week to start my car at the grocery store and must have left it in the parking lot by accident. The universe is playing a cruel joke on me.

I look for other cars in the area and there isn't a single one to be found. It's past 2 A.M. on a Tuesday morning. No one is out right now, and I refuse to go back in and face Tripp. I get back in the driver's seat and tap my fingers on the steering wheel, deciding what I should do next. I know who would want to help me, I'm just not ready to face him. I sit for a few more minutes listening to the rain pour down on my car before I pick up my phone and reluctantly hit the caller ID for the only person I know who will be awake right now.

Hunter answers on the second ring, his voice laced with concern. "Olive? What's wrong?"

"I need help. My car won't start," is all I can say.

"Are you at work?"

"Yes."

"I'll be there in fifteen minutes." Hunter hangs up then, I'm sure to rush out the door, to be my knight in shining armor once more.

He must think I'm pathetic. Always coming to rescue me. I can't do this to him anymore.

Chapter 51

Hunter

I was editing some skate footage for a local brand, my insomnia getting the best of me tonight, when my phone lit up with an incoming call. Seeing that it was Olive, I instantly felt concerned. She usually doesn't reach out to me late, and especially not in the past few weeks. I knew something was bad, and from the sound of her voice on the call, today didn't go as planned. Her voice was curt and distant on the other end, almost robotic. And I surmised all that before she even mentioned the reason for her call.

My stomach drops now as I pull into the parking lot of Whiskey Jane's. It's pouring down rain, but I can see Olive outside. I park next to her and jog over to her driver's side where she's leaning against the door.

"Why are you standing out in the rain?" I shout as it pours onto us.

"I was hot in the car," she says back. "It won't start."

"Do you think it's the battery?"

"Yes," she responds, still robotic in her responses.

I stand next to her, just as drenched now. "I have cables.

Let's see if the rain will die down a little bit before we jump it. Just to be safe."

Olive nods her head and crosses her arms. She's staring at her feet, her body language completely closed off.

"Let's go sit in my truck while we wait."

"No. I need air," she quietly responds.

"Okay." I stand next to her, waiting to see if she wants to say anything else. A few minutes later she speaks.

"Tripp is selling the bar for two million dollars. He said the land is worth more now. He even laughed in my face when I asked him about buying it."

Anger consumes me. I clench my hand at my side. "That piece of shit."

Olive continues, "He said he has known about our attempt to raise the money this whole time. That it only helped him sell the bar for more money. He goes under contract tomorrow with the investor. The bar will be closed in less than a month."

She sounds like she is reading off a script, not describing her own life. She's detached. The way she is acting scares me; her lack of emotion with everything she tells me paralyzes my own thoughts.

"Are you okay?" I ask, instantly feeling like a dumbass because of course she's not. Who would be okay in her situation right now?

Olive shrugs her shoulders. "Oh well. We tried." She looks up at me blankly.

"Olive, we can raise the money. Let's figure this out. I will help you."

She starts shaking her head quickly. "No, no. This is over, there's nothing else to be done. This was my problem, and you did your best to help me."

I try to reason with her. "Let me help. Maybe I could get a loan?"

Olive recoils back from me. "*No*, Hunter, stop. Stop trying to save me!" she yells out and turns away. "It's done."

I refuse to let her give up. I know she means more than just the bar when she says this; she means us, too. She's trying to push me away.

She is still standing with her back to me, looking across the street, when she says, "I'm moving."

"What?" I whisper breathlessly. The earth feels like it's dropped out from below me.

She turns back towards me and speaks softer now, a note of sorrow in her expression. "Curls, I'm leaving. I'm going to move to Atlanta to live with Ivy. I need to figure my life out now." I can't believe my ears as she continues, "There's nothing left for me here."

"You have me," I quietly say.

"Yeah, and if I stayed here just to be with you, you would leave me, too, one day. Everyone leaves me eventually," she tells me. "Don't you get it? No one has ever chosen me in my life." Her voice raises with every word. "My dad didn't stick around, and my mom never cared enough to put me first instead of her love life. I was always a choice to them, not a priority. The people that were supposed to love me more than anything in the world didn't give a shit about me. This has caused me to feel neglected and unattached towards other people. I promised myself that I wouldn't get close to anyone. Wouldn't allow myself to feel love. The only person I really let in was Jane, and it took years for her to crack my hard exterior." She throws her hands in the air. "Now look at where that got me. I let someone love me and now I'm more alone than ever. I lost my job, and I am trying to figure my life out without her. I'm a lost cause, Hunter. You need to forget about me."

I grow angry now. "That's bullshit, Olive, and you know it.

You have so many people that love you. Ivy, Rob, Missy, Mr. Ray, Mrs. Sonjia, Rick, Johnny."

She stares at me and seems taken aback at my burst of anger. The only other time she has seen me upset is when I punched Dennis, but I can't stop the passion as the words pour out of me.

"Olive, *I love you*. I choose you. I want to be with you every second of the day. I can't stop thinking about you and it's driving me insane. I want to be the person you call home. I want to kiss your soft lips and hold your beautiful face close to mine. I'm out of my mind every time I leave you, trying to think of any excuse to come see you. I would never abandon you." My voice cracks with emotion as I say it a second time, "I love you."

She stands looking at me, speechless as the rain continues to cascade down on us.

I don't stop talking, "I know you love me, too, Olive."

She nods her head slowly, like she's in a trance, her eyes finally shining with a hint of emotion. "I do," she whispers, the phrase pouring out of her lips, like a confession.

Hearing those words, I step towards her quickly, and she meets me halfway. Our lips meet instantly, both of us kissing each other with longing. The emotion between us encompasses me. Olive grabs at my hair as I frantically kiss up and down her neck. I breathe in her floral scent and groan. Her admission that she loves me fills me with warmth, even though we are both soaking wet. I never want this moment to end as she draws back and whispers to my mouth, "Be with me one time before I leave."

"Don't leave me," I plead.

She looks at me, her large eyes filled with sadness. "I'm not the girl for you, Hunter. Please just be with me tonight."

Before I can respond and tell her that she is wrong, that she is the only girl for me, her lips crash back into mine. Her kisses become more sensual and deepen, and my own need for her takes over before my brain can tell my heart to stop. I know it will hurt even more when she leaves, taking this next step together. But I can't seem to care.

I pull back, running my thumb over her plump bottom lip, as I softly tell her, "Okay, Olive."

I realize the rain has stopped so I walk her to my truck and grab a picnic blanket from the back seat. It's the same blanket we sat on together at Onilley Lake and the thought doesn't leave me as I lay it out in the bed of my truck. I turn to her and sheepishly say, "This is all I've got."

Her lips crash back into mine in response and I can't help but moan as she starts to feel for my body under my shirt. I pick her up in my arms and gently lay her in the truck bed. I climb on top of her, and I lean over. Looking down, I push a damp strand of hair out of her face and gently kiss the tip of her nose. She giggles softly; her eyes finally look full of life as she pulls me towards her.

"Thank you for everything, Hunter. I will never forget you," she whispers into my ear. My throat is tight with emotion, so all I can do is nod in response.

Then I make love to the woman I cherish under the stars.

Chapter 52

Olive

Three weeks later

I toss a few more items into a box laying on my apartment floor and decide that's the last of what I'm bringing to Atlanta. I've spent the past few weeks saying goodbye to the people I treasure most. I finally got a new battery for my car and had some maintenance done on it, so it will be ready for the move. It drained the small savings I had to fix Barney up, but I plan to look for a job as soon as I get to Atlanta.

I will be leaving Clairesville for good in a few days when my lease for the month is up. I want to get out of here before the deal closes on Whiskey Jane's. I can't handle seeing them bulldoze the place. I feel sick just thinking about it, knowing the bad guy won in the end. Tripp is getting exactly what he wanted all along. I have constantly wondered why Jane handed the bar over to him without even mentioning it to me, but I guess she didn't have to explain. She was his mother, no matter how he treated her in return.

I look over to the corner of my room and see something

under my dresser. I bend down and pick it up. It's a note from Hunter. When I first lost Jane, he used to leave me notes constantly. I sit on the floor and read it.

Olive,
You are strong.
You are beautiful.
You are important.
You are loved.
You are unique.
You are a gift.

My eyes well with tears as I read the words over and over again. Deciding I like the mantra, I tuck his note in the back pocket of my jeans.

Hunter saw deeply into my soul. He knew that I loved him back, and he called me out on it during our last night together. There hasn't been an hour that's gone by since we said goodbye that I haven't thought of him. I begged him that night, after we slept together, to end it there. I told him I would be leaving in a few days, and I couldn't handle seeing him anymore. That it would put salt in the wound to say goodbye to each other another time after that magical night. I told him that we needed to end contact completely, let the time together be what it was, and that he needed to move on with his life without me.

Hunter honored my wishes and hasn't reached out to me again. The sadness in his eyes as he listened to me and agreed, even though I could tell he didn't want to, just shows how good of a guy he is. I never deserved his love, not for a minute.

Whiskey Jane's has been sitting vacant since I quit. Sonjia called two weeks ago to inform me. After I left, it caused a snowball effect and Rob walked out, then our regulars stopped showing up, too. Without us, Tripp was unable to run the place alone, but he didn't seem to care either way, so he closed the bar. I'm sure he hasn't lost an ounce of sleep since he shut off the lights for good. Jane and Seymour would be devastated. I feel ashamed of myself for letting them down, but push the thought away.

My phone rings in my pocket, and I pull it out. Seeing Missy's name on the caller ID, I answer.

"Hey, Missy."

"Olive, turn on the news *now*," Missy commands from the other side of the call. "Channel 24."

"Um, what?" I laugh.

"Do it!" she shouts.

"Okay, one sec." I walk out to my living room, which is packed with boxes, and shuffle around for the remote control. When I find it under a couch pillow, I click it on as Missy says, "Hurry, hurry."

I punch in the channel number. "Okay—" I start to chuckle but end up speechless when I see what's on the screen.

Tripp's face is there, with an *arrested* banner running across the top of the screen. I click the volume up to listen to the male news anchor.

"Local man Tripp Fern is under arrest after allegedly stealing money from clients in business dealings in New York. A viral YouTube video helped police discover his whereabouts when they found out that the bar where it was filmed belonged to his parents before their passing. He was arrested this morning outside of the bar, Whiskey Jane's, and he has been charged with eight counts of investment fraud and two counts of fleeing law enforcement. He is also being charged with four counts of fraud for allegedly forging documents stating he owned his late parents' business. He is currently being held at the Clairesville Detention Center. Bail and hearing details are unknown."

The next news story starts to play and I silence the TV. My hand holding my phone begins to shake. "Holy shit."

Missy says quietly—for once—on the other line, "He faked the deed to the bar, Olive. Jane never signed the business over to him. He doesn't own it."

I have no words to respond, and my legs give out from under me at the news.

Chapter 53

Hunter

I have tried to stay as busy as possible since the night I last saw Olive. I've buried myself in work and left town twice to film for brands. No matter how much I have busied myself, though, the emptiness still consumes me. I know in my heart that Olive is the only woman for me. My parents *just knew* about each other and that's exactly how I feel about her. But while she may love me as much as I love her, she doesn't want to be with me, so I just have to accept that.

I look at the time and motivate myself to get up from the couch and throw on a snapback. I was supposed to meet Wes at the skate park twenty minutes ago. Shit. I shoot him a quick text that I'm on my way, knowing he probably won't read it, but just in case. He always keeps his phone in his car while he skates so he doesn't fall on it and break it.

I head out my front door and jog to my truck. Once I'm seated, I scroll through my playlist and click the song that Olive and I listened to together lying in the bed of my truck, our hands entwined, after we had sex. "Nights in White Satin" by

The Moody Blues plays through my speakers, and I'm transported back to the moment. Her smooth skin brushing against my own. Our limbs twisted together like a puzzle. I've never felt a moment more intimate or perfect.

I pull up to a stoplight and run my hands over my face. I hope she's doing okay in Atlanta. There have been so many times recently where I have started to text her and then decided it's a bad idea. I won't disrespect the boundary she set. She wants to move on from Clairesville and I understand that.

I pull up to the skate park and see it's empty other than Wes and one other guy, which I'm thankful for right now, because I would prefer not to be in a crowd. I grab my board out of my passenger seat and walk up the concrete steps to greet Wes. He is skating some ramps on the other side of the park, so I get on my board and skate over to him. He gives me a "sup" motion with his head and continues to ride around. I do the same, my mind clearing as I focus on only two things: the board and my movements on it.

After attempting a nollie heelflip and hitting the pavement multiple times, I decide to take a break. I ride over to a bench and Wes follows. He daps me up and then walks to another vacant metal bench next to mine and picks up a bottle of Gatorade. He chugs the container and wipes his mouth, then walks back towards me.

"How's it going, buddy?" Wes asks.

"It's going," I respond, looking up at him from bench. My board's resting between my feet and I push it back and forth.

"Nice to see you on the ol' board, old man."

"Yeah, I almost broke a hip. I'm rusty."

Wes sits next to me and nudges me with his shoulder. "Come skate more. It's good for you."

"Yeah, I know," I tell him.

"You've been working a lot recently, I feel like I've barely heard from you, dude."

"Yeah, just accepting more jobs now. Staying busy."

"To block out your feelings for Olive, right?" He raises an eyebrow.

I look over at him. "Right."

"That's what I thought." He nods. "Understandable, man. I could tell you were really into her."

"Still am," I say.

"I'm sorry the bar thing didn't work out for you two, that place was really sweet. I liked the vibe."

"Yeah, we tried the best we could. I just wanted to help."

"You're a great dude, Hunter. A way better man than me."

I tip my head in thanks.

"I meant to ask you, what are you two going to do with all the money now? The money you raised?"

"We talked about it the last night I saw her, after Olive found out she couldn't buy the bar. She said she wanted to make sure that the money was returned to everyone who donated so I told her I would handle it. I've refunded every single person that has donated at this point; so, it's really over now." I look down at my hands.

"It's going to be okay," Wes says, and puts a hand on my back in support.

"That's what everyone keeps saying," I respond. My attitude has been unusually pessimistic since losing her.

"Don't let this get you down. You will find someone new. Like I always say, 'The best way to get over someone is to get under someone else.'"

"I'm not like you, man," I tell him.

"I know and that's why I said you'll always be better than

me." Wes chuckles and smacks me on the back. "Come on, let's go get some food. I'm paying."

I nod my head and follow him out of the park.

Chapter 54

Olive

After the news breaks about Tripp having no legal ownership of the bar, I decide to stick around town to see what happens. I know I don't have the money from the fund anymore, but maybe if the bar goes up for auction at a cheaper price, I can try to work something out with the bank. I feel like this is a second chance and I'm trying to remain optimistic.

I'm heading to the grocery store to grab some food because my fridge is bare. I thought I would be leaving town by now and I'm down to nothing but baked beans in my pantry. I'm halfway to the store when Sonjia calls me.

"Hello?" I sing into the phone.

"Olive," Sonjia responds. "Where are you?"

"Huh?"

"Are you not coming? Jane specifically requested your attendance for this."

"What are you talking about?"

Sonjia whispers on the other line, "The reading of her will.

We are all here waiting on you, hun. Jane didn't want it read without your presence."

"I have no idea what you're talking about," I tell her.

"We all received letters from the holder of her estate that the will reading was supposed to take place today. Everyone is here, except Tripp, of course. But you need to get up here now. We can't start without you."

"I never got one. I mean, I never check my mailbox at the complex, but no one ever sends me snail mail, so..." I drift off and glance at my clock. My stomach is rumbling as I make up my mind. "I'm coming."

"Rob said he will text you the address," Sonjia responds. "See you soon, sweetie."

Ten minutes later I pull up in front of a big, official-looking brick building and glance down at my yoga pants and band tee. Great. I get out of my car and head inside. There are numerous rooms, and I'm greeted by a kind, elderly lady behind a desk. I tell her that I'm here for Jane's will reading and she guides me in the right direction towards an office.

I knock on the door and a man greets me. He is tall with salt-and-pepper hair and introduces himself as Mark, saying he is the executor of Jane's estate. He moves out of the way for me to enter and I look around to see Rob, Missy, and Sonjia smiling back at me. Missy pats the seat next to herself, motioning for me to join her on a small, suede couch.

I take a seat, and the man clears his throat. He steps behind his desk and picks up some reading glasses before resting them on his nose. He looks across at us and sits in his chair.

"Now that everyone is here, I will read Jane Fern's last will and testament. Jane changed her will with me the day she found out she was sick. She was of sound mind when she wrote and signed this will. These are her final words and wishes for you all."

He lifts a printed document from his desk and begins to read the first page. "'Well, I'll be dammed, I died.'"

Rob snorts to my left as Mark continues to read. "'I wasn't able to outsmart the clock of life—we all know time is a thief. But don't you worry. There isn't a single moment in my life that I would change. I lived the greatest life I possibly could and each and every one of you changed me in a way words can't describe. Look at each other and know, you all are my favorite people, and I want you to look out for each other.

"'Now, don't you worry about what has happened to me. I'm up in heaven with my soulmate now. I'm happy. I'm more worried about y'all being okay. I know how much you all loved me. I really was the *greatest*.'" Sonjia lets out a teary laugh at Jane's playful words. Even from the afterlife, she can make us smile.

Mark flips the page and continues reading. "'Since I can't tell you I love you anymore, I want to do something for each of you. Let's start with my son, Tripp.'"

Mark looks up at us. "I will still read what Mrs. Fern has written, per her wishes that the whole letter be read out loud, but due to Tripp's recent arrest, he will not be in attendance for his portion."

We nod our heads, and he continues.

"'Tripp, I leave my life insurance policy to you, in its entirety. I hope you can use the money to create the life you always wanted. The life your dad and I could never give you.'"

I bite my tongue so hard I taste blood when I hear this. The last thing Tripp deserves from his parents is a cent, but they were always good people, so I expect nothing less from them. Of course, she wouldn't leave her son high and dry after they both passed. I hear Rob exhale a breath and I know he feels upset, too.

Mark looks up at us, making eye contact with each of us and then continues on.

"'To my teddy bear, Rob, and sweet Missy, I leave our house. It is completely paid off and waiting for you. Please do whatever you'd like with it. Turn it into your home. Please just be happy in it; you two deserve it.'"

Missy puts a hand to her mouth and begins to shake next to me. Rob sits with his mouth wide open, shocked. I know they have always wanted to buy a home, but could never afford it. Jane just handed them one, paid off. My eyes fill with happy tears for them. I reach over and squeeze Missy's empty hand, which is shaking in her lap. We make eye contact, and I nod and smile and then do the same to Rob. "Congrats, you two."

She reaches over and hugs me tightly, still quaking in disbelief.

"Continuing on," Mark says, clearing his throat. "'To my dear friend Sonjia, I leave my diamond wedding ring. My favorite jewel belongs on Jewel Mountain with my best friend. I leave all of my clothing and the rest of my jewelry to Sonjia, as well. Do with it what you want: wear it, sell it, turn it into bee homes. I don't care. Just enjoy it. I also leave my cherry red '62 Oldsmobile Starfire to you, Sonjia. Put on some hot pants and take the town while you're still alive, lady.'"

Sonjia smiles deeply, puts her hands together, and looks up to the sky. "Thank you, friend."

Mark flips the paper again and you could hear a pin drop as he starts to read off the final page.

"'Now for my Olive, my daughter.'" I intake a breath when I hear the word *daughter*. "'Our years together were cut short; there were so many more things I wanted to see you do. I know you will accomplish every single one of your dreams. I knew you were special from the second you walked through the bar door at eighteen years old. I leave to you something I cherish immensely. Something I know only you will treasure as much as I did. I am so proud of the woman you have become; you have grown up before my eyes. I will watch down from heaven and cheer you on every step of the way.

"'My sweet girl, I leave you Whiskey Jane's.'"

Chapter 55

Hunter

Six months later

The weather is starting to warm up again, finally. This winter felt never-ending; there was even some snow up on Jewel Mountain this year. I head out of my house and smile over at my garden as I pass; the flowers have started to bloom. I look over at the extra petunias I planted last week and think about her.

It's been seven months since I've seen or heard from Olive and there isn't a day that goes by that I don't think of her. Eddie told me a few months ago that he drove by Whiskey's and the bar was open. He went inside and said Olive was running it. She told him that Jane gave the bar to her in her will.

I was thrilled for Olive, hearing this, but I can't lie that I wasn't also hurt. Knowing she has been in town and that she hasn't even bothered to reach out to me crushes me. I haven't worked up the courage to visit her. I can't handle the pain of seeing her at this point. It's obvious that the love I have for her isn't reciprocated anymore.

I haven't wanted to travel as much recently, so I've started taking on local filming gigs. I've shot some commercials for local businesses and even filmed a few weddings. I have enjoyed the slower pace of the work. I was losing my spark trying to stay busy working for brands after Olive first left. My heart wasn't in any of it. But the feeling of helping a mom and pop shop with their advertising, or recording a couple's most important day, like their wedding, has given me a sense of purpose again.

After we finished the video series on Whiskey Jane's, I was lost for a while. I felt like what I was filming was meaningless in comparison to what we did for the bar. So when my mom told me that her friend's daughter was getting married but couldn't afford anyone to film it, and asked if I would do it, I took a chance.

I sat there in awe behind the camera as I watched a young couple pour their hearts out to each other, the raw vulnerability of the moment. They expressed their love in front of everyone, and it inspired me. I finally felt passionate about filming once more. I wanted to chase that feeling again so I started getting the word out to people and sure enough, I've been able to take many local projects on.

Right now, I'm headed to Bricks to talk with Savannah about shooting a commercial for the restaurant. She told me she has a few ideas, so she is going to meet with me instead of her dad, even though he's the owner. I told her, "No problem." Savannah has always been kind to me, just a little intense with her flirty eye contact at times.

I roll all my windows down and shuffle my playlist. "Heart in a Cage" by The Strokes starts playing as I leave my neighborhood. I pass Mrs. Bodart walking Pebbles on the side of the road and give her a wave. She gives me a curt nod and continues her walk. She hasn't seemed to like me ever since the night Eddie drunkenly yelled on his birthday in front of my house. The night I met Olive.

No matter what I do, everything brings me back to her. A flower, a funny story, a handwritten note, *butter*, for god's sake. I can't get away from thinking about her. I try to switch my brain into work mode as I pull up into the parking lot of Bricks and shut off my truck.

Chapter 56

Olive

I stand in the bright sun, shielding my eyes from the light as I look up at the bar sign that's being lifted by a crane. Once it's in the right spot by the main road, I smile as I read the words.

Whiskey Jane's

Est. 1979

Seymour & Jane's place

I look around at the exterior improvements I have made over the past few months, thanks to Mr. Purngast's generosity. When he found out that I was the new owner of the bar, he told me he wanted to still donate the $500,000 that he originally was going to, so I could fix the place up.

I tried denying him many times, but he pleaded, saying he wanted to do this for Jane and Seymour, and for me. We have developed a friendship over the past few months, and I genuinely enjoy his company. I know that Rick and Johnny do, too. They have many stories to swap from their youth, and I love hearing about each of their adventures.

"That looks amazing!" I shout out to the construction crew that placed the sign and then head back inside. I look around at the full bar and feel my heart swell with gratitude. The series with Hunter ended up bringing a ton of business to Whiskey's and I owe it all to him. There are many times I have wanted to reach out to him over the past months, in moments of weakness. But I also wanted to wait till I was sure I was ready to give him the love he deserves.

I've been seeing a therapist weekly since I opened the bar. I was dealing with a lot of childhood trauma, and after the loss of Jane, it pushed me over the edge mentally. I was horrible to Hunter, I see that now. He deserved way more than I ever gave him. My therapist, Anna, told me that I am suffering from parentification trauma, so we have been working through it together. I finally feel like I am in a good headspace and I'm proud of the growth I've made. I've worked really hard to get my shit together.

I wave to one of our new barbacks, Tate, as he wipes down the counter of the bar.

"Hey, boss!" He smiles at me. His floppy hair covers one eye before he pushes it back. He is young and goofy; he just turned eighteen and this is his first job. His lack of work experience almost made me write him off, but then I decided to take a chance on him, just like Jane did for me. He's been a hard worker so far.

"Hey, Tate." I smile back. "How's it going?"

"Great! Rob let me drop a few racks of fries in the fryer earlier!"

Rob peers at me from the side of the kitchen window and shrugs. "The kid's a natural."

"He told me I might be able to prep salads next shift if I have time!" Tate continues.

I laugh. "Awesome. Maybe we need to start letting you take a few kitchen shifts."

Tate's face lights up. "That would be great, boss! Thanks!"

His enthusiasm is refreshing and I'm happy to have him at the bar with us.

I hear the bar door jingle and turn around to see Sonjia walking in. Her long, green, floral skirt swishes as she saunters towards me. She has a large pair of chunky earrings on today that I realize are Jane's. I feel a pang of sadness, missing her.

"Hey, sweetie, ready to go grab some lunch?" Sonjia asks.

"Yup! Let me just get my purse. I'll meet you outside," I tell her and quickly head to the office so I can grab my bag. I pick it up off the chair and then glance at the picture of Jane that Hunter's mom painted. I hung it up on the wall the day I was handed the keys to the bar. "Thank you," I whisper to it, like I do many times a week. I can't believe this place is mine; I'm living my dream.

The only thing missing now is Hunter. I'm sure he has moved on by now, though. I can't expect him to wait on me forever, especially when I told him not to.

I head outside and get in the passenger seat of Sonjia's Oldsmobile, which used to be Jane's.

"Looking good, Sonjia," I tell her and wiggle my eyebrows. "Very extravagant."

"Oh, this old thing?" She laughs and pretends to smooth her skirt in an uppity motion.

"Where do you want to go for lunch?" I ask her, feeling my stomach grumble with hunger.

"Let's go to this pizza place, Bricks. Mr. Ray took me there last week and you would love it. Everything is cool and hip, like you young people."

"Okay, sounds good to me. I could totally go for some pizza right now."

We pull up to the restaurant shortly after and Sonjia is right, the place looks super unique. It's huge and looks like a converted airplane hangar.

We walk inside and order some slices of pizza from a man at the front counter. He tells us to take a seat anywhere, and that he will bring us the food when it's ready. I ask Sonjia what she wants to drink and go fill up our fountain cups while she chooses a table.

I take a seat across from her and notice a couple sitting a few tables behind us. The guy has his back to me, but he has curly dark hair that instantly makes me think of Hunter for a moment. But this guy's hair is longer. There's a woman with long blonde hair facing my direction, and she's so beautiful, I can't help but stare at her as she reaches over and pushes some hair back from his face.

I miss that intimacy. I miss Hunter. I feel an ache for him deep inside suddenly and decide that I am going to try to call him tonight. I think I'm ready now to be the best possible woman for him and for myself.

Seconds after my moment of realization, though, the guy stands up to excuse himself to the bathroom and I think I might be sick. It *is* Hunter. He's here with this beautiful woman. I'm too late.

I quickly turn to Sonjia. "I'm so sorry, but I'm actually feeling really sick suddenly. Is there any way we could get our pizza to go?"

She looks at me with concern and reaches a hand over to lay it against my forehead. "You poor thing. Of course, hun. You go wait in my car; I will get it."

She hands me the keys and I rush out the front door before Hunter can notice me.

I get outside and now know it is *definitely* him inside; his truck is right in front of me. How did I not notice it when I walked in?

I'm too late, he moved on. *Hunter doesn't love me anymore.*

I can't help it as my stomach betrays me, and I bend over and throw up in the street. I guess I don't even have to fake being sick.

Chapter 57

Olive

Four months later

It's now July and I can't believe the differences in my life over the past year. One year ago, I thought I was going to lose Whiskey's and that there was no hope; now, I'm the owner.

I'm busier than ever at work, I'm still attending therapy weekly, and I even joined a book club that Missy runs at the library once a month. I've made some new friends there, too. I've also hung out with Eddie's sister, Leena, a few times and she's a breath of fresh air. She has never mentioned Hunter around me and I'm grateful for how insightful she is.

It's nice to have more friends now, but I can't lie and say I don't miss Ivy desperately. She's living her best life in Atlanta, though, so I'm happy for her. I plan to visit her around Christmas time, so we can spend the holiday together. We FaceTime at least three times a week so we don't miss anything that each other is experiencing. She is kicking butt at the bridal salon and seems like she is in line to get a promotion soon. I couldn't be prouder of her.

I'm also proud of the fact she has put herself first and hasn't dated anyone. For the first time in our friendship, she has been single for longer than a month and she said she's learned to love herself again. Last night we stayed up till 3 A.M on FaceTime, watching *The Vampire Diaries* together. Our tradition that used to be centered around heartbreak is now just for fun. We can feel close to each other from thousands of miles away, without it being about a man.

That said...she has told me that she sees a tremendous change in me numerous times, and that I should just try to reach out to Hunter, to see if he responds. I picture him in that pizza place with the hot blonde girl every single time she encourages me to talk to him, and I just can't do it. I want him to be happy, and he looked happy with whoever that woman was.

I'm in my office writing checks for payroll when Rob knocks on the door frame.

"There's someone at the bar asking for you." He smiles at me.

"Who?" I question.

"Not telling. A friend of yours." He raises an eyebrow and pushes away from the door.

I blow out a breath and back away from my desk chair, setting the checks down. I give myself a quick once-over in the mirror and smooth down my simple black dress. Every day I'm thankful I never have to wear that stupid uniform ever again. Missy and I burned ours ceremoniously in the back dumpster after I was given the bar deed. I felt victorious after.

Tripp is still awaiting sentencing, but I have a feeling he will be behind bars for a long time, thanks to his crimes. I guess it makes sense that he was trying to sell Whiskey's off with no remorse, because he owed a lot of powerful men a *lot* of money. He stole millions from businessmen who trusted him, and it seems like his plan was to get the money from selling the bar and flee. Unfortunately, the life insurance money that his parents left him will probably all be used for legal fees and restitution. Not unfortunate for his sake, but for his parents', who were trying to provide for him, even after they passed.

I push through the kitchen door and see Wes standing across from me, smiling at the counter.

"Well, aren't you a sight for sore eyes," he jokes with me. "I miss that old uniform, though."

I look down at my dress, and scoff sarcastically, "Well, thanks. Are you here to tease me or order something?" I put my hands on my hips playfully.

"My buddy is meeting me here for lunch. We were in the area skating and got hungry, so we decided to stop in. He will be here any second." He smirks.

My breath hitches as he says this. What if it's Hunter? Is he messing with me? I feel like he would just say it's Hunter if he was coming. But *he* wouldn't come here.

As my thoughts are spiraling, Eddie walks through the front door and I whoosh out a breath. I can feel Wes eyeing me quizzically as I greet Eddie.

Eddie slides onto a bar stool next to Wes.

"Were you expecting someone else?" Wes says, his eyes practically sparkling with mischief.

"Stop, Wes, don't give her a hard time," Eddie says. "Hey, Olive. How are you doing?"

"I'm great." I smile at him and turn to Wes. "Yeah, don't give me a hard time. I can throw you out." I lean in and whisper, "I'm the owner now."

"Oh yeah! I heard you're the big boss now, very exciting."

Wes nods and then murmurs under his breath, "And too busy to give Hunter a call, apparently."

"Wes, I said *stop*." Eddie gives him a serious look. "I just wanted to grab a burger and beer in peace. You told me you wouldn't start something."

"No, say what you want to say." I cross my arms and look at Wes. "I can take it, I know I was a bitch."

"Okay." Wes stares back at me, challenging me. "You really fucked up my friend. I have never seen him so in love in my life and you didn't care about him as soon as your video project was done. As soon as he couldn't help give you what you wanted"— Wes motions around the bar—"you left him like it meant nothing."

Eddie gives me an apologetic look, but I can't fault Wes for being protective and angry over his best friend.

"Wes, I know it seems like I just left him for no reason, but I had a good one. My whole life fell apart, and I couldn't have been a good partner to Hunter if I tried. My head was not on straight. I had a lot of trauma from my childhood and I was terrified to love him." I feel myself getting choked up and I hate it, but continue, "By the time I was sure I could be a woman that deserves his love, it was too late."

"What do you mean, too late?" Eddie asks.

"I saw him with a girl a few months ago. They looked cozy." I shrug. "She was beautiful. I'm assuming a girlfriend."

Eddie and Wes look at each other, completely confused.

Eddie speaks first. "Um, Hunter hasn't dated anyone since way before he met you. I'm sure of it."

"I saw him with her at Bricks, the pizza place."

Wes bursts out laughing and then pipes up, "Was she blonde with huge boobs?"

"Uh, I guess?" I wince at the thought of that day.

"That was Savannah, the owner's daughter," Eddie says.

"He shot a commercial for them. I'm sure he was there meeting with her about that."

"Their body language seemed really into each other, though," I say.

"Theirs, or *hers*?" Eddie responds.

Wes adds, "Savannah has always been obsessed with him. Hunter has never liked her back. He's just polite to her."

I think back to the moments I saw them together, her brushing a hair away from his face, him getting up and heading to the bathroom shortly after. Maybe I assumed he was into her, but I never saw his expression at the table. Maybe he actually stepped away because he was uncomfortable. His smile when I saw his face could've been professional, not genuine. I'm an idiot.

"So he doesn't have a girlfriend?" I ask quickly.

"No," Wes snorts, "he's still madly in love with you."

"Holy shit," I say under my breath.

This changes everything. I want to run to him; I want to shout it from the rooftops that I love him. I want to profess my love in some grand gesture. My hands shake at my sides and I hug myself.

"He still loves me," I say to myself.

"Yup." Eddie laughs.

"I want to go see him, right now," I tell them.

"Well, he's out of town till tomorrow for a wedding he's filming."

That's when I get an idea. I don't want to wait another second to tell him how I feel about him and a simple phone call won't suffice after everything we have been through.

"Eddie, you're really good at tech stuff, right?" I ask.

"Uh, yes. Why?"

"I'm going to need your help."

Chapter 58

Hunter

I 'm currently driving to my hotel room after filming the McClaine's wedding at a small country club in a rural area of Tennessee, when I hear my phone start to blow up with notifications from the passenger seat. *What the hell?* I pick it up for a second and see notifications for comments that say stuff like "Omg!" or "This is amazing." I toss my phone back into the seat, assuming one of the skate videos I filmed a while ago is going viral right now. Sometimes they will randomly get a lot of interest, even years later.

It's not until I drive for twenty more minutes, my phone lighting up the whole ride, that I start to get confused. I pull off the dirt road into the parking lot of the small hotel I've been staying at this weekend and put my truck in park. I'm exhausted from filming the entire day, start to finish, of another wedding, but I am also happy and fulfilled by how my time was spent.

I push wild strands of my hair out of my face. It's grown almost to my shoulders in the past year, and I have thought about cutting it off many times, but then I hear the nickname

293

Curls in my head and I can't do it. Anything to keep her in my mind.

My phone screen flashes for the millionth time, and I let out an exasperated noise as I pick it up again. I swipe open my home screen and open the YouTube app to see hundreds of notifications pouring in. *I wonder which video it was*, I think to myself as I open the tab to read the recent comments.

"This is the cutest thing I've ever seen."

Wait, what?

"I want a love like this."

I keep scrolling to see multiple people have written things with a similar sentiment. I click on one of the comments and it takes me to the video.

The video loads slowly on my screen; the service isn't great out here and I curse silently at the fact that I don't recognize the title, "It's You." It shows it was uploaded just thirty minutes ago. I wonder if I'm hacked when the screen finally loads.

My breath is taken away as the song "Baby It's You" by Smith starts to play and I'm instantly transported back to that moment with Olive in my truck, with her singing the lyrics on our ride to Onilley Lake. The number of times that I've listened to this song since losing her, relating deeply to the lyrics, makes me feel stunned in this moment.

Olive appears on the screen suddenly and my heart races seeing her. It looks like she's standing outside somewhere, against a wall. She looks stunning, her eyes bright and lively. She looks healthy and carefree, like she has put on some needed weight following the stress of last year. I reach out and run my finger across her face, while on the screen she begins to speak.

"Hi! Some of you may recognize me from a video series Hunter did last year. Crazy to say that was an entire year ago, but it was. I own the bar now, which is great, uhm, so Whiskey

Jane's lives on!" She pauses and looks nervous; it seems like someone encourages her from behind the camera to keep going and she starts to talk again.

"Sorry, I'm not used to being on camera like this." She laughs. "But I have something that I would like to share. So here it goes. A while ago when we were working on the video project together—Hunter and me, that is—he asked me if I wanted to film an episode talking about my relationship with Jane. I told him yes, but never got around to it because I was so consumed in losing her, I couldn't even speak about it. But when it's all said and done, I don't even think my stories with Jane were needed. Our relationship spoke for itself. She was a mother to me in every single way but biologically." Olive looks sad for a second and then lights up as she says, "Jane was looking out for me, though. She knowingly blessed me one last time after she passed away by giving me the bar. But she also blessed me in another way, without knowing it. Without the bar, without Jane's legacy, I never would have met Hunter Rowe."

She looks directly at the camera now, confident, like she is speaking to me only. "He is the most incredible person I have ever met. He is selfless, loving, intelligent, creative, and not to mention, *so* beautiful to look at." Olive chuckles slightly and then grows serious again. "I seriously fucked up a chance with a perfect man, big time. Oops, sorry! Can I swear?" she asks the person behind the camera, and I hear Eddie's laugh.

"It's fine," he says in the background.

Wow, I guess the fact that my YouTube email and password has been the same since I started the channel when we were all kids has caught up to me. I chuckle to myself. Need to change my password, noted.

Olive continues to speak, "There isn't a day that goes by that my thoughts aren't consumed with my love for Hunter.

This part is for him only." She grins and scoots closer to the camera. "Curls, I am so sorry for the way I treated you. I was horrible and I didn't appreciate you when I had you. I used your kindness and didn't thank you when I should have.

"I am so thankful for everything you did for me. You always showed up for me when I needed you. I have spent a long time getting to the place I needed to be at, so I can show up for you, too. I am ready to love you for the rest of my life, if you will accept my apology. There is no one else in the world I want to be with. I am madly in love with you, Hunter. I choose you. *Baby, it's you.*"

The video fades to black and I stare at my phone in shock before quickly snapping out of it, dialing Eddie.

He answers, "Yello?"

"Where is she?" I breathe out.

"She's at her apartment."

I hang up without even responding and throw my truck in reverse.

I'm going to get my girl.

Chapter 59

Olive

It's past midnight when I finally sit on my couch after a long shift and hold my phone in front of my face as Ivy talks to me.

"You still haven't heard anything from him?"

"Nope."

"I'm sure you will soon. That video was super sweet and way out of your comfort zone," she says, trying to reassure me.

"Yeah, I don't know. Maybe it is too late for us. I know I broke his heart."

"Don't give up hope," she says. "Maybe he hasn't seen the video yet."

"It's been six hours, Ivy. I'm sure he's seen it by now." I blow out a breath. "It's late. I'm going to shower and try to sleep."

"Alright, well call me tomorrow. I love you," she tells me.

"Love you, too."

I click off my phone screen and toss it aside. I get up, walk to my bathroom, and turn the shower handle to the hottest setting before beginning to undress. I connect my phone to my small speaker and select "My Own Summer" by Deftones from my nighttime playlist. The music surrounds me as the steam begins to fill up the bathroom and I roll my neck, releasing the tension from today.

I can't help but feel like a failure that Hunter didn't even send me a text after I made the video pouring my heart out to him. Maybe he's angry that Eddie helped me upload it on his account. I thought maybe he would be moved by the gesture— me putting my heart on the line for everyone to see since I was always so reluctant to show him love before. I guess I thought wrong. I will try to call him and apologize tomorrow.

I'm about to step in the shower when I hear someone knocking on the door repeatedly. I'm not expecting any visitors, especially at this late hour. I wrap a nearby towel around my body and head towards my front door. I grow more anxious as the knocking aggressively continues and look around for an object to protect me, in case it's an intruder. I guess an intruder probably wouldn't knock, though? I see the butter knife that Hunter bought me sitting on my kitchen counter and snag it as I walk past. I don't have a peephole, so I open the door a crack first, gripping the knife, to find out who's repeatedly banging on my door at 1 A.M.

As soon as I pull the door open, I make eye contact with Hunter. He looks at me and then down at the knife and smirks a little. "Hello, Olive," he says in his deep voice.

I drop the knife to the floor in shock and before I can even process what's happening, his lips are on mine. I moan into his mouth as he sweeps me up into his arms and I wrap both my legs around his waist, my towel falling to the ground. He carries me into my apartment and slams my front door with his foot without breaking our kiss. My heart starts to pound wildly out of my chest.

I pull away from his lips and cradle both sides of his face in my hands. "Holy shit, you're here."

He smiles at me. "I'm here, baby, and I'm never letting you go again."

"Please don't," I whisper and then pull him back into me.

We continue to kiss while our hands explore each other, unable to get enough. I get down from his hold and pull his hand to lead him towards the bathroom.

"Would you like to join me in the shower?" I tease him.

Hunter quickly nods and begins to rip his shirt off over his head, kick his sneakers off, and then pull off his pants. I stand in the middle of the bathroom, watching him. Seeing him undress is foreplay on its own; his tan, muscular body, ready to be kissed, ready to be touched. I pull back the shower curtain and step in; he follows.

The second the water touches his body, he flinches and reaches for the handle. "Are you trying to burn me alive, woman?" he jokes as he turns it cooler.

I shrug. "I like a hot shower."

He stands right above me now, leaning over me. "I like *you*," he whispers.

"I love you," I boldly say back, never breaking his eye contact.

His eyes burn with intensity as he responds. "Fuck, Olive. I love you so much. I can't believe this moment is real." He touches my hair and cups the back of my head. Hunter pulls me in and kisses me deeply. In this moment, I finally feel like the final puzzle piece of my life has been found.

I am whole.

Epilogue

Olive

Fifteen months later

It's a Saturday night, four days before Halloween, and we are having a big party at Whiskey Jane's. I decided to do a Halloween Mask or Task theme for fun. I've kept most of Jane's traditions around; it's part of the charm that makes everyone love Whiskey's.

The bar crowd is decked out in masks and Halloween costumes and there has been a huge turnout for the event. Whiskey's is packed, and every single person I'm close to is here for the party. Ivy even flew in for the week, saying she couldn't turn down a good Halloween party. She walks by me dressed as a cat, with a mask covering the top half of her face, her eyes shining through, mysterious. She has on a black spandex bodysuit, and I've seen her get hit on about ten times already in the past hour.

Ivy walks backwards, noticing me. "Nice boobs. Where's Hunter?"

I look down at my ample cleavage, which usually doesn't

exist, and smooth down my costume. I am dressed as Christine from *The Phantom of the Opera*, with a masquerade mask. The pink gown has a corset that has sucked in and pushed up my chest. Not the best choice for a long night, I'm now realizing in hindsight. I thought it would be a cute couple's costume, because I made Hunter dress up as the Phantom. Everyone knows he's better than Raoul.

"He should be here soon; he told me he had to stop by our house and grab something he forgot." I shrug.

"Our *house.*" Ivy smiles at me, her eyebrows raised as she flutters her eyelashes dramatically. "How cute."

"Oh, shut up." I push her playfully, but I also love the way it sounds: our house. Together. I moved into Hunter's house a few months after we started seriously dating and we haven't looked back since. He told me I could change anything I wanted, so it felt like my space, too, not just his. I liked it just the way it was, though. I only added a few cool pieces of furniture that I found from local art markets and the framed photo of Jane and I singing Abba. It now rests on the wall right above Hunter's record player.

"He's kind of cute," Ivy whispers into my ear, motioning to Wes playing lead guitar up on the small stage. I hired his band, Rinse and Repeat, to play the party tonight. They have mostly done covers and taken requests from the crowd. Everyone seems to love them. I glare at Wes, who is wearing a TMNT mask—the whole band is dressed as the Ninja Turtles—and turn back to Ivy.

"You can't even see his face..." I snort.

"Yeah, but I just know he's hot. Look at that golden hair coming out from under his mask, look at his toned body, *dripping* with sweat as he sings. Woooo." She fans her face with her hand. "I can tell he's hot. And if for some reason he's not, I can just make him keep the mask on when I sleep with him tonight."

"Ivy!" I command. "That's Hunter's best friend. You're not going to take advantage of him."

"Why!" She pouts at me.

At that exact moment, Wes tells the crowd the band is going to take a five-minute break and lifts his mask to take a sip of his water. I can practically see Ivy's eyes bulge out of her head. "Your opinion is vetoed," she tells me and walks off.

I watch as she does a circle of the crowd and then makes her way over to him. She's like a lioness, stalking her prey.

I roll my eyes and laugh to myself.

A minute later, Sonjia, wearing a cute mask in a shape of a strawberry, comes towards me. When she gets to the bar counter, she gives me a smile.

"It's nice to see you girls together again," she says, knowingly.

"Yeah, I really miss her being local," I agree.

Rick chimes in from the bar, "Tell her to open a bridal salon here."

"I'm trying." I laugh.

"Tell her I'll buy the first dress from her," Johnny playfully adds.

I glance at him and chuckle. He's made a lot of changes in the past year, too; I'm not the only one. Johnny is now a grand-father to two little ones and no longer wears his iconic top hat. He stopped wearing it after his first grandson was born because he was terrified of it. Every time he saw it, he would burst into tears.

So, it turns out that the "what" under Johnny's hat is: *nothing*. Literally, he's bald. I told him it was an anticlimactic reveal after he made us all have a sit-down dinner at the bar, just for him to take off his top hat. He has always had a flare for the dramatic, though, and loves a good story. Johnny then told me that he had bright orange hair as a kid and it was a huge insecurity of his because everyone called him "ginger Johnny." One day he decided he would rather have people stare at a ridiculous hat instead of his hair. Over the years he lost his hair but said he kept the top hat on because it was just something he was used to wearing. His security blanket of sorts. Johnny keeps the hat off now, even when he's not around his grandson. He said once he felt the breeze on his head, there was no going back.

One thing that hasn't changed is that he still refers to Hunter as bar stool boy, even though the night happened over two years ago. It always makes me laugh, but I can tell the nickname still makes Hunter cringe because it reminds him of my injury each time it's said.

As if he has been summoned by my thoughts, I see the entrance door open, and Hunter steps through. He looks gorgeous as ever, his dark hair cascading around his face in waves, his muscular body causing the white shirt he has on to pull taut. I love this man. Realizing his outfit is missing something, I make a disappointed expression and put my hands on my hips when I see he doesn't have his Phantom mask on.

"Don't tell me you forgot your mask," I loudly say and half the bar turns.

Oh shit.

I see the crowd give each other knowing looks before exclaiming, "Task! Task! Task!" in a chant. Hunter has no one to blame but himself. He knows we take themes seriously at Whiskey Jane's.

Hunter laughs and puts his hands up in surrender. "Okay, okay! My fate is sealed."

He's a good sport, just like the first night we met. Everyone quiets as he walks over to the bucket and pulls out a slip of paper. He looks down at it and smiles.

"Come up on stage, buddy, and read us your task," Wes calls out from the mic. "Just like old times. But no one give this man a bar stool!" he jokes.

The crowd laughs at the comment. Everyone that wasn't here the night we met knows our story by now.

Hunter steps up on the stage and clears his throat as he looks down at the small, crumpled sheet of paper again.

"Oh my. It looks like I'm going to need Olive's help for this one," he says into the microphone, gesturing for me to come over to him.

My eyes grow large. "No, no, no! I'm not a part of this. I wore my costume!" I point to my face.

"Come on, baby." Hunter smiles, his eyes crinkling with delight. "Get up here." He looks so sexy up on the stage, I want to lick the grin off his face.

The crowd begins to chant my name repeatedly next. I groan, but I finally start to walk forward after some coaxing from Sonjia and a very pregnant Missy. I can't deny a pregnant woman's wishes.

I weave through people and end up making eye contact with Mr. Purngast as I walk past him to the stage. He winks at me, and I give him a big smile in response. I'm surrounded by people I love in a bar that I've always dreamed of owning. My life is everything that I dreamed of, and in this moment, I'm so grateful.

Hunter reaches out his hand from the stage and pulls me up to him. I notice he's shaking a little and feel bad because I know he gets anxious when a lot of eyes are on him. I reach out and touch his cheek to soothe him, and he leans into my touch in response. Then he takes both of my hands in his; we are standing connected on stage now. He's smiling down at me, and

I feel the warmth of his affection engulf me, like it always does. Suddenly, Wes's band begins to play "Sleepwalk" by Santo & Johnny behind us, and I look at Hunter quickly.

"This is my favorite song, my comfort song," I say in a faint voice, shocked.

"I know," he says and pushes a strand of hair behind my ear.

The bar is completely still other than the music. The energy in the room feels different right now and I turn to look out at the crowd. They are all just smiling and staring at us.

I turn back to Hunter, confused. "So, what's your task?" I nervously laugh.

Hunter reaches into his pocket and then holds the piece of paper out towards me without breaking our eye contact. I take the small sheet in my hand and look down to read it.

Ask the girl of your dreams to marry you.

I gasp and look back up as Hunter gets down on one knee.

The story doesn't end here.

Ivy is up next...

* * *

Book 2 of the Clairesville series will be out 2026.

Acknowledgments

First, I want to thank, YOU, the reader. Without you picking up this book, the story wouldn't be told. Thank you for taking a chance and deciding to read *Baby, It's You*. As someone that loves reading just as much as I love writing, I thank you.

* * *

I want to thank my family. Without my husband's support I wouldn't be able to carry out this crazy dream of writing a book.

Jordan- Thank you for constantly letting me bounce skateboarding questions off you and for being my sounding board. I know I get crazy ideas- thanks for just going with the flow.

Mom- Thank you for taking the time to read this manuscript before anyone else. Back when it was in its first draft- now that's a mother's love- because it was a doozy. As always, thanks for your honest feedback.

Jesse- Thank you for constantly being my cheerleader through this process. Without your uplifting advice, I would have talked myself out of writing this book 12 times already. I know you usually enjoy reading fantasy, so you reading my romance novel just to help me out, means a lot.

Katie- Thanks for walking into my life on a random Saturday night. You have been exactly what I needed in a friend during the process of writing a book. You listened to my bitching and offered me advice. Also, thanks for watching reality TV with me, you're a real one.

Edith- Thank you for being all authors dream reader. You read the manuscript quickly and were a breath of fresh air to discuss everything with. Thanks for taking a chance on me.

Jennifer- Thank you for your honest and helpful feedback. Without you, the book wouldn't be where it is today. I'm so grateful for your help.

Danielle Barthel- If I could host an award ceremony in your honor I would. You are amazing. I mean, what a task you had before you- you made my book readable. I promise to work on my commas and periods, but no guarantees. You're the best.

Last but not least, thank you to all the girls in my book club. I am blessed and lucky to have women like you in my corner.

Holy shit, I wrote a book!

About the Author

Nicole Mikell lives in sunny Florida with her husband, three kids, and two dogs. When she's not busy reading, you can find her thrift shopping or watching K-pop music videos with her daughter. Nicole loves reality TV, anything artsy, and a good Youtube dance workout.

She also really loves music, so send her some song suggestions.

You can follow her for future book updates on Instagram and TikTok:

@nicolemikellauthor

www.ingramcontent.com/pod-product-compliance
Lightning Source LLC
Chambersburg PA
CBHW010531100726
47903CB00011B/2967